GIOVANNI

THE COUGARS AND CUBS SERIES 💋 BOOK #3

GIGI MEIER

GiGi Meier

Cover Design by GiGi Meier

Developmental Editing by Jessica Lessor

Editing by Robyne Hunt

Author Photograph by Tara L. Grundemeier

ISBN: 978-1-9636250-2-8 (e)

ISBN: 978-1-9636250-3-5 (pb)

GiGi Meier Media LLC

ALSO BY GIGI MEIER

Standalone Book

Coyote

Sammie and Carlos's forced proximity

cartel, kidnapped, Military hero, dark romance

The Cañon Series

Tomlin

The start of Dani and Tomlin's

slow burn, enemies-to-almost-lovers

Tomlin Takahashi Duet #1

The Cañon Series, Book #1

Takahashi

The conclusion of Dani and Tomlin's

friends-to-lovers, happily ever after

Tomlin Takahashi Duet #2

The Cañon Series, Book #2

Hamilton

Hamilton and Molli's second chance,

small town, police officer romance

The Cañon Series, Book #3

Isla

Isla and Gabe's opposites attract,

age gap, forbidden love romance

The Cañon Series, Book #4

The Cougars and Cubs Series 💋

Paolo

Taylor and Paolo's reverse age gap,

forced proximity, office romance

The Cougars and Cubs Series 💋, Book #1

Sebastian

Sebastian and Chloe's reverse age gap,

opposites attract, Christmas romance

The Cougars and Cubs Series 💋, Book #2

Giovanni

Giovanni and Kacie's reverse age gap,

protector, Alpha male romance

The Cougars and Cubs Series 💋, Book #3

Kadus

Kadus and Bex's reverse age gap,

best friend's brother, rockstar romance

The Cougars and Cubs Series 💋, Book #4

Marco

Marco and Victoria's reverse age gap,

steamy Latin couple, soulmates romance

The Cougars and Cubs Series 💋, Book #5

Gods and Goddesses Anthology

Eternal Reign

Hades and Persephone Modern Retelling

Russian bratva, kidnapping, touch her and die, slow burn.

GET TWO FREE BOOKS

The Cañon Series 🖤
is deliciously dark and intensely traumatic.

DOWNLOAD FOR FREE ON MY WEBSITE
www.gigimeier.com

Dani and Tomlin's story is a single POV, slow burn, enemies-to-lovers, forced proximity romance. Check my website for a list of content and trigger warnings.

DEDICATION

To my beloved mom, who passed during the creation of this book.
Her unwavering support was a cornerstone of my writing journey,
yet her traditional beliefs humorously insisted that women aren't
fond of books with shirtless men on the cover and open-door romance
on the pages. Bless her heart. I believe she might have been mistaken.
Among the many cherished conversations we shared, this one always
brings a smile to my face in the midst of my mourning.

GIOVANNI

1

GIOVANNI

The throb of the bass beats with my heart as I power through another set. I'm in my zone. Lifting the cool barbells is a breeze today, like I'm in sync with the universe or something. I'm chasing something bigger than just muscle—my dreams. Each lift is a step closer to the Mr. Olympia stage, where the gods of iron battle. I glance at Marco, my training partner, mirroring my movements on the bench press.

"All about consistency, brother," I shout over the music. Marco flashes a grin and hoists the barbell up with a grunt.

"Pure beast mode, Gio," he pants, the bar hitting the rack with a satisfying clang that resonates through the gym crowded with all the new members conquering their New Year's resolution of getting in shape. He mops the sweat off his forehead.

I start moving to the beat, dancing between sets. The gym's my playground, and the mirrors are my cheering crowd. I throw in a flex here and there, watching the light dance across my biceps. It's not vanity—it's artistry. Analyzing the various muscle groups to see which need further development and which are on track thus far. This is what the crowd will see when I step on that Mr. Olympia stage and what will set me apart.

"Easy on the showboating," Marco chides, the lower half of his face hidden in the towel, still catching his sweat.

"Not showboating," I quip back, arms flexing into a perfect double biceps pose. "Studying my progress. Seeing it from different angles is important, especially since I'm still working through my posing routine. If I miss something, it costs me points, and I must be perfect on stage, or else the guy next to me will be."

I wink at him, twisting my hat backward as my curls jut out the sides. Curls for the girls is what my mamma always used to say. Not sure if that's ever been true, especially with my hair too long and looking a little ragged. An Italian Ronald McDonald, according to Seb. With his straight blonde hair, he gives me grief over my chocolate curls, even more grief about my thick 'stauche. He hates it. What does he know?

I'm not telling him, but I'm thinking about cutting my hair. This African American dude comes in with lines on the side of his head. His curls are tighter than mine, but the sides are trimmed close with designs on the edges.

It would be pretty cool if I did something like that, but I have yet to talk to the guy to see where he goes to get that done. I doubt my dad's barber, where I've gone my whole life, would know how to do it.

"Showboating, studying, it's all the same thing with the number of women that stare at you in this pace."

He chuckles before laying back and killing another set. His good nature keeps him from being jealous of anything about me besides my height. His definition is more pronounced as his frame is thinner and shorter in stature. He competes in the lightweight category and wins most of the local shows. I asked if he'd ever compete with me at Mr. Olympia, but he mumbled some nonsense about enjoying being a big fish in a small pond —unwilling to become a tiny fish in a world pond.

I don't take him seriously as I finish dancing and flexing to the song. I examine my arms and chest muscles as I do different poses. I have my problem areas, specific muscle groups that are taking longer to grow than I'd like, but what's life if you're not having fun doing it?

I return to the bench, balancing the barbells on my thighs before easing backward. Today is about reps, not heavy weights. If the reverse were the case, I'd spot Marco and vice versa. I'm easily pumping out another set when Jenna enters my line of sight. The cold air conditioning does nothing to cool my heated skin.

I glance down at my cock to make sure it doesn't pop up like it does every time she's around. I've been crushing on her for months, thinking we were getting closer until last month when she slid that big ring on her finger, and I found out she was married or getting married, whichever. I didn't hear much of what she said, too focused on the ring and the crushing disappointment that killed my growing love for her.

"Happy New Year, Gio," she calls out, her voice slicing through the music and the clatter of weights. "Hey, Marco."

"Happy New Year, Jenna." My voice is steady despite the adrenaline from my workout. I pound out an extra set, trying to look calm while my heart does its best impression of a jackhammer.

"Wow, you've really got some gains since the last time I saw you."

I don't allow my face to crack with emotion, but my stomach is doing flips at her compliment. If she only knew how much I like her, she'd probably never talk to me again.

"No days off."

I finish my set, lean forward, and dump the weights on the ground. The pump flowing through my biceps is insane, causing her to reach out to touch them. This is why I thought she was single. All the flirting and touching sends me mixed signals.

"I haven't seen you around."

I hate myself for asking. I also hate myself for looking for her whenever I set foot in here. A guilty smile and pink flush cover her skin, making her look adorable.

"It's been busy between the holidays and our engagement photos in Cancun."

My heart drops into my stomach. Marco glares at me from behind her, shooting me a warning look, which I ignore. He knows how I feel about her, having busted me getting a woodie when I spotted her working out. An awkward pause lingers, and I adjust the Velcro straps on my wrists.

"Any resolutions for 2024?" she asks, following me as I rack the dumbbells for others to use.

"To stand on the Mr. Olympia stage," I say without hesitation. This gym is where my dreams will come true. "To show them what I'm made of."

Jenna's eyes hold mine, and there's a flicker of something like admiration—or is it challenge?

"Wow! That would be something. I believe you can do it."

"I believe I can too."

Her words stoke the already burning fire in my belly. I'm not just building a body. I'm sculpting a legacy. Every drop of sweat, every weight I push, pull, or lift, every meal measured down to the last macro—it's all for that moment under the bright lights.

"So, what did you do for New Year's Eve?" Jenna asks, beginning her workout ritual.

Marco pipes up about his wild night on 20th Street and falling off the swings at McIntyre's. He's sporting a cut above his eye because of it, and she awws at him like he's a damn baby. He is a big fucking drunk baby and not the cute ones that coo and shit their pants.

I stay silent for a beat. With Paolo and Taylor attending a hotel party downtown and Seb taking Chloe to New York to see the ball drop, I was left in my own company on the last night of the year. Not that I'd admit this to her, but I got too fucked up over her last month. Getting trashed and Seb taking care of me on more than one occasion was stupid and not something I want to repeat. The hand on the clock hitting a new year was just what I needed to reset my life.

"I was here," I admit, the echo of the empty gym still vivid in my mind. "Just me, the weights, and a midnight toast of my protein drink." And a decision to compete in Mr. Olympia.

Jenna pauses, the dumbbells in her hands forgotten for a moment.

"You weren't lonely?"

I duck my head behind the squat rack, grab a forty-five-pound plate, and put on my poker face. She hit the nail right on the head, and I feel a twinge in my gut that I'm not keen to divulge to her.

"Loneliness is for people who don't have goals," I deflect with a half-smile as I slide the plate onto the bar with a clang that I hope sounds more confident than I feel. "Wasn't lonely, just focused."

She's watching me, her gaze kind of piercing in a way that says she's not buying it, but she lets it go when her eyes flash to Marco.

"Focused is good," Jenna concedes, resuming her reps. "Especially with a goal like Mr. Olympia on the line."

There's a beat where I just watch the smooth control of her movements, the determination in each lift that mirrors my own.

5

It's clear she understands the grind, the sacrifice, the tunnel vision I need to have if I'm going to make it to the top of anything.

I step under the squat rack, feeling the familiar weight settle across my shoulders.

"What about you?" I ask, pushing up the weight in a steady rhythm. "Your New Year's was good?"

She nods, setting down the dumbbells and taking a sip of water.

"It was quiet. Just family and some reflection on the past year. Made some resolutions, too."

"Resolutions, huh?" I grunt out another rep. "Like what?"

Jenna laughs a sound that makes the gym feel less empty. "Not telling. It's bad luck to share them too early."

I rack the weight, turning to face her, curious despite myself.

"Since when?"

"Since I decided it's a new rule," she teases, picking up her towel. I can't help but laugh, the tension from her loneliness question fading.

"Fair enough. I'll just have to wait and see then."

She gives me that smile again, the one that's too knowing, too warm. The twinge in my gut turns into a stabbing of my heart. This is why I like the girl. She's nice and friendly and always has this sweet side about her.

"Guess you will."

I glance down at her left hand, the ringless ring finger without so much an indent or tan line indicating she's taken. Fucking mixed signals.

As she moves to the next part of her workout, I find myself watching her again. Jenna's got this way about her, an open honesty that makes me want to spill all my secrets and plans. But I've learned the hard way that the less people know about my inner battles, the better. My family being some of them.

I turn back to the mirror, to the weights, to the silent promise of a new year and a new start. I've got a title to win, a physique to perfect, and a heart to protect—getting fucked up over anyone or anything isn't part of the plan. Not this year.

This year is about discipline, about reclaiming every piece of myself that I let slip away last year. As I lift, I can almost feel the burden of past poor decisions being eliminated with each rep. I sink into another squat, muscles burning with the sweet agony of growth and determination.

"You're really gunning for it, huh?" Jenna's teasing voice cuts through my concentration.

"Absolutely." I push up, locking my knees with a slight jerk. "Mr. Olympia isn't just a competition. It's the pinnacle of everything I'm working toward."

She nods, appreciative, her eyes reflecting a respect that makes me feel proud of my choice to compete.

"I can see that. Your dedication is kind of . . . inspiring."

"Inspiring, huh?" I can't help the smirk that plays on my lips. "I could say the same about you."

She's ripped herself. She could easily compete in a bikini competition or even fitness if she added more bulk. Either way, she is perfect, and her glutes are something I can't help but stare at. Jenna picks up another set of weights, the motion fluid and deliberate.

"We all have our mountains to climb."

She's right. We all have our mountains, our giants to slay. And here, in this temple of transformation, we're all warriors in our own right. I move on to the next set, adrenaline pumping through me while the energetic music pulsates around me.

"You're pushing hard today, Gio," Marco observes, coming over with his water bottle. He takes a swig, his eyes never leaving mine.

"Got to, man." I pause, breathless, as Jenna starts chatting with a female trainer. "New year. New goals."

He casts a curious eye over his shoulder at her. "Wouldn't have anything to do with her, would it?"

"No."

Marco chuckles, downing more water before replying, "*Sure*. Just don't burn out, yeah?"

I give him a nod, but the hunger inside won't be tamed, regardless of who's around me. "No chance of that. It's all about pacing, brother."

My eyes catch Jenna's reflection as she talks animatedly with her hands. Marco follows my gaze, his eyes narrowing slightly.

"Just remember, she's got a rock on her finger even if she doesn't wear it," he murmurs a hint of protectiveness in his tone. I look away, a twinge of something—loneliness or longing —pulling at my chest. "I'm not looking to start anything, Marco. Just friendly talk, that's all."

He raises an eyebrow, unconvinced.

"Friendly talk can lead to . . . complications."

I jerk the plate from the bar, ready to rack it and move away from my greatest temptation—Jenna.

"I know, I know," I reply, keeping my voice even. "No complications."

Marco claps me on the shoulder, a silent show of camaraderie.

"Just looking out for you, Giovanni. You've got a good thing going. Don't want to see you get hurt."

I glance her way again, the ladies' conversation still flowing, before I turn my back.

"I won't," I assure him and myself, more than anything. "I've got too much riding on this year to get sidetracked."

My gaze doesn't stray again. The rest of my workout passes in a blur of focus and determination. The space around me narrows when I concentrate on the rest of my training. The music, Jenna, and even Marco fade into the background as I finish with a heaving chest and a sweaty sheen coating my skin.

As I head for the locker room, I don't look back. There's nothing for me there—not in the past, not in distractions, not in the blue of Jenna's eyes. There's only the path forward. I've got a title to win. And nothing, not even the soft curve of Jenna's smile or the sweet melody of her voice will stand in my way.

2

KACIE

The fluorescent lights of my office flicker overhead, casting a clinical glow over the chaos of my desk. Right now, I feel more like a ringmaster at the world's most disorganized circus than an assistant district attorney for the fourth largest city in the nation. My fingers drum impatiently on the mountain of files that stand between me and a semblance of order.

I'm on the phone with Dr. Bennett, our go-to forensic expert, trying to nail down a time for him to testify. He's as busy as I am, and we do this awkward dance around our calendars.

"I understand, Dr. Bennett, but Judge Warner announced his retirement today, and now everything's been pushed up."

He sighs, a sound that carries his weariness.

"Kacie, I can do the fifteenth or nothing at all. You know how it is."

I pinch the bridge of my nose, feeling the start of a headache.

"Fifteenth it is. I'll rearrange the docket. Again."

"If you can get this case, the Brown murder, and the Flores assault moved to that date, it would help me out."

His voice rattles through the phone with a seemingly impossible request. Instead of being a ringleader, I'd need to be a magician to make that magic happen. It would also help me, but those cases fall across three presiding judges, two with the most impossible schedules.

"I'll see what I can do."

It's the best commitment I can make at the moment. The phone call ends, and I'm left staring at the mess in my office. It's a reflection of my life. Takeout containers from this morning and yesterday are stacked precariously on the corner of my desk, a testament to the many nights spent working late. My case files are a jigsaw puzzle of criminal charges, witness statements, and plea bargains waiting to be struck.

A knock at my door barely registers before Ethan, my fellow ADA, steps inside. He's holding the Jackson file, a high-profile murder case that's become my waking nightmare.

"Kacie, we need to go over this."

His tone is urgent, and his face pinches with worry. I gesture to the chair opposite my desk, and he sits, sprawling the Jackson file across my desk.

"The defense is going to argue self-defense based on the knife wounds on his hands. We need to be prepared to counter that."

I nod, my mind racing through the evidence photos, the angles of the wounds, the blood spatter patterns, and other notes.

"The knife was in the defendant's hand when Mr. Jackson, the victim, was stabbed. It doesn't make sense for self-defense. The defendant was the aggressor."

Ethan leans forward, his eyes intense.

"I agree, but we need to make the jury see that. The defense is going to play up the victim's military background and his PTSD. They'll say Jackson was a trained government killer, confusing the defendant with an insurgent from his time over-seas. They'll flip this and paint the defendant as the victim."

I rake a hand over my curly black hair, a strand catching on my watch.

"We'll highlight the premeditation, the threats he made. We've got the text messages and the emails."

"We'll dissect the narrative they're trying to sell. Show motive and opportunity and expose every inconsistency in their self-defense claim."

Ethan's nod is sharp and decisive.

"I'm working to bring in our expert to discuss the nature of the wounds and reenact the scene. Make it clear that the wounds on the defendant don't match the story they're peddling."

I swipe at a stack of folders, searching for a specific report, my fingers brushing against the cool plastic of my keyboard.

"The transcript from the message is the most damning. It paints a picture to clear intent. Ethan."

He leans forward, his gaze meeting mine when his elbows hit the edge of the desk.

"We'll need to prep our witnesses again, ensure they're solid on the stand. The defense will be gunning to discredit them."

I nod, aware of the monumental task ahead.

"They'll be ready," I assure him, more a promise to myself than anything. "We're not letting this guy walk. Not after what he did to the victim."

I gather the content of the Jackson file to shove in the folder, the edges frayed from handling, and push it toward him. He stands, his eyes roaming stacks of documents for current cases, my notebooks scribbled with daily to-dos, and the collection of half-drunk coffee cups that I'm too lazy to wash out in the breakroom.

"We've got a strong case, Kacie." Ethan lingers in the doorway, clutching the file and tapping the frame. "Another late night for you?"

"You know it. Bennett is only giving me one day this month. He's off on some safari the following month, so everything is getting double booked. Not to mention Judge Warner's retirement announcement. Did you hear about that?"

He frowns, his finger tightening over the worn wood of the door trim.

"I did. It's no wonder we'll never catch up. If we could get more funding out of the city."

He sighs, and I roll my eyes. The fight with the mayor's office is recurring, resulting in the same old excuses. Bipartisan politics, corruption investigations, and failed voter amendments.

"Until then, I'll need to decide which place I'm ordering dinner from tonight." I lean back in my chair, going over the usual places in my mind. "You staying late?"

"No, it's the science fair at the school tonight. I've got to see how well the volcano *my son built* erupts."

His use of finger quotes to drive home the point that he made the volcano makes me chuckle. I don't have kids, married to my career of pursuing justice for the victims, but I hear enough stories from my colleagues to know that most parents construct their kids' science and history projects.

"Didn't you build a replica of the Alamo out of popsicle sticks last year?"

"Sugar cubes. And yes, it never ends." He groans in frustration. "Well, don't stay too late. I'll see ya in the morning."

I'm still chuckling when he leaves, relishing the simplicity of my life. Me and work are all I have to focus on. The former is severely neglected. The latter monopolizes my waking hours. I wouldn't have it any other way.

The door closes with a soft click, leaving me in the quiet

aftermath. I stand and stretch, my body stiff from hours of sitting, and my eyes burn with screen fatigue. I down the cold remains of my coffee and tidy up to create an open spot on my desk. The rest of my office is too overwhelming to even bother with.

I collapse in my chair, my hips hurting and my back aching from the hours hunched over my computer. Reaching for the phone, I dial the familiar number of the barbeque place down the street.

"The usual but lean brisket this time and an extra fried okra."

I change my order ahead of my doctor's appointment tomorrow morning. It's no secret that I've gained weight over the years. The size four I used to be in college progressed to a size eight in law school, which turned into a size twelve with all my years here.

Not that I like the weight gain. The rolls collecting around my middle don't make me feel confident being naked in relationships, so I avoid them. Every new year is paved with good intentions of losing weight, so I feel comfortable starting dating. My procrastination and lack of discipline in putting myself first always win, resulting in me staying married to my work and putting on the pounds.

The food arrives as delicious as ever, and I continue working. Hours slip past, marked only by the rhythmic tap of my keyboard and the occasional murmur of the janitors as they make their rounds. They're the witnesses to my relentless routine and the evidence of me living in my office.

When I finally call it a night, my eyes are dry, my veins vibrate with too much coffee, and my body slumps with exhaustion. The janitors nod as I pass with a wave. Night security stopped acknowledging me leave long ago, even though I mutter goodnight every time I exit. The streets are cold and empty. The synchronized traffic lights are the only signs of life around me. By the time I get home, I'm walking dead and can't even muster the energy to do anything more than brush my teeth and go to sleep.

The phone wails from my living room, where I dumped my purse last night. I peel my eyes open, regretting not washing my face and removing my stinging contacts. My eyes have difficulty focusing when I sit in bed to look at my alarm clock, seeing it's well past 8 am.

I set an early doctor's appointment to avoid missing work. When I realize I only have thirty minutes to shower, get ready, and be in the medical center, I fly out of bed, stubbing my toe and cussing up a storm.

Panic gives way to a flurry of activity as I make do with the minimalist effort in my appearance and dash out the door to race into rush hour traffic. I honk my horn, cut people off, and am a general asshole to get to his office fifteen minutes late.

The receptionist gives me a tremendous attitude about my tardiness before the nurse calls me back to that dreaded machine that tells the real story of my weight gain. I nearly faint when the scale climbs over one hundred and sixty pounds, only to be made worse when she takes my blood pressure. Both results are dizzying. My heart throbs in my chest when she guides me to the room, catching up on my medical history and medications since last year's appointment.

Once that's complete, she leaves me alone with my thoughts, wondering how I let it get this bad. Dr. Patel slips into the room with a grim look, and I immediately apologize for my tardiness. He shakes his head, humming at the results on the tablet, sitting on the stool the nurse vacated. Suddenly, I don't think his look has anything to do with my late arrival.

"Kacie, your blood pressure is high. Too high," he starts, not bothering with preambles. "And the weight gain is alarming. We'll run some labs today, but I suspect they'll confirm that you're on the verge of becoming prediabetic."

None of this is what I want to hear. I appreciate Dr. Patel's bluntness as I usually deal with the facts of the case, not emotions. This time, I wish he'd soften the blow.

"I've watched your health parameters climb steadily each year. It's time we talk about your lifestyle. Please walk me through a typical day. Work, diet, and exercise."

Oh no.

He asks me this every year. I have forgotten how much I dread the interview portion before the examination. It's always bad when he makes me account for my lack of work-life balance.

"Well," I begin, clearing my throat. "I'm at the office early, often skipping breakfast or grabbing something quick like a bagel from the cart in the tunnel. Lunch is . . . whenever I can fit it in, usually something fast."

He scribbles his notes on his tablet, waiting for me to continue.

"Dinner." I hesitate, the image of my overflowing trash bin of takeout containers flashing in my mind. "Is often the same. As for exercise, it's . . . sporadic at best."

"Are you eating out all three meals of the day? Is that what I am hearing?"

He knows this. I know he knows this. It's the same question he asked last year and the year before. It didn't start that way when I first got the job at the District Attorney's Office, but it sure is that way now.

"Um . . . yes."

Dr. Patel's lips press into a thin line.

"Kacie, this can't continue. Your career is important, but you're heading toward the edge of a cliff if you continue. High blood pressure, prediabetes—these are serious conditions that can lead to life-threatening events like heart attacks or strokes."

His words are startling, sending chills into my hair. I'm always good when put on the spot in the courtroom, but my usual defense mechanisms fail me in the doctor's office.

"Wow, that's hard, given my job. The demands are unrelenting. And with the DA election this year, we're getting a lot of pressure to clear up the case backlog."

He straightens his posture, regarding me with a blend of professional detachment and personal concern.

"I know you work hard, Kacie. You have an impressive record. You're one of the best prosecutors this city has. Your name is always in the paper, but what's the point if you're not around to enjoy the fruits of your labor? It would be best if you made some changes. *Immediately.*"

"What do I need to do? I mean, specifically. I can't exactly quit my job."

I feel glum as I thought I had more time to get this under control. The reality that I'm only thirty-seven years old and facing these health issues is upsetting. From the sound of it, things will only worsen if I don't get a handle on this. Dr. Patel leans forward, arms draped over his crossed legs.

"First, we need to address your diet. More whole foods, less processed meals. That means preparing food at home, which I know is a challenge with your schedule, but it's vital—and portion control. Cut back on the takeout. Reduce sodium and increase your intake of fruits, vegetables, and lean proteins. Small, frequent meals to stabilize your blood sugar."

I release an overwhelming breath—needing a personal chef. The simplicity of the advice belying its difficulty.

"And what else?"

"Exercise. At least thirty minutes a day. Walking, swimming, anything to get your heart rate up. A combination of cardio for your heart and weights for muscle strength. Find an activity you enjoy. It's not just about weight loss. It's about your heart health and managing stress."

Stress. I almost laugh. The concept is a familiar companion, an ever-present shadow in my life as an ADA. I can't help but think of my crammed schedule.

"I'll have to carve out the time, I guess."

The thought is as daunting as the high-profile cases under my charge.

Dr. Patel smiles, but it's a serious one.

"You must. It's non-negotiable. Meditation, yoga, deep-breathing exercises. Anything that can help you decompress. Stress exacerbates every condition you're facing."

All that sounds foreign to me, but the fear of having a heart attack or stroke is a powerful motivator.

"And about the pressure from your office," he adds, standing and moving close for the examination part. "Remember, your health won't wait for anyone's reelection. You're no good to anyone if you're hospitalized or worse." Dead. He doesn't have to say it. It's strongly implied, and my heart races in my chest as he places the stethoscope against it. "Deep breaths, please."

I need the deep breaths to calm down more than he needs them to hear my lungs. Worry settles into the pit of my stomach. The urgency of the situation is apparent. This isn't a closing argument I can charm my way through. This is my life, my well-being hanging in the balance.

"Okay." I steel myself with my newfound reality. "I'll make the changes. More home-cooked meals, more exercise. Less . . . everything else."

The examination continues, checking my ears, eyes, nose, and throat and confirming if I got my flu shot.

"Good."

Dr. Patel steps back, indicating the appointment is over.

"I want to see you back here in three months. We'll check

your progress and adjust if needed. And Kacie," he adds, pausing by the door. "Start today. There's no time to waste. The front desk will send the bloodwork order to the lab. They are right next door, so get that done."

"I will."

This day has to get better.

3

GIOVANNI

The bass thumps through the air, echoes off the gym walls, and goes straight into my head as I hum the song. Frank, one of our regular bodybuilding clients, discusses his limitations of obtaining a perfect deadlift in mid-conversation.

"It's all about the hips, the pull, and timing," I explain, my body moving instinctively to demonstrate the fluid motion required. I watch him while he does them, seeing the resistance in his hip hinge. "We need to work on your hip mobility. It's preventing you from going as low as you need to."

I point out my hinge compared to his, adjusting his posture as it wobbles against the resistance he encounters from that joint. All things he knows but slips into bad form to compensate for. I throw in a little dance, nothing much, just a bit of flair to lighten the mood. Frank chuckles, shaking his head.

"Gio, if I had half your moves, my wife would be a happy woman."

Happy is this place. It's my second home—a comfort amongst the free weights and treadmills. I chuckle, giving him a playful shove when my name is announced over the gym's intercom system.

"Continue that set, then move on to good mornings."

I immediately straighten, morphing into something more professional and more restrained as I stride to the front, where the management offices are.

Mr. Daniels is sitting at his desk, a guy twice my age yet absolutely shredded. Across from him is a woman, clutching her purse, looking uneasy with her shoulders raised to her ears. He stands upon my entry, leaving her to scramble to her feet when I face them.

"You need me?"

The question is directed at him, but my eyes linger on her. Her skin is a smooth canvas of caramel, unadorned by makeup, and honestly, it's refreshing. There are a lot of women in here who cake on the makeup to sweat it off when they work out. I never understand it.

And those eyes—the lightest green I've ever seen. They're trained on me with unnerving intensity as if demanding my best without uttering a word.

Her hair is black and luxuriant. The curls are free and wild around her face, with no attempt to straighten or tame them. I'm curious about what products she uses as I could use some advice for mine.

She's older and curvy, and her head tilts when my gaze lingers for too long. Under the harsh fluorescent lights, there's an understated beauty that doesn't scream for the attention of every man like those Instagram girls dragging their film equipment in here and monopolizing the machines.

"Gio, this is Kacie. She's new to the club."

Mr. Daniels extends a hand toward her while making introductions, drawing her eyes to him. I step forward, extending a hand, trying to channel my usual confidence under those watchful eyes.

"Nice to meet you, I'm Giovanni Marconi."

Her hand is soft and smooth when it slips into mine. Her eyebrows lift slightly when she looks up at me, the height difference between us mighty given her short stature.

"Kacie Yacob." I'm struck by the contrast between her light voice and her hard gaze. "It's my pleasure."

Mr. Daniels is all smiles.

"Kacie's looking to make some lifestyle changes, and I immediately thought of you. The best personal trainer we've got," he boasts, rounding the desk to clap a hand on my shoulder.

I can't help but glance at her again, hoping to catch a flicker of amusement, something to break the ice. But she's all business, her eyes still fixed on me with an unreadable expression.

"Personal training. I'm not sure I'm the gym type," she says, more a statement than a question. I smile, trying to ease her worries.

"Everyone's a gym type. You just don't know it yet. It's all about finding the right approach to working out. And I'm here to help with that."

Her expression remains unreadable, and after an awkward silence with her finally nodding, she looks at Mr. Daniels again.

"If you need anything else, Kacie, you know where to find me. Otherwise, you're in good hands."

Mr. Daniels is oblivious to his word choice, but I don't miss the rise of her dark eyebrows. Suddenly, it's just Kacie and me, her seriousness, my embarrassment for Mr. Daniels's comment, and the echo of the music still playing as I usher her out of his office.

I lead her to a quieter part of the gym, where the row of trainer's desks is situated along the glass front of the building. Offering her another seat, she sinks into it slowly, gazing around the crowded gym with a doubtful look.

"So, what are your goals?" I ask, pulling out a clipboard and attaching our questionnaire for all new personal training clients.

She hesitates, her gaze returning to mine while releasing a breath.

"To get healthier, I suppose. My doctor . . . well, let's just say he gave me quite the wake-up call."

I nod, understanding the subtext. The gym is full of wake-up calls and folks with New Year resolutions that will stop coming by mid-February.

"You've come to the right place then." My professionalism creeps back in now that my embarrassment has disappeared. "Do you mind if I ask you a few questions??"

She shakes her head rather than answering in that light voice of hers.

"Tell me what you hope to achieve. Both from what your doctor advised and what you'd like to see for yourself?"

Another long sigh loosens from her before she tells me about her doctor's visit and the changes she wants to make. As I jot down notes, I can feel her eyes on me, and I become acutely aware of every move I make. She's studying me but for what I don't know.

"Giovanni?"

Her intensity falters, her eyes darting around as she leans forward.

"I don't want you to think I always looked like this. I used to be . . . better."

Her face is etched in embarrassment, looking down and unwilling to meet my eyes. I've seen this look many times before and understand where it comes from. Societal norms say curvy women are unhealthy or unkept. Having been in the gym since I was a young teenager, I know there's not an ounce of truth in it.

"Honestly, Kacie, you're a very attractive lady. *Very.*" Her eyes lift to mine, curious to measure if I'm lying. "If you hadn't just told me about what your doctor said, I'd say you are perfect the way you are."

I come right out and say part of what I think. I refrain from saying she has a great ass and thick thighs, keeping it clean and classy. It crosses the line of professionalism, but with the slight smile sliding onto her lips, I doubt she'll report me.

"But feeling good about yourself and being healthy is far more important than what I or anyone else thinks."

Her smile broadens.

"Thank you. I appreciate that."

The glimmer of insecurity shifts the dynamic between us. Her shoulders relax, and the tension in her body fades when she leans back. The questions become easier and answered quickly, forming a general camaraderie between us.

"We'll start where you are and build from there. It's more than just fitness. It's a quest for overall health and wellness, crafting a sustainable lifestyle."

While we converse, the bustle of the gym vanishes into the background. It becomes just the two of us, lost in our own world. Her earnestness captivates me, and I am driven by a newfound desire to guide and impress her. I want to prove that placing her trust in me is the right choice.

"Now, tell me about your work."

As Kacie opens about her work, every sentence carves a scene in my mind. The early mornings are spent running the courthouse halls from one docket to another, sometimes overlapping, other times running past lunch, with meals skipped and cups of coffee suppressing her appetite. The late nights juggling emails and calls to the victims' families, confirming witnesses, chasing down evidence, and field experts.

When she speaks of her career, fierceness and passion are the opposite of her soft voice. Her dedication to her career resonates deeply with me, as I'm just as committed to my goal as hers. Not that bodybuilding is as important as her work, but the intensity and dedication are the same—something I respect.

I find myself leaning back, my clipboard forgotten, my role as her trainer momentarily set aside. I'm caught up in how she lights up when discussing a recent case she won. She's not just another client looking to shed pounds. She's doing compelling work with numerous people counting on her. It's worlds away from my day-to-day. I'm supposed to be crafting a fitness plan, but for a moment, I can only listen and be impressed.

"Your job . . . it's incredible, Kacie," I finally say, my voice tinged with genuine admiration. "The impact you have, the responsibility you carry—I can't imagine. Mad respect."

She gives a soft laugh, a sound that seems the opposite of her cold, harsh reality and sometimes underbelly of society's dealings.

"It's not what I expected when I first went to law school, but I wouldn't have it any other way. And thank you, Giovanni. It means a lot."

And it does. I can see it in how her posture loosens and the subtle lowering of her guard that invites me into her trusted space. I pick up my pen, scribbling notes on how I can train her while supporting her energy, stamina, and weight loss goals.

"Let's make sure your fitness regime supports your schedule, not competes with it," I suggest, already strategizing ways to integrate stress relief and functional strength into her program. "What you do is important, Kacie. I want to help you do it even better."

"I'd appreciate that. To be fully honest, I've never had a trainer before, so I don't know how this works."

I hear that a lot. She took the hard initial step of coming here. The rest is up to me to keep her coming.

"Now that I understand your busy lifestyle and where you want to be, we need to do the fitness assessment."

She immediately looks worried, her gaze leaving mine to circulate the busy gym again. I lean forward, touching her arm resting on the edge of the desk to draw her attention back to me.

"It's nothing to worry about, just a few simple tests to set a benchmark of where we need to start, and with consistency, you'll have a place to look back to showing your growth."

She looks unconvinced as I say it but nods all the same. I clutch the clipboard as I stand, intending to get her started with measurements before she bolts out the door. If that were to happen, I'd feel terrible.

"Tell you what, we have a room with most of the equipment we'll need for the assessment. Would you like to do it there? It's more private," I offer while she slowly stands, her hands still curled around her purse strap. Seeing how she's dressed in conservative leggings and a baggy T-shirt, I think the private room would be best.

"Please."

I flash her a reassuring smile and then guide her across the gym to the cluster of group fitness classes underway while explaining the place's layout. She remains silent, her keen eyes taking it all in as if listening to the facts of a case.

Quiet observance seems to be her modus operandi. I swing open the door to an assessment room, the shock of cold air causing her to shiver. That won't last long once she warms up by the movements.

"Alrighty, it's just me and you in here. Like Vegas, what happens here stays here."

She chuckles. Her smile is bright and a stunning contrast to her darker skin. It catches me off guard in the best way. I'm attracted to all races of women. It's quality over quantity for me. Having been in the gym for several years, I see all shapes, sizes, and skin tones. But that laugh and smile are hard to come by, and now that I got it, I want to hear more of it.

"I've never been to Vegas, so I'll take your word for it," she says quietly, lowering her purse to a box step and facing me.

I think back to my birthday last year when Seb flew a bunch of us to Vegas and had strippers waiting in the penthouse suite for us. It was shocking and not something I wanted to partake in. Even though it was my twenty-first birthday, and everyone was getting shit-faced, partying with the girls, I left to go gamble.

"You're not missing much, trust me." The sour taste from Sin City is still fresh in my mind. "Alright, let's start with the basics—your weight and measurements."

I lead the way to the scale, but when I glance back, she's rooted to the same spot, her body language screaming her uncomfortableness.

"Kacie." I soften my voice and extend a hand as an invitation. "This is just our starting line. Where we begin doesn't matter. It's where we're going that counts, okay?"

She nods, taking a deep breath that seems to steel her insides as she walks toward me. This is the first uncomfortable step of many more to come. She steps onto the scale with a determined readiness on her face. The digital figures flicker into place, but I keep my expression neutral and professional.

"Got it," I say, clicking my pen and scribbling on the clipboard without showing any sign of judgment. "This is just a number, Kacie. It's not the full story. Not by a long shot."

She exhales, her shoulders dropping when she sees the scale's display.

"Okay, what's next?"

"We'll take some basic measurements," I explain, pulling out the measuring tape. "It helps to track your progress. And remember, progress isn't always about the numbers. It's about how you feel, how much stronger and healthier you become, your energy level, and what your bloodwork says."

As I guide her through the process, I keep the conversation

light, tossing in a joke here and there, anything to keep her smile in place. And it works. Her laughter comes easier, and her nervous edge fades. I take her through five exercises to assess her general health. When we're done, she collapses on the floor, her back plastered to the mat as labored breaths pour out of her.

I plop down beside her with my trusty clipboard to detail what is happening now. I can't help glancing at her heaving chest, the shirt compressing, to get an idea as to the size of her breasts. Usually, I'm an ass man, but with how large they are, I could easily switch.

I shake my head, scolding myself for reducing this intelligent and accomplished woman to body parts. Thankfully, she doesn't notice when she sits up, mentions her schedule, and asks how to integrate a fitness routine.

"Fitness can be a great stress reliever. A way to clear your head after a day of . . . well, doing all the kick-ass stuff lawyers like you do."

She laughs, and it's music to my ears.

"I could use some stress relief. Between the trials and the paperwork, it's non-stop."

"That's what I'm here for. To relieve stress."

I didn't mean for it to sound as suggestive as it does, and my cheeks heat up. She doesn't flinch or pull back. Instead, she leans forward, a curious tilt to her head, and her light green eyes seem to flicker with interest.

There's a pause, an inhalation, and her gaze momentarily flickers to my lips. It's a heartbeat, maybe two, but it's enough to send a charge through me that no amount of weightlifting could match. I clear my throat, suddenly conscious of the space closing around us, the gym walls receding until it feels like we're in a tiny box.

"I mean, fitness to combat the stress of work," I clarify, my voice a touch more gravelly than intended. Her smile widens, and she sits back, breaking the momentary tension.

"Of course."

Her tone is light, yet that flicker of interest is new and can't be ignored.

We wrap up by setting a schedule that works with her court appearances and my sessions before walking her out. The door to the gym closes behind her, and I'm left with the echo of her laughter in my ears and the anticipation of seeing those green eyes again.

I might be here to help her relieve stress in more ways than one if she feels half of what I felt when she leaned in and gave me that look. Mr. Daniels gives me a friendly slap on the back as we watch her leave.

"How did it go?"

I can't help the grin that spreads across my face.

"Very promising."

The innuendo only known to me this time. Our training plan is solid, but the real question lies in what wasn't planned —the look, the lean-in, that spark. It's enough to make me look forward to our next session with a curiosity about more than sets and reps.

4

KACIE

As I push through the gym doors and step into the cool afternoon air, a wave of fatigue washes over me, tinged with a sense of accomplishment that's foreign and thrilling all at once. My muscles protest, already sore from Giovanni's carefully crafted torture. There's a fire within me, an exhilarating burn that murmurs of change. I couldn't be prouder of myself.

I'm doing this. I'm really doing this. The commitment, a promise made to myself in the sterile quiet of a doctor's office, now echoes in the beat of my heart and the sweat that cools on my back. I took the first step—literally and metaphorically—and didn't falter.

The gym lights fade behind me, but the memory of today's session lingers vividly and sharply. With his easy smile and confident nature, Giovanni pushed me further than I thought possible. He's good at what he does. Not just because he knows his way around the gym, there's kindness in his approach. A softness in his touch and a genuine desire to see me achieve my goals.

I can't help but replay that moment—the one that might

have been all in my head or the start of something unexpected. His words, an offer of stress relief, hung between us, intoxicating and inviting. His cheeks flushed with a color that matched the red of the gym's logo on his tight shirt, and for a second, time stood still.

Was it a pass? Was it the unintended slip of a tongue used in casual flirtation? I can't be sure, yet it piques my interest more than I care to admit. I can't remember the last time someone made a pass at me. The innocence with which it happened makes it more confusing.

Giovanni is handsome, the kind of handsome that's obvious to every woman who walks through the doors of his gym. His silky chocolate curls caught the light in that small workout room, and his thick mustache speaks to his carefree spirit. Something I find myself envious of.

I shake my head, trying to dislodge the image, the warm brown of his eyes, and the gold flakes close to his irises, but it's futile. He's made an impression that has my thoughts drifting to places they haven't wandered in far too long. Places involving him, me, and my bed.

The walk to my car combines limping from sore muscles and walking tall with pride. Each step reminds me of my work and the path I've now begun with the most attractive guy possible. And as I lower myself into the driver's seat and start the engine, the soreness of my body is a testament to a new beginning.

As I drive through the fast-food restaurant for the last time, a vow I make to myself, I can't shake the feeling that today marks a pivot. A shift in my life that's been too long about work and not enough about well-being. Maybe it's the endorphins talking, or perhaps it's the thought of those curls and that moment of shared attraction that left me feeling strangely . . . alive. I'm already looking forward to the next session, the burn, the push, and whatever it is that's sparking between Giovanni and me. There's a journey ahead, and I'm ready to see where it leads for the first time in a long while. With a smile tugging at the corner of my lips, I realize I'm eager for the week ahead.

⚖

Monday morning arrives faster than I had hoped. I'm acutely aware of every sore muscle as I navigate the familiar halls of the courthouse, each step a reminder of Saturday's physical exertions. The ache was so deeply set in my muscles the next day that I used my hands on the walls to lift off the toilet. I probably shouldn't have caught up on my sleep like I'm guilty of doing every Sunday. I probably should have walked off the soreness as he advised during my workout, but I didn't, and now I'm paying the price.

I'm shuffling papers on my desk, trying to focus on the cases before me, when Ethan saunters in, his brow furrowed as he holds his steaming cup of coffee.

"Good morning, Kacie."

He observes my careful movements as I rise to retrieve my notes from the round table across the room.

"Why are you moving like you just went ten rounds in the ring?"

I glance up, the corner of my mouth lifting.

"Started working out with a personal trainer at the gym," I confess, feeling pride and embarrassment at the admission. "I guess I'm more out of shape than I thought."

Ethan's eyes widen in mock horror.

"You? The woman who runs on a slow drip of coffee, carbs, and courtroom adrenaline. I don't believe it."

His tone is teasing, but there's a flicker of genuine surprise there. I can't resist rolling my eyes, but his question nudges my thoughts toward Giovanni—the burn of the workout, the heat of attraction, and the unexpected spark of connection.

"It was . . . interesting."

My words trail off as I realize just how true they are. The way Giovanni's curls fell across his forehead, the warmth of his smile, and the redness that crept up his cheeks flash back with vivid clarity.

"Interesting. How?"

Ever the investigator, he leans against my desk while sipping his coffee. I shake my head, flipping a file open to hide behind the pretense of work.

"Just different from what I'm used to," I deflect but smile at the papers in my hand.

I shouldn't be thinking of Giovanni as much as I am. I don't think it's normal to crush on a guy I just met. But maybe this happens with all new gym people. I'm sure I'm not the first woman to find him attractive. Between his easygoing personality, stunning dark eyes, and fantastic physique, he probably already has a girlfriend and many others waiting in the wings should they break up.

"It's good that you're getting back to it. I used to be a runner back in the day." He steps away from my desk when I walk over and sit down. "I've been thinking about starting again. I'm not getting any younger, and I could use a way to decompress from this place."

When he mentions stress and needing an outlet, my mind goes straight to Giovanni and working out stress with him. Not in the gym, but the dream I had of him and me making out at my place and then having sex on my bed. It was hot and steamy, something that would never happen in real life, but it was a delicious fantasy. A sneaky smile appears on my face, and I look away.

"What's so funny about that? I know I'm out of shape, but it's—" Ethan takes my smile as a slight against his reinstatement of running, and I quickly dissolve that.

"I'm not laughing at you. Just something that happened this weekend," I interrupt, easing over his bruised ego.

Something I can relate to as I'm overly sensitive about my fitness journey, so I would never criticize someone else.

"I think it's a great idea, and it would get you out of here earlier. That will be one of my goals, not working past six so I can get to the gym at a reasonable hour."

He relaxes, smoothing his shirt in a gesture of resettling his dignity.

"Right," he agrees, his stance more confident now.

I turn back to my files, but my mind lingers on Giovanni—the way he moved, his cheeks flush, the promise of what's to come. It's a new motivation to leave the office while there's still daylight.

"Did you want to review this week's cases and docket, Kacie?"

"Of course."

I shake away my lingering thoughts, motioning to the chair across from me and clearing some things off my desk. We spend the next two hours reviewing motions and countermotions to be filed, witnesses to be confirmed, and compiling emails to the various courts about the cases. It's productive and sets the course for a smoother day, especially with both of us intending to leave early.

I offered to include Ethan on my lunch delivery order, but his wife had already packed his lunch, something she does most days for him. Once he leaves my office, I pick up my phone to order my usual cheeseburger and fries when Giovanni's words about diet and nutrition float through my mind. He said every decision is a vote toward or away from my goals and everything in moderation.

With only coffee for breakfast and desperately craving my delicious, high-calorie meal, I sigh and choose health over taste. I order a salad with protein and put a tally mark on my telephone pad as a vote for my goals.

Work continues to pour in, filled with back-to-back meetings, calls, and the never-ending email inbox. My salad gets scarfed down through all of it, my stomach rumbling for more food, which I fill with a few unhealthy snacks from the vending machine and more coffee. When my alarm rings at six o'clock, I'm tired, my hips and back ache, and I dread committing to the gym. The only saving grace is Giovanni.

I lock the door to my office, change into my gym clothes, and drag my hair into a bun. I didn't work out in my makeup on Saturday, and I'm curious what Giovanni will think when he sees me with it today. Will he make another pass, or did I fabricate the whole thing? If he does it again, how should I respond?

That thought gets me out the door and over to the gym faster than it should, considering I'm cutting people off in traffic even though I have a dedicated hour with him. When I arrive at the gym, the atmosphere is high energy, with the music blasting and people all over. I place my purse in the locker and spin the dial, looking across the gym floor until I spot Giovanni. He's in his element, dancing to the music next to a petite blonde. His curls are an unruly dark halo around his head, bouncing with each movement.

There's an ease about him, an infectious freedom while the woman continues working out. She's fit, muscles evident in her back and arms as she pulls on the cable. Her thighs and butt are thick like mine, yet where she is curt with definition, I am not. A wave of insecurity ripples through me as I watch them interact casually. Of course, he'd be into someone who looks like her—a fitness model with her blonde ponytail and blue eyes, a perfect smile flashing at him, and him returning one of his own.

When he catches me looking at him, he straightens, the

professional façade falling into place and away from the playful, carefree version saved for her. It bothers me more than it should. He strides toward me.

"Hey, Kacie."

"Hey," I reply, trying to keep my tone light and casual. Inside, I'm anything but. I take him in—the lean muscles of his arms, the broad set of his shoulders, the way his gym shirt stretches across his chest, clinging just right. His butt is high and tight from doing a zillion squats, and his thighs are bulky and cut, peering out from the hem of his shorts. He's the kind of handsome man who doesn't need to try, he just is.

"Ready for today's torture?" he jokes, but there's a challenge in his eyes, a silent question of whether I'll rise to it.

"Bring it on," I say, more bravely than I feel remembering the challenge of getting off the toilet. He touches my shoulder, the warmth burning through the fabric of my shirt as he walks me over to something called a TRX.

"I'm kidding, of course. How do you feel?" His tone is serious, all business, and now the true torture begins.

"I'm sore but good."

His eyebrow lifts at my words as though they sound like an unintended innuendo of my own. He leans over, moving his ear toward my face. His cologne invades my senses, a clean fragrance that enhances my growing infatuation with him.

"Come again? I didn't hear that."

Thinking he does indeed hear it and wants me to repeat it, I change my word choice by raising my voice over the loud bass throbbing through the speaker directly overhead.

"Good. Ready for more."

He comes away with a smile, muttering something that gets lost in the music, but his expression says it all. He did hear me the first time, and my heart spikes at the thought of the flirting starting even earlier in the workout.

The moment passes as he turns toward the apparatus

fastened to the top of the bar, yelling the instructions and demonstrating them for me. When it's my turn, he adjusts the length to accommodate my short arms and taps the side of my tennis shoes for me to widen my feet.

Once my form is set, he counts the reps for me. I'm groaning all the way through, the burn in my arms growing as his enthusiasm for me grows too. With his encouragement, I push myself harder to earn his praise and feel accomplished.

Praise is my kryptonite.

Throughout college and law school, I strived for the teachers and professors praise to keep going through the most challenging struggles. It drove me more than the perfect grades and high scores I received. Respect as a minority is hard-earned sometimes. When it comes, I feel on top of the world.

Praise is not given in a courtroom or the endless hours I spend in my office. It's offered in the private chambers of grieving families when their loved ones receive justice by winning their case. Those are getting rarer with the backlog of cases due to the flooding of the criminal court building during Hurricane Harvey and the pandemic shutting down the courts for months. The backlog is well past three years and continues to grow with each new administration.

Sweat forms on my chest, forehead, and back. I dot the neckline of my shirt when I wipe my face on it, forgetting I'm wearing makeup. Shoot.

"Do we need to take a break?"

Giovanni's gorgeous dark eyes flash to mine with concern.

"No, we've barely just begun."

"Good, let's continue warming up, and then we'll move on to the workout," he explains, demonstrating another exercise while my mind cries.

This is only the warm-up. I'll be drenched by the time we're done, and he won't be flirting with me then.

He walks me through another two exercises, my breath

heaving in and out. I could have sworn he was staring at my chest before his eyes darted away when I caught him. I'll have to pay closer attention to see if he does it again.

When the warm-up is finally over, I'm ready to collapse on the stretching mat beside me until he suggests a water break. Forgetting to bring a water bottle, I make for the water fountain across the gym, away from Giovanni, so I can wipe the sweat from my face and try to fix my hair. Looking cute while working out is a lost cause, something the petite blonde does and makes look easy.

When I'm better assembled and can breathe again, I see Giovanni standing in a row of machines, bent over, getting things ready for us when she approaches him. I don't hesitate to make a beeline for him. I'm curious about what they are to each other, and I'm paying for this hour of his time. She isn't— even if that sounds a little possessive of me.

"You ready to go again?" Giovanni directs at me, and her eyes follow. She's very pretty, definitely his age. The familiarity of her hand on his arm speaks volumes.

"I am." I edge closer, my investigative skills getting the best of me. "Is this your girlfriend?"

The reaction is immediate. Giovanni's cheeks color with a flush, and the girl gives me a look that's hard to read before her hand falls away from him.

"I'll check on you tomorrow, Gio," she says, with a swift departure, leaving a tense silence in her wake.

I didn't intend to provoke such a harsh response, and a flicker of guilt passes through me for the blunt intrusion. But it's quickly replaced by a sharp spike of something else—relief and satisfaction. I push the feeling aside.

Giovanni clears his throat, looking anywhere but at me.

"No, she's not my girlfriend."

"But you like her."

His expression turns into misery when he raises those dark eyes to mine. I'm surprised by my forwardness and the impulse that drove the question. Yet here we are, standing in a sliver of honesty as raw as an exposed nerve.

"Is it that obvious?"

His lip catches in his teeth, and if I hadn't seen his charismatic, playful personality the other day, I wouldn't believe this version of him. The confident guy dancing in a packed gym looks both resigned and discouraged. I edge closer, intentionally using a gentler tone.

"Maybe to someone paying very close attention, but not really," I admit, still curious about the history between them. Those beautiful eyes of his turn piercing, as if trying to find an answer without asking.

"And you were paying very close attention?"

There it is. The same look as Saturday and the spark I've thought nonstop about. However, I can't give it much credo, as he just admitted to having feelings for someone else. Perhaps the spark I think I felt is only in my head.

"I'm trained to be observant. To see things that others don't."

It's the truth. Keen observation skills are required when picking my jurors, advising my investigators, and preparing my witnesses.

"Oh, of course, right," he says in a rush, his brown hair shaking as he nods.

My eyes search his face, watching a myriad of emotions play across it until he straightens and resumes his trainer mode. As we continue our session, I become more aware of Giovanni—the trainer and the man. There's a story there, and while curiosity tugs at me, I respect his privacy.

The hand on the clock races toward the top of the hour, signifying the end of my exclusive time with him. With the last lift completed, I collapse on the mat near where we started, him standing over me until he swings down to join me.

Sweat leaks from my pores as I lay on my back, staring at the ceiling tiles when his handsome face appears.

"Kacie?"

My gaze moves to him as he runs a finger over his mustache to straighten the hair.

"Yeah?"

"She's getting married."

I can't quite read the emotion in Giovanni's eyes as he confesses, but the fact that he shares this with me while I'm vulnerable and sprawled on a gym mat, looking sweaty and feeling gross, somehow bridges the gap that's sprung up between us. His admission hangs in the air, as heavy as the weights we've been lifting.

"She's getting married," he repeats, his voice carrying a tinge of something I can't place. Is it sorrow? Resignation?

I prop myself on my elbows and turn to face him fully.

"That must be tough," I offer, trying to provide a space for him to express whatever he's holding back. He shrugs, a casual lift of his shoulders that doesn't quite match the dense gravity in his eyes.

"Yeah, I never did shoot my shot."

There's an unspoken invitation in his words, a chance for me to ask more, to delve deeper into his personal life. But I hesitate, mindful of the boundaries that should exist between us. Since he likes another, I'm simply lusting after his good looks and fantastic body. I change the subject instead.

"Well, she's missing out," I say, mustering an encouraging tone to lighten the mood. "Any woman would be lucky to have you."

His eyes lock with mine, and there's a flicker of surprise, then something warmer that makes my heart skip a beat. He smiles at me, a genuine one this time, and I can't help but return it.

"Thanks, Kacie," he murmurs, his voice sounding deeper than before. "You did great today. Good job."

He juts out a tight fist between us, looking at me expectantly until it dawns on me.

"A fist bump?" I laugh, amused by this innocent gesture. I bump him once, and he does it in return. "I haven't done one of these in . . . I don't even know how long."

"Good. It will be our thing now."

His words are teasing, but they unexpectedly imprint on me.

Our thing.

A 'thing' that's just ours plays over in my mind. That petite blonde isn't the only one with a connection to him now. He swiftly stands, offering both hands to help me up. When my thighs give out from fatigue and I fall toward the floor, he swiftly catches me, making me feel weightless in his strong arms. His strength is a living testament to his profession and dedication. But in this moment, as I am suspended in his grip, it's incredibly personal.

"Gotcha."

His voice rumbles close to my ear. The warmth from his body is a stark contrast to the cool air of the gym, and I'm acutely aware of every point where we are touching.

"Thanks," I manage to say, my voice steadier than my legs. As he helps me back to my feet, I'm reluctant to let go of him. He smiles, that easy, disarming one.

"An Epsom salt bath will help with the soreness. Next time, we'll stop earlier and walk the treadmill together. That helps as well."

"Okay."

"And Kacie. I'm proud of the work you put into tonight. You should be too."

His eyes dance with the lightness I saw when he looked at her, warming my heart as his praise tickles my brain. I nod, unable to think of a witty retort as I wobble to the locker on tired legs that feel like I'm floating on air.

5

GIOVANNI

"I've got next," I holler over the sounds of explosions and gunfire as Seb hogs the controls for Call of Duty. I could play from my laptop. I brought my headset, but nothing beats playing on the big screen in his theater room. Seb grins, his eyes fixed on the game as he maneuvers through a virtual battlefield, his fingers rushing over the controller.

"You're just jealous because I'm owning this round," he brags, his eyes never leaving the screen.

He's always been competitive, but tonight, he's on another level. I grab a cold water bottle from the fridge and a bag of trail mix, waiting for my turn and watching him play.

"So, how was New York City with Chloe?" I ask, trying to sound casual.

I've been curious ever since he mentioned he was spending the holiday there. I can't recall if he's ever been as an adult. His mamma always flew there to shop during the holidays, but I don't think she ever took him. He pauses the game and turns to me with a faraway look.

"Man, it was incredible. Chloe knows the city like the back of her hand. We saw the ball drop at Times Square, the suite at

43

the hotel was cool, and the rooftop bar was even better. Out of respect for my girl, I won't say much, but let me tell you, she brought a suitcase full of lingerie. Lingerie, man! On vacation! Can you believe that? I almost died and went to Heaven when she opened that thing. Let's say she wasn't walking right the whole trip."

He's grinning ear to ear. I can only imagine how happy he was by the look on his face now.

"So better than Cabo?" I ask, and he lobs the controller at my head, which I easily dodge since he's slow and hasn't been to the gym in weeks.

"Fuck Cabo. And fuck you for bringing it up." He stands, getting all blowhard with me, and I laugh. "Now give me back my controller. It's still not your turn."

It's undoubtedly my turn since his character died when he thought he paused the game. I continue munching on my snack when he stomps over, grabs the controller, and slaps me on the back of my head.

"Chill, man. That hurt."

I rub the sore spot he left as he grumbles and walks back to his chair in front of the screen. Cabo and the whole ordeal with Veronica still bothers him. Chloe understood from what he told me, and they are together now, so he shouldn't be so upset over it.

I asked if it was the money he spent on Veronica that day he went to see my dad, that she lied to try to trap him, or the possibility of being a dad and having to grow up. He never answered me. Just told me to mind my own fucking business and has been snappish about it ever since.

"You know I don't want to talk about that shit, and here you're bringing it up when I was talking about my nice vacation."

His face is sour, and his tone is grumpy as he spreads out to play another round.

"Hey, what about you and Jenna?" Seb asks suddenly, a retaliatory glint in his eyes.

I shake my head a bit too quickly.

"Nah, let's not go there. She's getting married, and it's just a crush. Nothing more."

Seb raises an eyebrow but, unlike me, doesn't press further. He resumes his game, and I take the opportunity to shift the topic back to him and Chloe.

"How did you know an older woman would make you happy?"

I can't help but think about Kacie, who's much older than me. She's been on my mind lately, and I wonder if age makes a difference in relationships. It doesn't bother Paolo. Seb is happier and more stable than I've ever seen him. He pauses the game again and leans back, looking thoughtful.

"It isn't about her being older, dumbass. It's how she accepts me for me. She doesn't try to change me, tell me to calm down, or be quiet. But she also doesn't put up with any of my bullshit, and she's generally a very nice person. It doesn't hurt that she's hot as hell and a real tiger in the sheets."

He winks, finding another opportunity to brag about his sex life, which is not what I want to hear. Seb is very visual, and outside beauty is important to him. I'm different in that I must know the person first. It's the inside that I'm drawn to. Sure, an attractive woman catches my eye, but it's their thoughts, emotions, and feelings that make my cock hard.

Kacie didn't judge me when I confessed to liking an engaged woman. She looked sympathetic as if understanding how wanting someone I can't have feels. In her light voice, she said it was Jenna's loss, as if I'm worthy of something better, someone better. It changed my whole thinking around. Jenna and I had always gotten along, the touching and flirting making me think it meant something when it didn't by the ring on her finger. Now I have a spark with Kacie.

Twice. My flirting with Jenna is shallow and hollow compared to my honest conversations with Kacie about her career and life.

Kacie speaks for those who don't have a voice, the victims of heinous crimes. Prosecuting bad people who do bad things hasn't made her jaded or harsh. She's kind and empathetic with a seemingly soft heart. She wouldn't intentionally hurt anyone. It's not in her makeup or her profession to do so. It's an attractive quality I didn't even know I was drawn to. I nod, absorbing his words with my thoughts.

"But do you think someone older with more life experience is better at . . . protecting your heart?"

He chuckles, knowing where I am going with this. He always teases me about being too sensitive, but then he is the first to defend me if anyone else says that. It's a strange friendship we have at times.

"Again, not about the age. It's about the person. Are you asking if life kicks people in the ass and shapes them? Well, hell yeah. Life's a bitch sometimes. I didn't ask for my parents to die, but it happened and changed me in ways I don't want to talk about. No offense, man."

I never take offense to Seb's avoidance of talking about his parents. I never bring it up, and he rarely does, usually just a few comments each year around the date they died or the holidays.

"You gotta figure out what you need. And not what you *think* you need," he warns, his expression serious. "That's a big difference. I thought I wanted hot chicks all the time. Turns out I want my hot chick. Chloe's been through enough to know what she wants and how to handle a relationship, especially with me. She's straightforward, with no games and no drama. I always know where I stand with her. There's no guessing. Oh, and she's not out fucking other guys to decide who she likes better. That shit happens all the time with chicks our age, and I fucking hate it. Anyway, that's what I need. What you need is probably different."

I mull over his words. They make a lot of sense, and I can see the change in Seb. This whole conversation is a testament to her hand in his life. Before, he would have shoved me away and told me to stop acting like a pussy or to go eat some pussy. But now, he's thoughtful and a little introspective, both a nice surprise.

"But hey," he adds, picking up the controller again, "you gotta figure out what works for you."

It's not about chasing someone I can't have, like Jenna. It's about finding someone who resonates with me and what I need. Maybe that person is Kacie.

She's more grounded and sincere than women my age. Maybe I need someone who's seen more of the world and understands the value of honesty and depth in a relationship. Someone who understands my drive for the stage as she's just as driven in her career.

Kacie wouldn't lead me on like Jenna. She wouldn't flirt with me and be committed to another. No, Kacie has impeccable integrity.

"Who's the chick that has your panties in a wad, anyway? If not that Jenna chick, then who? Is she an older broad like mine? Is that why you're asking?"

His eyes never leave the screen when he yells out all his questions. I'm hesitant to answer as Seb can either be insulting or supportive.

"Not a broad, but yes, an older woman. I assume similar in age to yours, but not exactly sure."

I'd never dare ask how old his girlfriend is, or any woman for that matter. I'm certain they are in the same range, but does it matter if one is older or younger by a few years?

"Her name is Kacie. She's a new client of mine."

"Ah, dipping in the company ink. Don't get fired for that

shit. I still don't know how Paolo and his woman get away with it. Chloe tells me they hide it well, but I'd fire someone at my company if they did that shit."

The fact that he has no idea what happens at his company, only what's told to him at the board meetings, makes this statement laughable. Regardless, I get what he's saying. Being Mr. Daniels's favorite and most successful trainer, I doubt this will be an issue, especially since it's not in any employee handbook I've seen.

"Unless you already love this chick. Then that's different. I'd kill the guy that stands between me and my girl."

That statement speaks volumes about how he really feels. If I were to ask him outright if he loved her, he'd say, "Shut the fuck up," and probably try to beat my ass. He's a conundrum, stating exactly what he wants to anyone at any time, but direct confrontation gets met with massive avoidance. If I didn't know him as long as I have, I'd say he's a bully. Sometimes he is. Mostly, it's an avoidance of the hurt and pain he's been through and doesn't want to experience again. I can't blame the guy. He's had the worst of it.

"Yeah, thanks, Sebby, I appreciate it," I say, watching him play for a few more minutes.

"No problem, now go see if the pizza is ready. Ms. Martha said she's making one for each of us."

I've told him several times that I'm in training, but he doesn't seem to care. Food is his love language—he always wants to ply people with it. It's overbearing but still caring.

"It's supposed to be my turn."

I stand, collecting my trash to throw away as I down the remains of the water bottle.

"Go get the pizzas, and you can play after," he commands, never looking away, even though he can play on his gaming system all day on his own and could give me a chance instead. "And grab me a beer, but only one. I'm cutting back on the alcohol. Gotta lose some weight in my belly, so my dick looks bigger."

"I'm pretty sure that's not how it works."

Pizza, beer, the candy wrappers on the couch next to him. If he wants to lose weight, he needs to clean up his diet and increase his workouts with me. He shoots me the middle finger, then swears as he almost gets killed in his game.

"Fuck you, Gio. What do you know? Now go."

"I'm only a personal trainer with a degree in nutrition and health," I mumble over the racket of the machine gun he's using, knowing he can't hear me.

As I jog downstairs, I think about Kacie and the possibility of exploring something real with her. Maybe it's time to take a chance. Starting tomorrow at our next session.

I could hardly sleep last night, Kacie occupying my thoughts after leaving Seb's place and growing weary of his constant ribbing about already falling in love with her. That's not the case, even though love is something that I give freely compared to his stingy ass.

It's understandable, coming from a big, rambunctious family such as mine, whereas he's been alone for a few years and is still adjusting. Regardless, I left motivated and determined to see if there was something between us or if I was making it up in my head.

Without much to do this morning, I head to the gym early to get my workout in before my clients come in. Marco can't train today. He's helping his mamma move furniture. The gym regulars are sparse this morning.

Wednesdays are usually the quietest day of the week, which I normally like, except today, it makes the clock crawl toward my dedicated time with Kacie. I should get her number, not from the computer system, but from her, text her, and possibly pressure her to come in earlier.

I immediately dismiss that thought, knowing it's taking her away from her important job for my selfish reasons. She mentioned ordering a salad instead of her usual fast food the other day. Maybe I can coax her into coming over to learn about nutrition and meal prep together. She admitted not knowing how to cook when we did sit-ups on Saturday. Possibly kill two birds with one stone.

The day blurs once my clients arrive, with a couple of meal breaks in between. I shower before she comes, wanting to smell fresh with how close I'll get to her this workout. It's also another way to test if there's something between us and not look foolish like I did, crushing on Jenna. I'm already waiting by the door when I see her crossing the parking lot with a slight limp on her right foot and battling against the wind, pushing her dark curls into her face.

"Hey there," I greet as she approaches. She appears momentarily surprised. "Is your foot alright, Kacie?"

"Oh, hi."

She hesitates, a flicker of pain crossing her expression.

"Um, just missed a step at work. It's nothing," she assures, maintaining a tough front. I open the gym door wider, not convinced.

"You sure? We can ice it. Better to check it now than let it ruin your workout."

She nods, reluctantly agreeing as the wind whips another curl into her face.

"Alright, Giovanni, maybe just a quick ice then."

She limps to the nearest bench in the gym's entryway, close to the smoothie bar where we have crushed ice for drinks and freezer bags filled with ice for injuries on the floor. As she settles, I catch the scent of her shampoo, something fruity and great smelling.

The moment feels strangely intimate, contrasting with the metallic clangs and thuds from the gym floor. While I fetch the ice, the idea of meal prepping together resurfaces. The gym could be our starting point, not just for workouts but for building healthier habits for her and to see where it goes with us.

Returning with the ice, I hand it over, our fingers brushing momentarily. Hers are cold, whereas mine are warm. It makes me curious if she's a cuddler or not. I shake my head at those thoughts, not wanting to get ahead of myself, and end up having two crushes for unavailable women.

"Here you go. Just keep this on for a bit," I instruct, trying to keep my tone professional.

"Thanks." She presses the ice against her ankle. "I appreciate it."

I sit beside her, maintaining a respectful distance while observing her tentative smile.

"No problem at all. It's what I'm here for." I pause and then decide to shoot my shot. "You know, speaking of taking care, you mentioned wanting to eat healthier, right? Maybe we could try some meal prep. I could show you some simple recipes to help you get started."

Those light green eyes bore into me for several long seconds, and I begin to doubt my offering is a good idea.

"I'd like that." There's a warmth in her light voice that wasn't there before. "I'm clueless in the kitchen. Any help would be nice."

"Great," I say, more enthusiastically than I intended. "It's a date then. I mean—not a date, but a plan. A cooking plan."

She laughs, and the sound eases my nervousness.

"A cooking plan sounds perfect. But I must confess, I don't have the stuff to do meal prep." Her eyes look around the gym as if she's spilling state secrets and then return to mine with a crooked little smile. "Am I even allowed to say something like that in a place like this?"

It's adorable watching another side of her personality come out. Her confession brings a genuine smile to my face.

"Your secret is safe with me," I reassure her, resisting the urge to touch her. "We'll start from scratch. I'll make a list of everything you need. If you like, we'll go shopping together— make an adventure out of it."

She seems taken aback by the offer, but a twinkle in her eye wasn't there before.

"You'd help me with that?"

"Of course. Eating right is just as important as the workout. And let's be honest, navigating those grocery store aisles at this time of night is the real cardio."

Her laughter rings out again, and I can't help but feel a sense of accomplishment.

"I guess I'm in for a full fitness experience then."

"Absolutely. Plus, it'll be fun. I promise."

"Wait, did you mean tonight?"

Her eyebrows draw together as if something else could be on her schedule.

"You're my last client of the day." I shrug, trying to appear casual and not overly excited about where this might lead. "We can work out, go shopping, and then meal prep. Or is that too presumptuous of me to do in one night?"

I flash her my best smile, hoping to convince her to agree. She laughs, the ice slipping from her ankle in the process with a light thud to the floor. I reach over to pick it up as she does too. The neckline of her oversized t-shirt falls forward, exposing a sea of flawless caramel skin with a lot of spillage from her sports bra.

My cock immediately stiffens at the sight, and thinking about burying my face in them has me flushing when she catches me. The surprising thing is she doesn't rush to fix her shirt. Instead, she meets my gaze squarely, unembarrassed, with a trace of a smile still playing on her lips. Time freezes until I clear my throat and hand her the ice pack, our fingers brushing with electricity between them.

"So, what do you say?" I ask, once more striving for a casual tone.

She takes the ice pack back, holding my gaze for a moment longer than necessary, the air between us thick with the possibility of 'what if.' The corners of her mouth curving up in a decision that seems to be about more than just meal prep.

"Yes, Giovanni." Her voice is soft as my name falls from her glossy lips. "Working out, shopping, and *cooking* sounds like a perfect plan."

I shot my shot, and it worked. She's giving me a chance. She didn't falter or back away when I was ogling her, nor did she fix her shirt, which still shows more skin than usual. I wonder if that could have been intentional on her part. My mind races with possibilities.

"Perfect," I reply, my knee bouncing with barely contained excitement. "I'll make sure it's worth your while."

"I'm sure you will," she says with a wink, sliding the ice pack back onto her ankle.

I adjust on the bench next to her, that surprisingly sassy remark making me even harder than seeing that silky skin awaiting my touch, lips, and tongue. I clear my throat again and look down at my hands while calming myself. It's just meal prep, which could lead to other things but might not.

Besides, I might not like her, or she might not like me. Either way, I can't have casual sex like Seb. I tried, and it's literally the worst. No connection, no emotional intimacy, just physical bodies slapping together doesn't do it for me. But getting to know her more might be on the table tonight, depending on how much she flirts back.

"I guess we should get started since we have a long night ahead."

She removes the ice pack to rotate her still swollen ankle.

"Attagirl," I murmur as I help her up, mindful of her injury.

"Did you just praise me for wanting to work out?" she questions with my arm still clutching her side to ensure she doesn't hurt it worst and can't go through with our night. I flush at my word choice, hoping she doesn't think badly of me for saying it.

"It sort of just slipped out. If you don't like it—"

Her nails dig into my arm briefly, hinting at her strength or perhaps an inadvertent response.

"No, it's fine. I don't mind a bit of encouragement. It makes me feel like I'm doing something right."

Her words lift the embarrassment from my face, and I can't help the grin that forms in its place.

"Good, because you are."

It's not just about the workout. It's about her willingness to step outside her comfort zone to trust me with more than just her fitness goals—her nutrition too.

As we move toward the gym floor to focus on upper body exercises, I can sense the shift in our dynamic. The casual banter is still there, but there's a new layer, a shared anticipation for the evening ahead. And while I'm still her trainer, responsible for watching over her form and technique, I'm also becoming something else—a friend, hopefully even more.

6

KACIE

My mind is reeling. We're icing my ankle one minute, and Giovanni asks me out the next. Well, sort of. His quick backtrack to 'cooking plan' was almost as smooth as his recovery after getting caught staring a bit too long at my chest. The flush that crept up his neck told stories he couldn't hide, and honestly, I found it endearing.

How long has it been since someone looked at me with that kind of desire? Like last time he dropped an innuendo, I didn't back away, and I wasn't going to this time. I wanted to bask in the feeling of an attractive younger guy looking at me as he did on Saturday and Monday.

The workout flew by despite my throbbing ankle. The story of running for the elevator and getting tripped by my briefcase strap was too ridiculous to tell him. But come hell or high water, I wasn't missing my dedicated hour to see him. I'm even more happy to be here with him as he seems to be opening up to me. His smile flashes faster, his laugh is louder, and he throws in a couple of dance moves to distract me from the heavyweight he stacks on the machine.

I'm nearly about to collapse, pushing the last and heaviest

set of my bench presses, when my arms falter. His thighs surround the sides of the bench, grabbing the bar to lift off me and putting his tight crotch within eyeshot. For a split second, I get a perfect view of that long shaft tucked to one side of his compression shorts when I see up the leg of his shorts.

"Holy shit," slips past my lips, and I squirm, thinking about what that would feel like.

The last time I had a snake that size, I was in an orgasm coma for days. Blood surges to my privates at the memory of that efficient lover from long ago. I've had a few lovers since, but none as proficient and skilled as him. Indeed, Giovanni must have had some experience growing up with a thing that big. I'm so lost in my thoughts that I almost don't register the 'good girl' that slips from his lips.

With the bar firmly racked, he offers a hand to help me sit on the end of the bench to catch my breath. As a workout reference guide, he's logging stuff into my training app as he does every session in case I want to work out without him. I guarantee that's never happening. His words nag at my mind long enough that I have to ask.

"Did you just say, good girl? Or am I hearing things?"

His flush is immediate. The reddening of his skin is an admission of his guilt.

"I did."

His confession is swift, almost the same slip as the words themselves. His gaze holds mine for a few seconds, a strange tension coiling between us until he raises his shoulders, unsure what else to say.

Good girl.

No man has ever said that to me. The pragmatic and equalizing side of me hates it. How dare he call me a girl when I'm a woman. And an older woman at that. The judgment of being called good or bad is as condemning as growing up in the southern Delta in the 1950s and saying you don't attend church. It's archaic and chauvinistic.

The treat and reward side of my brain loves it. Those two words hit the orbitofrontal cortex with a smack, releasing dopamine that skims through my system and collects at my core. The heat rising from between my thighs is too powerful not to make the association. If he were to whisper it to me in a bedroom, I might be convinced to do everything he says.

It's really a conundrum. I hate it. I love it. Logically, I'm not exactly sure which side should win versus which side wants to win.

"I'm sorry," he murmurs, squatting to where I sit taller than him.

His lowering himself to me is equally unsettling, and I'm not sure I like this either. Power plays are very common at work. They set up the dynamic in the opening statements of both attorneys, lob power back and forth throughout the trial, and fight for it during closing statements. All to realize we never had it in the first place since the true power resides with the jury.

But this isn't a case to be tried or a courtroom to convince. This is him and I, not a battleground, and I don't want it to be. I've fought enough to be heard, to be the smartest in the room, and come out on top. That's why I walked into this gym, needing help—to relinquish control, be guided, and follow someone else's lead in my fitness journey.

"Don't be. I kind of like it."

I surprise myself with the admission. Part of me revels in the reprieve from constantly being in charge, while another is wary of yielding too much.

His smile blooms in response to my words, and the tension dissolves. He offers a fist for a bump, a gesture of solidarity, of equal ground. It's friendly, affirming, and nothing like the power play I'm so weary of engaging with him. And "our thing."

"So did I."

His honesty is disarming. The wink he gives me as he stands is playful, a promise that this—whatever it is—is something shared, not one-sided. He extends a hand to help me up, and I take it, letting him pull me to my feet.

"I need to grab my stuff from my desk. Meet you at the front?"

There's an undercurrent of something more in his voice, a hint of excitement, maybe even hope.

"Sure."

As he walks away, I watch the easy sway of his stride and realize that this is precisely what I need. Not a power struggle, not another competition, but a partnership of sorts, a mutual support system.

As I take my time getting to the front to wait for him, I can't help but feel a sense of anticipation for what the evening will bring—cooking, laughing, and maybe sharing a bit more of ourselves. And for the first time in a long while, I'm not concerned with who's in charge. Because with Giovanni, it feels like we're just two people figuring things out without a verdict hanging in the balance.

I lean against the cool wall, a brief respite as Giovanni disappears toward his boss's office. Alone for a moment, I glimpse myself in the reflection of the glass front. I'm a mess—a sweaty, flushed, endorphin-fueled mess. Smoothing back my hair, I try to tame the wild curls that seem to have grown bigger from the heat off my scalp. My makeup, what little I put on this morning, has mostly surrendered to the workout, but I dab at the smudges under my eyes. This isn't a date, I remind myself. Still, I want to look decent and presentable. Sexy would be better, but that was many months and thirty pounds ago.

Lost in my reflection, I almost don't notice Giovanni returning. He's got a backpack slung over one shoulder and a lunch box in the other hand.

"Sorry I didn't walk you to the front. I should have."

There's a note of genuine apology in his voice. I wave him off with a reassuring smile.

"It's fine. I needed a minute to collect myself anyway."

I gesture vaguely at my appearance, silently acknowledging my disheveled state. He chuckles, the sound warm and comforting.

"You look great. Really."

I roll my eyes but can't help the smile that rises on my face.

"Thanks. So, which grocery store are we meeting at?"

The question feels like a lifeline, steering us back to the plan, to the neutral ground where I feel more sure-footed than compliments and flirting.

"There's a great place near here with everything we need for meal prep. It's called Green Earth Groceries. Ever been?"

He adjusts the backpack on his shoulder, ready to go.

"Can't say I have, but I'm all for new experiences."

The words are more than just about the store. They're about this entire evening unfolding before me. I apply pressure on my foot, my ankle protesting. His hand cups my elbow to help even though I feel stronger with a renewed sense of purpose. This is good. This is what I need—a break from the norm.

A break from going through the fast-food drive-thru as I did after Saturday's workout, a reward for all my hard work. A break from my bad health habits. Who better to share it with than this attractive man who's already changing how I feel about myself and my wellness journey?

"Great, it's just a five-minute drive from here."

He helps me to my car, a sweet and caring gesture. Once I'm seated with the engine purring, he jogs to his truck, an easy athleticism in his movements. He throws his backpack and lunch box in, then jumps behind the wheel to pull out of the parking lot with a wave for me to follow.

The drive is quick. When we arrive at Green Earth

Groceries, Giovanni parks near the entrance. My ankle twinges as I step out of the car, and a flicker of doubt crosses my mind. How much walking can I manage?

"Um, I'm not sure this is a good idea after all."

I hobble toward him, my ankle swelling from the pressure I keep sporadically applying. Giovanni seems to read my thoughts. He's at my side instantly, gesturing to the store's motorized scooter, complete with a shopping basket.

"Why don't you use this? No point in straining your ankle further."

I hesitate, the idea of drawing attention to myself on the scooter makes me squirm.

"Oh no. I'd rather not. People might stare."

Before I can finish, Giovanni, with a mischievous glint in his eye, hops onto the scooter.

"Let people stare."

He drives in tight circles, the scooter humming under his weight. I can't help but laugh, the sound bubbling up despite my discomfort.

"You're ridiculous," I say, thoroughly charmed by his antics. He stops circling and looks at me, his smile wide.

"Come on, Kacie. It's either you or me on this thing, and I've got to say, I'm kind of liking it."

The playfulness in his voice is infectious.

"You're going to make me ride that thing, aren't you?"

"Absolutely. It's either ride in style or watch me parade around the store in this baby like I own the place."

I shake my head, a smile tugging at my lips.

"Fine, but you're pushing the cart then."

"Who needs a cart when you got this basket?" He pats the inside of the large basket, really trying to bring it home. "But if your basket runneth over, I'll get a cart," he replies, standing to offer me the scooter.

I take a deep breath and climb in, the scooter feeling

strange and more than humbling to my ego. This is just another example of why I need to get into shape, to keep me from needing to use one of these later in life. I hear him chuckle behind me as I start toward the store entrance.

"You're doing great."

I can hear the humor in his voice. I shake my head again but can't suppress my grin.

"Just for the record, I'm never living this down, am I?"

"Not a chance.

Giovanni's enthusiasm for nutrition is infectious. He's like a kid in a candy store, except the candies are organic fruits and vegetables. His passion for healthy living is evident in every word and every gesture. It's a side of him that's just as attractive as his playful humor and good looks.

"Okay, what do you think about trying some ancient grains? They're like the ancestors of all modern grains."

He holds up a bag of something that looks intriguing and slightly intimidating. I raise an eyebrow.

"Ancient grains? Sounds like something Indiana Jones would go hunting for."

He laughs, placing the bag in the basket.

"Exactly! Eating healthy can be an adventure. Next, we'll try finding the raiders of the lost ark of organic spices."

It's a terrible comeback, light and corny, as our banter continues while we move through the store. He makes a show of weighing two different kinds of apples, pretending to struggle with the life-altering decision.

"Kacie, this is crucial. Sweet or tart?"

I play along, taking it seriously.

"Hmm, the fate of our meal prep hangs in the balance. Let's live dangerously. Go tart."

He nods solemnly, adding the apples to our burgeoning collection of groceries.

"Brave choice. I knew you were a risk-taker."

Our laughter and jokes fill the space around us, turning what could have been a routine chore into a delightful experience. With Giovanni, every moment is airy and fun. He continues dumping different things into the scooter's basket. Most of the time, I have no idea what they are or what we are making, but when he makes a side comment to a guy about taking care of his old lady, the man chuckles. I clear my throat to get his attention.

"Hey, you got to admit, that was funny. Get it because you are older than me and in the scooter?"

He laughs again at his joke, no ill intent behind it. It is humorous, even if it's at my expense.

"Well, sonny, if you're a good boy and help with the groceries, I'll give you a quarter for the horsey ride out front."

I have no idea if they still have those coin-operated machines when I jab my finger into his side. He laughs so hard he grips the side of the basket, bent over with his eyes watering. I can't help the giggles that escape me.

"And I'll take you up on that offer. I never say no to a horsey ride."

His laughter, shifting seamlessly into that smoldering gaze, sends a thrill through me. The closeness, the intensity in his eyes, it's disarming. I find myself lost in the moment, the playful banter giving way to something deeper, something more charged. The air between us crackles with unspoken possibilities, and his glance, laden with meaning, makes my body flush and leaves me speechless.

His face moves away, those dark eyes glittering dangerously, and I know exactly what he wants. Not said in a vulgar or vile way, but playfully and plainly spoken that he wants me in the very way I want him. My curiosity about that shaft could be solved tonight, and I anxiously adjust in my seat.

My mind is still reeling with his sudden interest in me and the acceleration at which things are progressing. I've always been too busy to date seriously. My weight gain and docket attest to it. But a casual relationship with a young, hot trainer?

I'd be a fool to turn him down. It's been so long since I've allowed myself the luxury of such an indulgence. The thought of exploring this chemistry, of seeing where this could go without the pressure of something serious, is liberating.

My palm squeezes the handle to get the cart moving again. He's tossing food in the basket, claiming they are three shot points, and faking fans cheering for him at the end of the aisle. It's then that I decide to go all in, not turning back, and the next pass he makes at me, I'm taking action.

When we finally reach the front of the store, I park the scooter and stand, testing my weight on my ankle. It's sore but manageable. Giovanni is there instantly, his hand at my elbow, ready to support me.

"You good?"

His eyes scan my face for any sign of discomfort.

"Yeah, I'm good," I assure him, and it's more than just my ankle I'm referring to. I'm good because this evening has been about laughter, flirting, and a possible romantic connection—all things I need more of.

7

GIOVANNI

The moment Kacie steps into my downtown loft, excitement and anticipation settle in my chest as we drop the groceries on the counter. A part of me is curious to see if she's as open as I am to exploring what's between us. Her fierce determination to take her health seriously and the kindheartedness radiating from her make me feel like I can be myself around her. She's got this blend of career-driven focus and life experience that shapes her into someone who's both compassionate and patient, qualities I find incredibly appealing.

Kacie's response to my goofy nature is genuinely refreshing. When I was being a bit silly in the store, she played along instead of rolling her eyes or dismissing me. That spurred me on to raise the stakes. The way she laughs, with its gentle and musical quality, makes me happy. There's a comfort in her presence, a sense of ease that makes me feel good about myself, better than I usually do, especially with the demands from my family wanting me to go into medicine like my older brother.

They seem unable to grasp why I'm so passionate about health and fitness, bodybuilding, and competing. With both my father and brother being successful doctors, my family frequently nudges me toward following in their footsteps. They view my gap year after finishing my bachelor's degree as merely a hiatus before I inevitably commit to going to medical school.

Dealing with their constant pressure can be challenging, and I feel as though I must justify my passion every time I see them. However, Kacie's acceptance, even in the early stages of our acquaintance, offers much-needed support. Her understanding and non-judgmental attitude affirm that pursuing my dreams and passions is okay, not just conforming to my family's expectations.

"Wow, Giovanni, this place is incredible."

Her gaze sweeps the apartment before it's drawn to the large windows overlooking the city. Her footsteps are light as she crosses over to them. My apartment is a spacious expanse of modern elegance, the kind of place that I've put a lot of myself into. Polished hardwood floors gleam under the soft lighting. Industrial furniture contrasts with contemporary art pieces adorning the walls, splashes of color against my minimalist backdrop.

"It's a different world up here." There's a touch of pride in my voice when I join her. "Part of the hustle and bustle, yet away from it."

The view from the floor-to-ceiling windows always gets the best reaction. The neon-trimmed city skyline stretches before us. The bustling streets create a lively panoramic view. Buildings lit up against the night sky seem close enough to touch.

"That's my office over there. I've never seen it from this angle."

Kacie gazes in awe as she points to her brick office building amidst the urban steel and glass jungle, which reminds me why I fell in love with this place. I nod, understanding the allure.

"The view never gets old."

"It's so bright and beautiful."

Her palms press against the glass, taking it all in while I take her all in. The round curves of her full breasts, trimming to a snug waist and flaring back out to wide hips, a generous ass, and thick thighs. All more than a handful that I'd love to grab and squeeze. When discussing her goals at our first session, she mentioned wanting to lose weight to look better. If she were mine, she wouldn't need to lose weight for appearance. For better health, of course. More stamina for the bedroom, definitely. Something I'm more than happy to work with her on, starting tonight if possible.

"Yeah, it is," I murmur, unable to resist touching her back. Her shoulders lift in startled surprise, her smile covering her response at my unexpected touch. I honestly can't help myself. I've been itching to touch her more and more as this night progresses. "Ready to dive into some culinary exploration?"

"Lead the way, teacher."

Teacher.

If she only knew the things that I'd like to teach her. Teach her how to appreciate her body, as I certainly would. How to lay back and receive when I pleasure her orally. How to take my large cock down her throat. How to accept instructions and receive praise in return. Blood is pumping into my cock right now as I think of all the things I could teach her about my preferences. Dropping praise during the workout was a test to see how she'd react. When her face lit up, and she looked away with a secret smile, I knew she'd love what I was into.

I breathe deeply to calm down while turning from the view to the kitchen. The transition from one area to another is seamless, and I wish my thoughts were the same. The kitchen area is open and inviting, with sleek, stainless-steel appliances and a large island that serves as a workspace and a casual dining spot. The countertops are a pristine white, offering a blank slate for our culinary adventure and a place where I could take her if she is so inclined.

"Alright, where do we start?"

Kacie's enthusiasm is evident as she surveys the array of ingredients I began unpacking. I read into every word, converting it into a bedroom fantasy. Where would we start? With her naked in front of those windows, letting the world see a beautiful woman getting pleasured from behind. Then, the mirror, to have her watch her body enjoy what it's receiving. There are so many ways to start deconstructing that insecure view she has of her body.

"Giovanni? You okay? You look bothered."

Chill, man. Don't blow this. She could still say no and be out the door if I don't keep it together.

"Yeah, just thinking about the recipe."

The recipe of me and all that soft caramel skin.

"So, these ancient grains," she begins, eyeing the quinoa box she's unpacking from the bags. "How do we ensure they don't taste ancient?"

I laugh, appreciating the corny joke to take my mind off of putting her on her knees and placing my cock on her lips.

"It's all about the spices. A little flavor can make anything taste great."

"And is that your life philosophy too?"

The glint in her eye keeps the blood pumping into my balls now. She has the ingredients unpacked in no time while I move about the kitchen focusing on getting the pots and pans out and not on her plump ass bumping against my thigh when I pass her.

"A little spice makes everything better, especially when mixing salt and pepper."

My joke is as corny as hers, but the tone in which I said it has her catching her lip in her perfect white teeth. I will keep heating things up between us, never backing off unless she turns me down or tells me off.

As we start cooking, the kitchen becomes the dance floor

between us. I guide Kacie through the steps, our hands brushing as we pass ingredients back and forth. She asks questions openly and honestly with a sort of flirtiness that is ruining my resolve not to turn off the burners and take her into my bedroom. She's so eager to learn I turn away and look at the ceiling to keep my cock from popping out of my shorts. I drop more praise on her, watching her soak it up and knowing she will love the praise kink I hit her with later.

The sizzle of chicken hitting the hot pan fills the air, mixing with the aromatic spices I sprinkle liberally. But it's no comparison to the sizzle between us. And when my hand grazes her ass, I'm quick with an apology that gets stuck in my throat when she gives me a sultry look over her shoulder.

I raise the stakes, showing Kacie how to chop vegetables to maximize their texture and taste by trapping her against the counter and wrapping my hands over hers. She leans into my body, her soft hair brushing my chin, and her breathing becomes erratic.

When she tilts her face to look up at me, I dip my lips to hers in the softest kiss possible. It's brief, fleeting, and a measure to watch how she reacts. The corner of her mouth falls into a frown, and a small sigh leaves her body—all signs she wants more.

"Good job on the vegetables," I murmur close to her face, her forgotten perfume rising into my nostrils as they flare with desire. "But you're not done."

She immediately straightens and focuses on the task, following my lead until her movements are steady in each slice. I release her hands, my hard cock pressed firmly against her soft body, making my intentions known as I grip the countertop.

My light teasing counters the roaring desire coursing through my veins. One simple kiss. One prolonged touching of our bodies. Now it's her turn to give something of herself, to meet me halfway and confirm she's all in as I am.

When she approaches, I move away from her to stir the quinoa and turn down the heat on the chicken. Her hand on my arm is soft but firm, a gentle tug to get my attention. I turn to her, seeing the desire in her look, the upturn of her face wanting more.

"You're right. I'm not done."

Her hand slides up my arm, resting on my shoulder while the other cups my waist. Her light green eyes narrow while her full lips shimmer with traces of lip gloss I tasted a second ago.

"What do you want to do?"

I know exactly what she wants. Being the intelligent litigator she is, she must tell me exactly what she wants. The rest I'll get from her body when it speaks to me. She takes a shaky breath, feeling as turned on as I am. But that beautiful, upturned face is my undoing. I'd tell her to get down on her knees if we were together. But we're not there yet. The choice is hers.

I rest a hand on the countertop, the pan's contents bubbling as I await her answer. Her light emerald eyes look me up and down, narrowing on my cock that has failed to go down since we got into my domain, to the food makings scattered all over the kitchen and back to me.

"I want to do other things."

I smile, her dilemma evident in what she wants versus what she thinks she wants. It's obvious that no one has ever taken their time with her, waiting patiently for her timing to prevail. Her choice of words is enchanting too. I doubt she'd ever say fuck me in that soft voice of hers. Maybe that's what I should be coaxing out of her.

"*Other things*?" I unfairly emphasize my choice before continuing, "Not cooking or meal prep?"

Her fingers tighten in place, her long nails pressing into my flesh, and I give her a knowing smile. She counters it with one of her own.

"No."

I wrap my arms around her, her petite frame fitting snugly into the embrace. Her small stature only heightens my instinct to protect and care for her.

"Good girl."

I lower my chin, staring intently into her eyes when I say it to ensure we are on the same page. She glances away, her mouth tightening, and I tilt my head in inquiry.

"What's wrong, Kacie?"

My voice is laced with concern. It's vital that she feels comfortable and understood, especially before we proceed any further.

There's a complexity in her expression, emotions that she seems to be sorting through. My words or perhaps the moment's intensity have stirred something in her. I wait patiently, giving her the space to articulate her thoughts.

I'm reminded of the delicate balance in our budding relationship. There's a professional boundary as her trainer. But as a man, I'm increasingly drawn to her. There's a desire to connect on a deeper level. Navigating this terrain requires sensitivity and an awareness that what I see in her—strength, beauty, and worth—might be a journey she's still embarking on for herself.

"Is it bad that I like it when you say that?"

Her question catches me slightly off guard, her voice tinged with vulnerability. I pause for a moment, thinking. It's a glimpse into how she perceives our interactions. A hint at the dynamics in play.

"Not at all," I respond gently, wanting to reassure her when her gaze returns to mine. "It's perfectly okay."

"If we're to explore a relationship beyond our professional training, then it's important that you're comfortable with how I communicate. Privately, of course," I add, wanting her to know her feelings are valid. While she's still taking everything in, I relay my final point, "And those words are said with affection, meant to be fun and encouraging."

She gives me the sweetest smile possible.

"And I can tell you, good boy?"

I release a hearty laugh, hers echoing with mine and bringing levity to the conversation.

"Absolutely, you can. Fair is fair, right? I doubt it will have the same effect, though."

Praise kink is something I deliver, not receive. However, if that makes her feel more comfortable and is something she wants to try, then by all means, why not? We'll be testing many different things in the bedroom, what's one more?

8

KACIE

My flirting skills are rusty and terrible from a severe lack of use. It's apparent how awkward I feel trying to keep up with his frisky personality. His confidence and quick wit are refreshing but leave me not knowing how to respond. I like that he senses my uneasiness and counters it with humor. I did see a serious side to him professionally. His commitment to health and fitness is evident in his body and lifestyle, yet I much prefer his easygoing side.

As for calling him a good boy? I doubt I ever will. It's a retort with no merit. Not something I want to back up, but more of me testing the waters to ensure we're still on equal footing despite all this seeming as if I'm the student and he's the teacher. If we were in a courtroom, I'd be the senior, more experienced person, something I live day in and day out. The fact that I get to reset go all the way back to zero and be a newbie at something is exciting.

I want to lean into it as an escape from the expert prosecutor I need to be to my clients, the victims, and all parties in the courtroom. Giovanni's willingness to provide professional expertise and a personal escape is exactly what I need. Where the roles are versed, he's in charge, and I'm not, which is something my overactive brain and eager body are ready for.

"We'll have to see," I counter with a slight lift to my shoulder.

If he's expecting me to make the first move, that will not happen. It's his place, his bed, his world. I feel out of place, but I'm not letting that stop me.

His fingertips caress my arm, leaving a trail of goosebumps until he tugs at my shirt sleeve. My breath catches. This is what I have been waiting for, fantasizing about when lying in bed at night, my fingers swirling my clit. To say I'm nervous is an understatement. It's been so long since I had sex, even longer with a fantastic-looking guy like this.

"I'm nervous," I admit, the words slipping out in a hushed tone, revealing the flurry of butterflies in my stomach.

His head lowers, bringing those intense chocolate eyes level with mine. The gold specks in his irises catch the light, shining with a warmth and understanding that eases my anxiety.

"Me too." His voice is a soft echo of my apprehension. "Come on."

My hands slip from his body while his glides down my arm, interweaving our fingers. His grip tightens over mine when he turns off the stove and moves the pots to the cool back burners. Once everything is secure, he leads me down a dark hallway to his bedroom.

A soft light illuminates the room with a click of a button, casting a warm, ambient glow that softens the space. Like the rest of his loft, his bedroom is stylish yet inviting, with a large bed taking center stage, its linens crisp and neatly arranged.

Giovanni's grip on my hand is reassuring as he guides me further into the room. Nervousness runs from my stomach into my throat, but his gentle manner makes it more manageable. He turns to face me, a question in his eyes, a silent check-in to ensure I'm okay with this progression.

"Are you sure?"

His voice is barely above a whisper, an earnest desire to respect my boundaries. I take a deep breath, feeling a sense of certainty amidst the whirl of anticipation.

"Yes." My voice is steadier than I feel. "I'm very sure."

"Good. Now sit right there."

He guides me toward the edge of the bed, and I sit, watching him intently. Giovanni takes out his phone, his fingers swiftly navigating the screen. Moments later, the soft strains of music fill the room, a slow, sexy song that envelops us, adding another layer to the already intimate atmosphere.

"How about a little show?"

He cocks his head, flashes me a naughty little smile, and I can't help the circle my mouth forms when his hips start swaying in time with the melody. His gaze holds mine, intense and unyielding, as he begins a slow, deliberate striptease.

There's a confidence in his movements, an incredibly alluring boldness. He's baring himself, literally and figuratively, a gesture of vulnerability and trust that no man has ever shown me. It's not just his physical presence that's captivating. It's the intention behind it that this is for me, to make me feel comfortable, to show that he's just as open and willing to explore as I am.

"I hope you're enjoying your front row seat."

"Best show in town," I quip back with some sass. Staring at his perfectly defined chest with his brown nipples and a dark, happy trail disappearing into the waistline of his shorts has lust coursing through me.

"Well, I aim to please."

He spins around, effortlessly kicking off his shoes, and with a playful shake of his hips, he starts striking a series of body-building poses. Each movement showcases his well-defined physique, turning this into a light-hearted showcase of strength and flexibility.

His back muscles ripple impressively as he flexes, a landscape of curves and peaks that speaks volumes of his dedication and hard work. The muscles seem to dance under his skin, each pose highlighting a different aspect of his strength. His back tapers down to a remarkably narrow waist, emphasizing the broadness of his shoulders and the sculpted nature of his body.

"And please, I shall," he adds, leaning over to face me while removing his socks.

It's a boast and a promise. Both cause me to release a ragged breath as wetness collects at my core. I'm so ready for what he's offering I don't even bother feeling nervous anymore. It's apparent by the hard shaft outlined in his compression shorts that he wants me as much as I want him.

"Showing off all your hard work?" I tease, inching off the bed to stand before him, my hands eager to touch the smooth expanse of muscles before me.

His shoulders are broad, leading down to well-defined arms where the contours of his biceps and triceps are accentuated with every movement. His muscular and firm chest complements the solid build of his arms, showcasing the result of countless hours of training and dedication.

As he moves, his abs flex—a well-defined six-pack that speaks of rigorous core workouts and a disciplined diet. The muscles ripple with each motion, longing for my tongue to trace each line.

"Showing what you're in store for."

His legs are thick and muscular, resulting from heavy squats and lunges. His entire body is perfection. A marvel I once saw in the body exhibited at the Science Museum. I'm lucky to see him like this, vulnerable, open, and desiring me by the look on his face. His bottom lip catches in his teeth, a quick wink, and then he slips off his boxer to reveal that long, thick shaft. It's gorgeous and veiny, with a slight curve back to a tight tuft of trimmed curls.

"Oh my."

I breathe softly, my pussy tingling in anticipation as heat sweeps over my body. His cologne swirls about my senses, mixing with the music in a tantalizing feeling that draws me closer to his naked body.

"You like?"

His tone is teasing, his stare is blistering, and all I can think about is his tasting the pearl of precum on the mushroom head of his shaft. I gaze up at him, exhaling slowly before nodding. My cheeks are hot, my body is on fire, and my gym clothes stick to my excited skin.

"You're gorgeous, Giovanni."

I watch as his hand skims down his skin to grip his shaft, stroking it slowly and deliberately. The sight of him touching himself, his muscles flexing with each movement, is almost too much to handle. But I can't look away. I'm drawn to his raw masculinity and how he commands the room with his presence.

"Thank you. Now it's your turn," he murmurs with an unmistakable rasp.

He releases his shaft when he steps closer to me, his eyes never leaving mine, and my pulse quickens.

"I . . . I'm not a good dancer."

The uncertainty in my tone matches my words. I can quickly strip naked to have him sink into me, but dancing slow and seductively like him isn't me and wouldn't be sexy at all.

"That may be, but I sure enjoy watching you squat."

He grips the hem of my shirt, slowly collecting the fabric in his palms to raise it over my head. It's the first protective layer I shed, and a shiver runs over me as our eyes remain connected. A silent exchange of understanding, acceptance, and encouragement.

"I thought you only count my reps and fix my stance. I didn't know you were checking me out."

"I'm doing it all."

He places my shirt on the dresser behind him, raises my chin, and captures my lips in a searing kiss. His full lips are soft and pillowy against the sharp barbs of his mustache. The dichotomy of how he feels distracts my brain from worrying about him seeing my naked body and the extra weight I'm carrying when his fingers dip under the edges of my sports bra.

"Relax, Kacie," he beckons against my lips as the music changes to something smoother.

My mouth parts, wanting more when his lips move to my jawline, grazing my skin with his teeth before moving down my neck. I relish the feeling, be it pain, pleasure, or something else entirely. I'm not sure.

I enjoy his roaming lips a few moments more until I place my hands on his body, allowing them to skim over his rippling muscles. He groans against my flesh, the rumbling permeating into my fingertips.

"You smell good."

His mouth rests on my collarbone before his fingers roll my sports bra up my body and over my head, joining my shirt on the dresser. My nipples harden against the cool air, goosebumps appear on my skin, and an instinct to cover myself rises with my shoulders slouching forward.

"Don't hide from me. I've been dying to see this silky caramel skin."

I take a deep breath, slowly relaxing the tightness in my shoulders. His words wash over me, soothing my insecurities and igniting a flicker of confidence. My hands wander in their exploration the same as his eyes, greedily taking in every curve, every imperfection, with hunger and appreciation.

"Beautiful." A slow smile spreads as if he unwrapped the most precious gift. "Absolutely stunning."

His words resonate deep within me, awakening a part of myself that has long been dormant. This is not just about him seeing me naked. It's about being seen for who I truly am— vulnerable yet strong, imperfect yet deserving of lust and pleasure.

"I could say the same thing about you."

He groans when I grip his hard shaft, the thickness surprising against the soft curls of his pubic hair. I expected him to be hairless, as it seems to be the trend in the few pornographic films I've watched. However, seeing this small patch tight like mine makes me pleased as he'll see we match.

"Then we'll be beautiful together," he rasps when my thumb circles his precum over this head. His hands tightened at my waist, and his thumbs paused underneath my waistband while enjoying my grip on him.

"Kacie, if you don't stop, I'm going to come in your hand, and that's the last thing I want to do."

I release him, my hand sliding down his length back to his base as I lock my gaze with his.

"Patience," I whisper, a mischievous smile on my lips. "There's so much more I want to do before that."

He groans in response, the desire in his eyes mirroring my own. His hands move from my waist, gliding up my sides and over the curves of my breasts, causing a shiver to ripple through me. My breath hitches as his thumbs graze over my hardened nipples, sending jolts of pleasure straight to my core.

"I knew they would be perfect. Look at them."

His expression is full of adoration as he holds my heavy breasts in his hands, his thumbs stroking relentlessly back and forth.

"More than a handful. Damn, Kac."

Kac.

A shortening of my name said it whispered desperation. It's the only way I want to hear my name. Leaning in, he takes one of my nipples into his mouth, sucking gently before flicking it with his tongue. My back arches instinctively, urging him to explore further. He obliges, switching to the other nipple and lavishing it with the same attention. The sensations are heightened by the contrast of his scratchy mustache and his soft tongue.

Not usually one for facial hair, he's winning me over with his, and the tricks it can do. He catches me by surprise when he plasters his face into my cleavage and then pushes my breasts against the side of his face. A low growl rumbles out of him and into me, and I grip his shoulders to push him back. His face is heavy with desire. Those dark eyes bore into me.

"I could suffocate on them and die a happy man."

I laugh, and he winks, breaking his smolder with humor.

"Let's hope that doesn't happen."

"If I'm going to suffocate, it's going to be with you riding my face."

The certainty in his tone causes my breath to catch in my throat. Without warning, he scoops me in his arms and carries me to the bed, placing me gently on the soft bedding. His eyes burn with intensity as he hovers over me before capturing my lips in another searing kiss that strokes the fire within me.

Our tongues dance together, exploring each other's mouths with fervor. His hand slides down the curve of my waist, leaving trails of heat in its wake to tug at my gym pants.

I feel his hardness pressing against my hip, and the ache between my legs intensifies. My body craves his touch and yearns for the release only he can provide. I arch my back, pressing myself against him while the soft fabric of my pants slips past my knees. The kiss ends abruptly as he draws away from my body to finish undressing me. My shoes land with a thud, my socks to follow, and once my pants are on the floor, he stands at the edge of the bed, his gaze blistering as he drinks me in.

"Perfect."

His voice is barely a whisper as he gazes at me, a raw hunger in his expression. I feel confidence coursing through my veins as I lie there, fully exposed to him. I cast him a faint smile, thinking the exact same thing.

The bulging muscles on his arms, the defined abs that ripple with each movement, and the thick length between his legs that throbs with desire. He stands before me, completely bare, his raw masculinity on full display. He is perfect.

He moves closer, his hands tracing a path up my legs, and his touch sends shivers down my spine. With each caress, my body responds eagerly, arching into his touch. He lowers himself between my trembling thighs, his hot breath teasing against my core.

I gasp as his tongue dips between the folds of my lips, lapping at my wetness with expertise that sends shockwaves of pleasure through me. His touch is both gentle and demanding. His tongue is soft against my clit, his fingers hard in pinching my nipple.

Gentle and demanding, soft and hard. It's how I'd describe us. I'm demanding in the courtroom, gentle with him. He's demanding as my trainer but gentle as my lover. His body is rippled with hardness. Mine is soft with lusciousness. The duality is something I never knew I liked, let alone needed.

Yet here we are. It works on many levels like his bristly mustache working with his soft lips and tongue. I grip the bedding, the orgasm collecting deep within, ready to explode in seconds when he stops. He lifts his face from my core, the hair above his lip glistening with my wetness.

"Not yet, my beautiful Kac."

His eyebrow twists up, a silent command to follow his lead. My thighs clench, quivering at the sight of holding back what was almost a wave of pure pleasure.

"What?" I ask breathlessly, my hips rising to connect with that masterful tongue of his. "Why?"

"Because in here . . ."

He crawls up my body, his cock dragging against my leg as his lips seek out mine. They meld together in a feverish kiss that leaves no doubt about the intensity of his desire for me. When his lips leave mine, I lean up, chasing them until his fingers run through my short curls and separate my lips to push two fingers inside of me.

"I'm in charge."

I collapse onto the bed, reveling in the exploratory pushing against my walls, trying to find that perfect spot where my orgasm is still waiting. His fingers curl upward, a knowing grin hinting at his lips when I grind my mound into his hand to create more friction between us.

"You conquer the world on behalf of others out there. But with me, I conquer you."

He lifts his chin to align our gazes, his shaft digging into my hip as I pump harder and faster against his hand.

"Do you agree?"

I'm so close to coming. Closer than I was before when it was only his magic tongue on my clit. This is what he wants. This is mostly what I want. He hinted at it earlier. I hinted that I might be willing, and now that we are here, I must decide. Do I genuinely want to relinquish control and let him conquer me? To follow and not lead?

"You're so very wet. Does that mean yes?"

He levels his full lips inches from mine, yet slightly out of reach. If I lean forward for a kiss, his fingers move from the spot, and my orgasm slips away again. If I relent, let him conquer me however he wishes. I forgo a kiss but experience an orgasm.

The dichotomy again. What I'm learning is always in play between us. I can get one but not the other, eventually both, but

I'll have to be patient and wait for him to decide. It's different from what I've ever experienced, and it's becoming an addictive game. But play it, I shall.

"Yes."

The word passes my lips in a slur, and I'm rewarded with a brush of the lips and a deeper thrusting of his fingers in me until I'm bursting apart from the orgasm rocketing through my core. I squeeze my eyes shut, seeing yellow swirls as he continues finger fucking every last bit of it out of me. When I open my eyes, his face is serious, and his eyes are tense.

"Good girl. Now get on your hands and knees."

9

GIOVANNI

Those light green eyes narrow for a split second, unsure of my change in demeanor. I'd never hurt her. Aftercare is my specialty. But the intensity with which she came in my hand speaks to how pliable and responsive she is. We're going to have a lot of fun, and I will bring her more pleasure than she can ever imagine, so long as she agrees that I'm in charge behind closed doors.

Her light voice accepting this makes my cock that much harder, to the point that I'm about to drizzle my cum all over her leg like a teenager. My need to have her on her hands and knees without hesitation is overwhelming to the point that I'm off the bed and grabbing a condom while she's still recovering from her first orgasm of the night, with many, many more to come.

My hand circles her ankle, the contrast of her caramel skin against my olive drives my desire, and I can't wait to watch my cock pump in and out of her. My thumb caresses the outside of her ankle, waiting for her to comply.

"Kacie?"

She props herself up on her elbows, looking me straight in

GIGI MEIER

the eyes when she bites her lower lip. It's sexy without intending to be with the furrow of her brow.

"But that's not all the time, right? Like, sometimes I can conquer you too?"

Ah, this is like that good boy comment in the kitchen. Once I said she could, she felt more comfortable. This is similar to wanting to know the boundaries and expectations before we go any further. It's her investigative side, the need to understand everything, and accessing every detail before deciding. I never stop caressing her ankle when I answer her.

"Do you want to conquer me now?"

She laughs, the lightness music to my ears that she's not disgusted by what I like, and walks out the door.

"No, I don't want to, but just in case."

"Good."

I remove my hand from her ankle to roll the condom on my cock, which hasn't gone down in the slightest, while clarifying things.

"Hands and knees on the edge of the bed."

She gives me an exaggerated wink, then flips over and backs into me. My hands are on her hips in an instant, my thumbs pulling her ass cheeks apart to expose that sweet dark hole I have been fantasizing about every time she lies on her back for a lift.

Her caramel skin shimmers in the soft light, her dark curls getting tighter with the heat we're sending into the air. When she turns those glossy lips to me, asking what I'm waiting for, I grit my teeth and slowly push into her.

Her long moan matches mine, a shared pleasure as the tight ring of her pussy concedes to the intrusion of my long cock. Her soft folds welcome me in, sucking my cock deeper until I bottom out, and we both grunt in contentment.

"Taking me all in," I verbalize what I see and feel, and my hands grip her hips tighter.

The pause at the bottom of her pussy, trying to hold off my orgasm, has her wiggling her voluptuous ass. It's almost too much. I'm trying to hold off, hold back from pouring into her. When she starts to use my cock to fuck herself, I reward her in a way I know she already likes.

"Good girl."

My palm slides over her velvety skin around her waist to her heavy breast dipping toward my mattress. The feeling of her under and around me is awesome. My only regret is the lack of a mirror in my room to watch her face as her pussy swallows my cock.

I continue to thrust into her, the rhythm becoming more urgent and desperate with each movement. Our bodies slap against each other, the sound of her pleasure filling the room. She arches her back, granting me deeper access, and I take full advantage of it, causing her moans to become screams.

With an impulsive squeeze of her breast, my hand retreats, trailing down her stomach and feeling the slickness of her arousal coating her thighs. I tease her clit with my fingertips, earning a gasp and a moan from deep within her throat. Her walls tighten around me as she rides the waves of pleasure, and I know she's coming when she screams my name.

"I want to taste you again," I growl, pulling out of her dripping pussy and squatting to bury my face between her cheeks.

She jolts forward in surprise. My hands firmly clasp the front of her thighs to pull her back to me as I spread her wide to expose her wetness. My tongue dances over her folds, lapping up her sweet taste as if it were the finest delicacy. She writhes beneath me, her fingers briefly touching my hand as she lets out a string of pleas to go back to fucking her.

"Oh, G . . ."

Her body trembles, and another wave of pleasure courses through her. I hold her tightly, supporting her as she rides out her orgasm. I savor the taste of her on my lips, reveling in the knowledge that I could bring her such ecstasy. Her upper body sinks to the mattress, her chest heaving as she catches her breath. The movement thrusts her pussy into my nose. My face is soaked, drinking in her core and breathing in her essence.

She's putty in my hands. Her knees wobble, and her thighs tremble. The sensations vibrate through her, and I stand to slide back in with little resistance. Her multiple orgasms have opened her walls, creaming my dick and dripping out of her. It's sloppy and wet. The sound of my flesh hitting hers is intoxicating and fuels me to take her harder as I barrel toward my release.

Her face is turned to the side, her eyes hooded in pleasure, holding onto the sheets as best she can while lost in ecstasy, sending me over the edge.

"Scream my name," I command, my voice laced with a primal hunger. "Let the whole world know who's making you come."

I thrust into her one final time, feeling my climax tidal wave over me. My name doesn't come out as the roar I wanted. It seeps out in a breathless purr that sounds even better. With a guttural groan, I empty myself inside her, the warmth of my release soaking my cock inside the condom. My chin raises toward the ceiling as my eyes close, savoring the rush coursing through my veins that's better than any pump the gym can provide.

This is the feeling I'd chase every day if I could. Being intimately connected as one, a melding of bodies in pleasure while freeing my mind of its incessant chatter. The security of being inside someone I care for, placing my trust in them to be my authentic self, and finding acceptance in the process. This is what I want with Kacie. To be there for her as she'll be there for me. It's all I've ever wanted.

I open my eyes to catch her gaze when she moves underneath me.

"That was incredible."

My hands loosen as she pushes onto her hands and then upright onto her knees with a groan, not from pleasure but from achiness. They sound familiar to me with all my training clients. The action forces me out of her glorious body, and I deposit a kiss on her shoulder before catching her at the waist.

"You're incredible."

Our lips connect in the sweetest of kisses before her hand attempts to tame her unruly curls.

"Get comfortable, and I'll get you a warm towel."

I want to take care of her, to make her feel as comfortable and pampered as possible. Not waiting for a reply, I quickly click on the ceiling fan to cool down the room, then head into the bathroom. Grabbing a hand towel and tossing it into the sink to heat under the hot water, I take a moment to look at myself in the mirror. The reflection staring back at me is one of a man on the brink of something new and exciting, and I couldn't be happier about it.

As I head back to her, I'm filled with anticipation. Tonight has been about more than just physical attraction. It's been about connection, understanding, and acceptance. All things I want far more of with her. I return to see her nestled under the covers, her wild hair spread across my pillows, looking adorable if it weren't for the memory of what I just did to her sexy body. I gently lift the covers off her and lay the hot towel over her swollen lips. She sighs and closes her eyes briefly, a smile tugging at her lips.

"You're so sexy."

My cock attempts to rise but fails with how hard I come. It will only be a matter of minutes before I'm ready and hoping she wants another round, with her riding me this time.

I collapse on the bed beside her, forgoing the covers and relishing the swirl of the ceiling fan against my hot skin. Her eyes open from the movement, the towel remains where I put it, and a smile glides upon my face. If Kacie only knew the lengths I'd go to have her fully responsive and available to me, she might run right out that door. Then again, maybe I'm just what she needs to relieve the stress from her demanding career, both physically and mentally.

"Come here."

I slide my arm under her pillow to gather her toward me. She uses the towel for a quick clean-up and looks unsure what to do with it. I toss it on the floor without hesitation while she rolls on her side to snuggle against me. Her thigh rests against mine as our legs intertwine, and I stroke the goose-bumped flesh with my palm.

"If you're cold, then we can cover up."

My offer goes unanswered when she adjusts her head on my chest to gaze up at me.

"I'm not cold."

Her lips pucker for a chasten kiss, which I grant a couple of times before we both resume our positions.

"I'll say this, Giovanni. I'm thoroughly conquered."

I bark out a laugh, one that has me gazing from her to the ceiling and back as the soft music lost during sex now fills the room. Her smile is bright like her wit, and I couldn't be prouder that I shot my shot. When I offer her my fist to bump, she laughs and hits it with her.

"I'll conquer you every day if you'll let me. Just walk over from your office, and I'll be here waiting," I offer, and then I know I made a mistake when she frowns. "Sorry, I just meant that—"

"No, don't apologize. I don't want to think about work tomorrow. Not yet." Her finger traces my abdominal muscles, the touch almost ticklish with how light it is. "I want to stay in the cocoon that is this place."

As we lay there, basking in the aftermath of our passionate encounter, I can't help but feel lucky that she wants to stay in the sanctuary that I created for myself. That statement speaks to the safety she feels with me, and I know she won't race out of here now if I show her more of what I want with her.

"Just to clarify, I wasn't too hard or rough with you. The whole conquering thing and all?"

Her fingertips stop when she turns to me, her eyes filled with a new contentment.

"That was the best part."

"How so?"

She lifts off my chest, inching closer to me.

"I want to ensure you see us as equals, which I think you do."

"Of course I do. If anything, you're better than me. . ." I stop when she pats my chest with a deep frown.

"Not better, Giovanni. Equal. It's important that you view us as being on the same level."

She licks her lips, a hint of worry in her expression, until I run a soothing hand down her back and squeeze her ass. That playful action chases away that face when she smiles.

"If we agree that we are equals, then beyond that, I don't care about conquering you. If you want to call the shots, respectfully, of course, then by all means. I could use the mental break from decision-making all day. I take care of other people all day long. It'd be nice to be taken care of for once."

Her confession is the music to my ears. Relenting, submitting, whatever word I want to use, she's all in from the sounds of it, and my heart leaps in my chest.

"I must have died and gone to Heaven because I think you just said you'd submit to me, respectfully, of course," I confirm, using her word choice, which I fully agree with.

She laughs, light and airy, with a warning look.

"I'm not sure I like the word submit. I'd use softer language such as yield on most occasions, reserving the right to exercise my free will as needed and at any time."

Now I'm laughing, the heartiness bouncing her on my chest.

"Spoken like a true lawyer. Now, let's seal the deal with a kiss."

She winks and avoids my lips.

"How about sealing the deal with another round?"

"Yes, ma'am."

My cock rises against her leg. When I roll her over, hovering inches above her, I let it dangle against her stomach.

"By the way, did you call me O.G.?"

Her eyebrows wrinkle in confusion until her expression clears.

"I started to say, Oh, Giovanni, but everything felt so good that I didn't get it out."

"Ah, I was going to have you call me Sir from now on, but O.G. for original gangster works too."

Her laughter gets lost in my mouth as I take her tongue in deeply while flipping us over. She breaks the kiss when she settles on top of my stomach, the heat from her mound soaking into my skin.

"O.G. What do you know about that?"

She's still trying to contain her chuckles when I grab her hips and slide her down to my awaiting cock. A small gasp escapes her mouth as she clutches my chest to hold on while I adjust her.

"I know Shorty wanna ride, so get to it."

Her nails dig into my skin as she moves my cock away from the crack of her ass, much to my displeasure. If she cooperated, she could slide down it, and I could watch her reaction to taking me all in again.

"Did you just quote Young Buck?"

She adjusts her legs to tuck her ankles under my hamstrings. My hands slide from her hips to circle her ass, pulling her cheeks apart and nestling my cock in between them as she frowns.

"I did. Now, are you going to be a good girl and ride me?"

She bites her lip at the challenge, forging sliding on my cock but starting to grind her slick pussy against my short pubes.

"Were you even born when that song came out?" she asks with a coy grin, knowing exactly what she's doing by not listening even though I asked nicely and used praise. This is what she's talking about, having a little control to tease me as I tease her.

"No idea. Now are you going to get on O.G.'s cock, or am I going to have to take you from behind again?"

Her fingernails dig into my abdomen while she twists around and strokes my cock. It's nice, her grip tight and firm, but hand jobs don't satisfy my craving to be back inside her.

"Maybe I will, and maybe I won't. What are you going to do about it?"

Her green eyes sparkle, her hips grind, and her hand tickles my balls, causing me to jump at the unexpected intrusion. Her unexpected sass is fast becoming one of my favorite things about her, outside of her light voice and caring disposition.

My heart races with anticipation as I watch her expression turn mischievous. I can't resist the challenge in her voice, the hunger in her gaze. I grab her wrist, stopping her teasing touch.

"Oh, you have no idea what you're in for."

With a swift motion, I flip her onto her back and pin her to the mattress with my fit body. She gasps, surprise on her face and excitement dancing in her eyes. Our bodies are tangled together, our breaths shared as the sexual tension intensifies between us.

"Maybe I do," she smirks, pinching my ass with a flirty attitude. I love what is emerging from her. A naughty side that will pair nicely with my dominant side.

"Tonight," I growl, my voice low and commanding. "I'm going to give you a preview."

She pinches my ass again, my body weight sinking further into her when I grab her hand and interweave our fingers. She looks from our hands back to me and smiles, pleased at my actions.

"If holding hands is as bad as it gets, then I like it already."

She lets out a light chuckle, the vibrations rumbling through me. It's so easy to like this woman. Aside from the respect and admiration I have for her career, the different facets of her personality coming to life in the privacy of my place have me falling for her. She's everything I've wanted—caring, patient, understanding, non-judgmental and fun. I dip my head to plant a long, sweet kiss on her plump lips, relishing the softness against mine. When a sigh of contentment escapes her mouth and floods mine, I know she's also feeling something for me.

I end the kiss, wanting to confess how I feel, as I suddenly want to hear her say how she feels about me. Not one for being insecure about myself with women, far from it, but in this intimate moment, I would like to hear the words. Receive verbal confirmation that it's not just one-sided like my gym crush. Maybe in places I don't care to admit, I want validation before it goes too far, and I'm getting hurt again.

"I like you, Kacie," I whisper, searching her face for what I'm looking for and need before we continue forward. Her grip tightens, her other hand suddenly cupping my face as her expression softens.

"I like you too."

Simple words that kids use to describe their feelings. Yet it's all I need to dip my head and take her mouth in the most passionate and powerful way I know how. My tongue twists with hers, infiltrating her mouth with unbridled need after confirming the feelings I have are being equally reciprocated. Something that hasn't happened in a very long time.

Her fingertips slide to my neck, resting there as I begin to grind my cock into her soft stomach. Her moans join my grunts, both of us wanting more of what is being freely given. She's matching my vigor with her own, her hips moving with mine until I suddenly push off her to grab another condom.

"This is going to be much faster this time."

My need to be back inside the warm walls of her pussy, cloud any consideration for being slow and patient.

"Good."

She spreads her legs wider and plucks at a breast while I mess with the wrapper. My gaze fights between rolling the tight ring on and watching her fingers slide down her belly to swirl that beautifully dark clit. What I won't admit to her is how visually attractive our contrasting skin tones are to me. Her caramel, my olive, is something that fucks with my mind in the best damn way and makes my cock hard enough to explode the second I'm in her.

"I love how you're looking at me right now."

My gaze shifts from her sensual thighs and the puffy mound between them to those stunning green irises. The heat coursing through me is blistering, causing me to start sweating in anticipation of taking her hard and fast.

"Then you're going to love how I fuck you."

The vulgarity of my words raises her eyebrows, but she only opens her legs further in an invitation to take what I want and give her what she needs.

"Conquer me, O.G."

The humor in her words is lost on both of us when her eyelids partly close, and she blows me the sexiest air kiss. She barely has time to register the shift between us when I throw her legs over my shoulders and push into her tight pussy again.

"Oh, yes," she mumbles as I slide all the way in, hitting the end and stopping to enjoy being enveloped in warm, soft wetness. She impatiently starts to move, her body creating the necessary friction while I need a few more seconds to not burst this condom by coming too early. Her thighs act as a weight to hold me back when I need more, and I need to remain as deep as possible to pull the biggest orgasm out of her tonight.

"Giovanni, get to plundering me."

Her word choice would be funny if it weren't for the pleading seriousness in her tone. Another thing I like is the need for me and me alone. It's intoxicating and could become addictive.

My upper body presses into her legs. They buckle slightly, and I wrap an arm around them to keep them on my shoulders as I leverage my weight on my knees. My thighs clench, and my ass tightens, holding back the tingle building in my balls as I pump hard and fast into her.

"Your wish is my command."

Her moans grow louder. Sounds of slapping flesh mix with the music in the room as I continue to thrust into her depths. Her nails dig into my back, leaving marks that spur me on. The sting only heightens the intensity of my desire for her.

Her expressive eyes close, cutting me from seeing her emotions. I rely upon the sounds forced out of her, her hands contracting and releasing my flesh, and the tightening of her body as an orgasm overtakes her.

"Remember what I said about screaming my name?" I remind her, my voice dripping with authority. "I want to hear who's plundering you now."

Her eyes flash open, full of lust as she concentrates on riding out her climax. My body is on fire by watching her enjoy the pleasure I'm giving her. She gives me a breathless O.G. after a few shorter thrusts, and then her body sags into relief.

Her legs relax, her hands fall to the mattress, and her cum drips onto my balls. She spent. Perspiration collects along her hairline and around her nose. A testament to the pounding she's taking like the good girl she is, and I remember to reward her with hard-earned praise.

"You're taking it like such a good girl."

She looks down at our bodies, where they connect, and watches what I'm doing to her.

"You love my big cock, don't you?"

"Oh, yes."

Her light voice is barely audible over my hips, slapping against her ass cheeks. I change the angle, practically bending her in half to capture her lips. She groans at the tension on her hamstrings but otherwise lifts off the pillow to meet my lips. The kiss is powerful, her hand lifting into my head, pulling at my curls in a demand of her own, while our tongues battle for dominance and our bodies move in perfect harmony.

I want to stretch her out, the same as I want to stretch her pussy. I'm already big for her, that much I can tell, but opening her up wider, having her drenched from yet another orgasm coursing through her, is chasing mine to the forefront.

She falls back to the pillow, her hand caressing through my hair to clasp my shoulder as I pick up the speed. I'm barreling toward the edge when she screams my name over and over, her back arching while her walls clench tightly. It's the last movement to have me fall into the precipitous ecstasy with her.

I praise her repeatedly, words spoken without considering how hard I'm coming. My nerve endings are on fire with bursts of pulsating pleasure while her pussy milks every last drop out of me.

I collapse next to her, my ribcage rising and falling rapidly as she swipes a hand across the sweat that has dripped onto her breasts. Marked by my sweat and cum. How beautiful she would look with a pearl necklace nestled against the folds of her neck. Her legs are splayed to each side, her pants coming softer than mine. When I reach for her hand to intertwine them, I'm met with a limp wrist.

"I'm floating."

Her eyes close tightly, and a loose smile is on her face when I turn my head to look at her. I plant a soft kiss on her breasts, the generous mounds having slipped toward the side of her body and looking good enough to bite. I nip at her flesh, the temptation too great when she yips, opens her eyes, and pushes my face away.

"You're taking away from my good feelings."

I bark out a laugh, knowing she's dead wrong. Pleasure and pain are fun contradictions. I'm no sadist, having tried that once with a college girl who loved it. But little playful smacks to the ass or mark-less bites are harmless fun.

"I'm enhancing it."

I offer her a fist bump, which she returns with a smile. For a few seconds, we are left staring at each other. A deep bond forms between us. I can't resist scooping her up into my arms and having her lying against my chest. We're hot, sweaty, and sticky. I can't think of a better combination. Her hair is wild and frizzy from sex, brushing against my chin, and the fragrant scent rising into my nostrils.

"Giovanni, I don't know why, but I feel like thanking you. For the fitness training, the meal prep, and this too. I feel more alive than I have in years." She moves her head to gaze up at me from her position on my chest. "Is that odd?"

"Not a bit. Because I know exactly how you feel."

She gives me an indiscernible look, but little does she know, I feel the best I have in a long time. New year, a new goal, and now a new woman. She says more alive, I say, I'm finally living.

10

KACIE

He gently kisses my lips before adjusting the pillow behind his head. The music selection pumping through his surround sound switched to classical. It's an interesting selection and not something I expected him to like. I scoot closer, his hand encouraging me with the pressure applied to my butt when he pats it. The condom tightly sealed against his cock is shrinking and drying out, looking very uncomfortable by the reddish-purple tip.

"Do you need to do something with that?"

I move my thigh to settle over his and narrowly avoid touching it with my knee.

"Probably, but I enjoy holding you too much to move."

He squeezes me before removing and dropping the thing on the floor. Problem solved. Silence settles between us as I relish feeling content, sated, and a little achy from the rigorous activity he just put me through.

"Kacie, will you look at me?"

His tone is serious. When I use his chest to adjust my body to look at him, a small exhalation leaves his. His expression matches his tone, and I'm slightly nervous about what is happening.

"Everything okay?"

"Sort of. I just want you to know that this isn't a one-time thing. I really like you and want to keep seeing you both as your trainer and your man."

His words hang in the air, heavy with sincerity. I search his face, looking for any sign of uncertainty, but all I find is earnestness. Giovanni's expression is open and vulnerable as he lays his feelings bare. He reaches out to brush my sweaty hair, his touch gentle yet electrifying.

"Trainer and my man," I repeat softly, testing out the words on my lips.

The thought of continuing this thrilling experience with him is tempting and precisely what I had hoped for. Surprise, happiness, a touch of apprehension—all swirling inside me.

"Really?" I manage to say, my voice a whisper.

His hand gives my ass a quick squeeze as confirmation.

"Really. I wouldn't say it if I didn't mean it. I've felt something between us since the beginning, and tonight . . . it just confirmed what I've been feeling."

His confession sends a warm rush through me. Hearing that he wants more than just a fleeting night of passion, that he sees this as something ongoing, is both thrilling and overwhelming. Looking into his eyes, I see his genuine affection and care for me, easing any lingering doubts.

"I want to keep seeing where this goes."

My voice grows steadier with each word.

His face breaks into a relieved smile, and he pulls me close for another kiss. This one is different from the first—it's a kiss filled with promise, with the excitement of a future we're both eager to explore. When he leaves me breathless, we settle back into our same positions, intertwined in each other.

"I feel as if I can tell you anything, and you'd understand," he says with a spontaneity that makes me a little cautious.

Men generally feel closer to women after coitus, having been witness to enough criminal confessions where it's usually after the act when dark secrets are revealed. I wait with bated breath.

"I attempt to reserve judgment until I know all the facts."

I keep my answer neutral with a hint of support, wondering where this leads and hoping it's not illicit or illegal. The silence grows between us as I stare into his dark eyes, which flicker to something behind me. Long seconds pass, and just as I'm about to press him on it, he starts talking.

"I don't want to be a doctor. There I said it."

A huge exhalation rumbles out of him and caresses my face. Not exactly what I was expecting, probably better than where my mind usually goes, but I'm missing all the facts to understand why this weighs so heavily on him.

"Um, okay."

I roll my lips together as my mind decides how to take this.

"Why don't you tell me more about this."

Putting my interrogator hat on, I balance on one elbow as I flip onto my stomach for a more comfortable position. The ceiling fan, necessary while we were going at it, is becoming cool against my skin, and I reach for the covers.

He picks up on my discomfort immediately and pulls them up to my nape while he remains uncovered. His body's heat is extraordinary. I think it has to do with all his muscles keeping him warm outside of the intense physical activity we just conducted.

"I'm taking a gap year. You know what that is, right?"

His thumb slides across my bottom lip, stopping at the corner of my mouth before smiling.

"Sorry, your lips are perfect, and I just wanted to feel how soft they were again."

I pucker my lips and kiss the pad of his thumb before he removes it.

"Yes, I do know about gap years. I didn't know you were taking one, though."

If I could have afforded to take one, I would have. The time spent going from my undergraduate directly into law school while working was exhausting and racking up far more hours than I put in now at the office. I don't blame him for taking one, whether he's going to medical school or not, from the sounds of it.

"Yeah, but my family keeps pressuring me about the MCAT, and I haven't taken it yet. I don't want to even though I did well in school, graduating summa cum laude."

He takes a deep breath before diving deeper into his deliberation.

"It's more complicated than just taking a gap year," he continues, his gaze returning to that fixed point behind me. "My dad, he's been financing my lifestyle—school, this apartment, my car, bills, everything. Like a loan or an investment in my future as a doctor."

"So, he's expecting a return on that investment eventually?"

I piece together the unspoken pressure he must be feeling and the complexity of his situation. Will his father stop supporting him if he doesn't attend medical school? Stop providing for his son because he didn't follow his plan?

"Exactly," Giovanni replies, turning to look at me. "He's always talking about legacy, about continuing the family tradition in medicine. And here I am, passionate about a career that couldn't be more different."

He talks about his commitment to bodybuilding, outlining his goals to participate in as many competitions as possible, leading up to his ultimate aim—competing in Mr. Olympia in the fall. His eyes light up with the vision of triumphing in such a prestigious event, a dream close to his heart.

He then shifts to his plans beyond the competition stage, revealing his entrepreneurial spirit of launching his chain of gyms. Possibly starting a line of supplements after deep diving into his study of nutrition and biometrics to understand what works best for the body. It's all very impressive. He's passionate as he talks until he directs it back to his family.

I can see the conflict in his eyes—the desire to follow his own path weighed against the guilt of defying family expectations and the fear of losing financial support.

"Have you tried talking to him about how you feel?"

He runs a hand through his hair, tucking it behind his head with a frustrated expression.

"I've tried, but it always ends up in arguments. Christmas was a nightmare because my brother was there and joined my dad's side. Unlike medicine, he doesn't see fitness and health as a viable career. It's like he's got this one-track mind about what success looks like."

The room grows silent for a moment as we both ponder his predicament.

"Why does your brother being there make it worse?" I adjust my upper body to lay on his chest, putting my hand in the center and resting my chin atop it. "If anything, I'd think he would have chosen your side. Siblings often do."

He lets out a small, humorless laugh at my comment.

"You'd think that, right? But my brother has always been our family's golden child. He followed my dad's path straight into medicine, excelling at it."

He pauses momentarily, his chest rising and falling under my chin with each breath.

"When he's around, he reinforces my dad's expectations. He's living proof that the path they want for me is the 'right' one. And he doesn't get why I'd choose anything different. They both tell me to grow up."

I can feel the heaviness in him, the pressure of living in the shadow of a successful older sibling. Family dynamics are an integral part of life. I see it all the time in my court cases. A fleeting thought as to if my little brother feels that way about me. I doubt it. I hear he's doing just fine in Atlanta from my mother.

"That sounds really tough, being compared like that."

I raise my chin and move my hand in small circles on his chest to comfort him.

"Yeah, it is. And it's not that I'm not proud of him or anything. It's just . . . I want them to see that I can be successful in my own way, doing something I love."

His eyes roam my face and hair as his lips pull together tightly.

"It's hard when you feel like you're not living up to your family's expectations, especially regarding something as personal as your career choice."

I understand his struggle. I've always had to fight to prove my worth to people. They see a short, curvy woman with darker skin and often jump to all sorts of incorrect assumptions about me. I've had to work twice as hard as everyone else to get where I am. He nods, grateful for my understanding.

"Exactly. And I love what I do. Helping people achieve their fitness goals and becoming healthier and happier is rewarding in a way I can't explain. I just wish my family could see that and be okay with it."

"You're a wonderful trainer, very caring and attentive. It's one of the first attributes about you I noticed. That and your great looks."

He smiles slightly, my compliment falling short as it doesn't have the same weight as his family's expectations.

"What about your mom? What does she think?" I ask, curious about the other influential figure in his life.

My mother has always been proud of me, having been the first to finish high school, college, and law school. When I go back home, she practically throws a party and invites the neighborhood so they can see her 'successful lawyer daughter.'

"She's more understanding but not one to go against my dad's wishes. She's always been the mediator, trying to smooth things over. But he's the law of the house, and she acquiesces to him."

Hearing him talk about traditional roles in marriage leaves me a bit taken aback. The concept of a conventional marriage, with its often-rigid roles, has always been something I've struggled to understand, let alone embrace. As an undergrad, my time delving into women's studies opened my eyes to the many ways traditional structures can be limiting, especially for women.

I've always pictured a different kind of relationship for myself. One where I could maintain my sense of self and independence and not be confined by outdated expectations. I believe a committed partnership should be about mutual respect and support, where both individuals can thrive independently and together.

"Mothers have their own ways of showing support, I guess. Maybe she's doing what she thinks is best to keep the family together, even if it means not rocking the boat to keep the peace in a more traditional home."

Giovanni looks thoughtful, absorbing my perspective.

"It's interesting to hear you say that," he says slowly. "I guess I've always been surrounded by those traditional expectations, so much so that thinking outside of that box never really occurred to me until I moved out. Now those expectations are stifling."

I nod, feeling connected in our shared understanding of wanting something different from the norm.

"It's all about breaking the mold sometimes, right? Create a path that works for you, not just follow the one laid out by others. You must be true to yourself, or else it can be a miserable existence."

He smiles, a genuine appreciation in his eyes.

"I like that. Breaking the mold. I guess that's what I'm trying to do with my career, and maybe in other aspects of my life too."

Encouraged by his openness, I continue, "It's not always easy going against the grain, especially with family. But I think it's worth it to pursue what truly makes you happy, to build a life that's authentic to who you are."

I slide my hand over his chest, reaching for his to interlace our fingers in solidarity.

"Have you ever tried breaking out of the norm yourself? Going against what others expected of you?"

"Yeah, I have, in many ways. Going to college out of state, for starters. It wasn't exactly what my mom expected or could afford, so I put myself through. She's very proud of me, but it wasn't ever something we spoke of growing up in my house. She didn't encourage me like other parents because she knew she couldn't afford it and didn't want to put pipe dreams in my head."

He listens intently, nodding for me to continue.

"And becoming a lawyer, especially focusing on criminal law, and working for the city isn't exactly most people's idea of a 'successful career.' They're impressed with oil and gas or corporate law, something more lucrative. But I wanted to make a real difference, work on cases that matter on a personal level."

Giovanni's expression softens, respect evident in his gaze.

"That's pretty courageous, Kacie. I find it hard to stand up for my beliefs, especially when it goes against the grain. And here you are going against it every time, like a warrior."

I smile, feeling a sense of kinship in our shared experiences.

"It's not always easy, but I've learned that staying true to myself is the most important thing. It was more than just choosing a different academic path or career. Being an African American woman supporting myself, working, and paying for law school came with its own set of unique challenges."

His grip on my hand tightens, a gesture of support.

"I faced the academic pressure of a rigorous program and battled stereotypes and biases. Sometimes, I had to work twice as hard just to be seen on the same level as my peers or even called on in class."

"That's incredibly unfair."

His voice carries a hint of anger at the injustice.

"It was, but it also made me more determined. You know, my journey was made possible by the feminist movement, by powerful women who broke so many barriers. And I have this dream, you see, of giving back. I want to become a law professor, to guide and empower others who come from backgrounds like mine, to show them that they cannot only succeed but also excel and leave their own indelible mark."

I am taken aback by my openness, articulating thoughts and dreams I've never shared with anyone before. It's a candid admission, revealing parts of my aspirations and inner reflections that have remained unspoken until now. He's shaking his head, his eyes dancing with admiration, making me feel warm and accepted now that my dreams are out in this intimate world.

"That's really powerful, Kacie. Your strength and determination are incredible. And the fact that you want to use your experiences to help others? That's just amazing."

"Thank you, Giovanni."

I smile brightly at him, this day and night full of surprises as we find what we need in each other. He gives my hand a gentle squeeze, in time with the ending of a lazy jazz song.

"You're going to make an incredible professor one day, Kac. Your students will be lucky to have someone as passionate and insightful as you to guide them."

I kiss his chest, one after another, until he growls and rolls me on my back. An implicit invitation that seems to hang between us as he hovers over me. His proximity, the warmth of his body on mine, sends a thrill of anticipation through me.

"Is this okay?" His voice is a gentle murmur that matches the intimate atmosphere of the room. My heart beats a little faster, and my core heats with desire.

"It's more than okay,"

He lowers himself, his body melting into mine, the weight pushing me deeper into the mattress while his hard shaft settles against my stomach. His lips meet mine in a kiss filled with the promise of more to come, weaving together the emotional intimacy of our confessions with the physical attraction that has been building between us.

"Conquer me again, O.G."

11

GIOVANNI

The day starts early for me, with a morning filled with client training sessions at the gym. Despite the busy schedule, there's an underlying thrill about the evening I have planned for Kacie. Before heading to the gym, I make my first move of the day—ordering a bouquet of red roses and white lilies to be delivered to her office. I imagine the surprise and happiness on her face when she receives them, a bright spot in her busy workday.

After placing the flower order, I scarf down breakfast and head to the gym. The sessions go well, but my mind drifts back to last night and how awesome it was. Her skin was velvety under my touch, glowing in the dim light of my bedroom. The sweat on both our bodies from how hard we were going at it makes my cock spring to life every time I think about it. She complained about her hair, seeing it out of her peripheral vision and frowning at what our heat was doing to it when she finally left my bed. I thought it looked great, and I even told her so.

Going three rounds with her was far more than I expected, and when she complained of being sore from the workout and sore from my large cock, I couldn't hide the look of pride on my face. I would have taken her again this morning if she had agreed to spend the night, something she's doing tomorrow night.

With her around, I doubt I'll be sated, my cock hardening in my shorts while sitting at my desk attesting to it. Aside from our physical fun, I dwell on the emotional connection and how quickly we delved deep into that. When I blurted out about medical school, I wanted her to know my struggles. Something that weighs on me every day as I prove to my family that I can have a successful bodybuilding career and support myself.

Despite the wary look on her face, when I continued to unburden myself, her natural caring demeanor took over, and she asked great questions. Ones that demonstrated she was listening, willing to hear me out and wanted to know more. Although she didn't offer me any solutions, it was nice to have someone to talk to who could relate to me better than girls I have dated in the past. Kacie's reaction was everything I wanted and needed, making me want to be back inside her and as close to her as humanly possible.

The warmth of her body next to mine, the cadence of her soft laughter filling the room, and the depth of our conversations made the night feel surreal, almost like a dream. Every moment with Kacie feels like a step into a future filled with potential and shared dreams, making even the most ordinary days feel extraordinary.

Grinning, I glance around the gym, embracing a new lightness and a more positive outlook. It's a refreshing feeling, this optimism about my path and the direction things are taking with Kacie.

I take time for my workout once my client sessions are wrapped up. Marco isn't here today, and my regular, Frank, is traveling to his competition this week to get his IFBB Pro Card at one of the NPC national-level events. Something I need to ask him about when he returns to jump start my competition circuit.

I'm convinced I could win one now with how dedicated and disciplined I've been over the past year, aside from a few cheat days and my drunken stupor over Jenna. With how fast things have accelerated between Kacie and me, Jenna is so far in my rearview mirror that I didn't even notice her when she walked in today. My mind is cemented on my girl and the places we're going.

Pushing through my routine with a stellar efficiency rate, I dial down the dancing and posing in the mirror, eager to get out of here. I have a long list of things to get done to make tonight special, and wasting time at the gym is not one of them.

Post-workout, I head to my favorite health-conscious restaurant. Something I thought of doing ever since Kacie went home starving last night after declining my offer to finish dinner for her, seeing it was too late to eat. My overriding guilt, ever since, decided always to prioritize food over sex, thus spawning the idea for tonight's surprise.

The staff knows me well and is happy to prepare a takeout order of signature dishes. Grilled salmon, calamari, zucchini fritté, peanut lime chickpea salad, and mushroom risotto. These are my favorite dishes and soon to be hers, I hope. I thank them and head back to my loft, affectionately dubbed 'the cocoon' by Kacie, with our dinner in tow.

Back at the loft, I transform the space into a perfect evening setting. I carefully set the dining table, placed the scented candles around the room, and ensured the jazz playlist was queued up and ready to go.

As the time for her arrival draws closer, I send her a text. My first one today, thanking her for a wonderful night, was met with a short but concise response about how she enjoyed it too but had to run to court. I plan to reach out more now that I have a caring woman.

> Hey, hope your day is going well. Can I pick
> you up from the office?

Her response is immediate which surprises me given her busy schedule. But I smile at my screen when she answers.

> The flowers are gorgeous! My office smells like
> a florist. Ethan was nosy about who had sent
> them.

Ethan.

A streak of possessiveness surges through me, wiping the smile from my face. My thumbs fly across the screen, trying to get to the bottom of this Ethan guy being close enough to her to dig in her flowers.

> Who's Ethan?

My pulse spikes, wanting to know who this guy is and why I'm just now hearing his name.

> You've never mentioned him. Why is he so
> curious about your flowers?

It's not like me to feel this way, but something about the mention of this Ethan guy being so close to Kacie's personal space makes me uneasy. I wait, my eyes glued on the screen, eager for her response. The seconds tick by slowly, heightening my anxiety. I remind myself to stay calm that there's probably a simple explanation, but the wait feels interminable, and I start to pace the loft. Finally, her response comes through, and I brace myself, hoping to clarify who Ethan is and why his curiosity about the flowers has unsettled me so much.

> Ethan's my colleague. He's overly curious
> about everyone's business.

Why? Were you worried you had some
competition?

The wave of relief is short-lived when she mentions competition. Instead of responding directly to her question, I find myself typing my own, driven by a flicker of worry about this guy or anyone else who might come between what Kacie and I are starting.

Should I be worried?

No, O.G. I've only got eyes for you.

That she's using my bedroom nickname pleases me, chasing away my doubts and solidifying that we're on the same page.

Good girl.

I stroll over to the wall of windows, watching as the setting sun casts a golden glow on the office buildings opposite mine. Below, a steady stream of cars and buses hustle through the downtown streets, everyone eager to leave the city behind for their evening commutes home.

Can I pick you up?

I'm eager to see her, flicking my wrist to check the time and noticing it's a little after five. The first day I met her, she said she often worked past the janitorial staff cleaning the building. I hope she can tear herself away from the office to join me.

I've got a little surprise for you.

I add to my text to entice her. We did talk about seeing each other tonight when I walked her to her car last night, but I failed to set a time. Something I regret and will be more diligent in doing.

When?

Now!

I stare at her building in the distance, willing her to leave it and head straight here. If she needs to continue working after dinner, I'll clear off my office desk for her. I just want to be around her, spend time with her, and kiss those luscious lips. Maybe convince her to go a round or two to release some stress. It's all on the table if she would just get here.

I'm excited to see you.

I follow up my demand with a softer text. The dinner is fine in the warming drawer for another hour but won't taste as good. The wine is open and breathing as we speak. All I'm missing is her.

Let me finish a few things, and then I'll walk over.

Walk?

With the sun setting and crime at an all-time high in this city, I certainly don't like the idea of her walking over. Despite the traffic continuing to pour out of downtown for the next hour, there was a stabbing in broad daylight a couple of blocks from here, in between her building and mine, so walking is out of the question.

I'll pick you up. Be outside in 30 minutes.

I don't mean for it to come out as a command, but when she replies:

> Yes, Sir!

I realize I came off a little intense. I quickly send another message, hoping to soften the tone of my last text.

> Didn't mean to sound bossy. Just concerned about you walking the streets. Not safe.

Her reply is swift, which I appreciate.

> I walk the streets at night all the time. See you in a bit.

That doesn't absolve my worry. It only heightens it. I plan on asking her more about this over dinner. I just got her. I don't want anything happening to her, especially with the types of criminals she puts away. It makes me wonder if she carries a handgun for protection. Maybe this is something else we can do together, as I've had my license since I turned eighteen. Having grown up around guns, I'm well-versed in gun safety. I make a mental note to add that to the list.

I start preparing to leave, double-checking everything for our evening and blowing out the candles. The thought of Kacie walking through the door, seeing her smile as she takes in the surprise, keeps playing in my mind as I head out.

The drive to her office is quick, the streets still bustling with the evening commute. I pull up to the curb at the front of her building, my eyes scanning the entrance for her. Finally, I see her stepping out, a sight that instantly brings a smile to my face.

She spots me and waves, heading toward the truck where I have the seat heat waiting for her. Her arms are loaded with her purse, a briefcase, and another bag, more than she should be straddled with in her high heels and still swollen ankle.

I jump out the door, round the car, and take everything from her. The sigh of relief and the brief kiss on her lips yields a grateful smile from her. I open her door, help her in and then place all her items in the seat behind her. Once she's secured, with her seat belt fastened, I close the door and round the truck to jump in beside her.

"That was sweet of you to help. Thank you."

As I pull into the line of traffic back to my place, I can't help but feel satisfaction at her appreciation of my chivalrous gesture.

"Always happy to help."

She will love my dinner surprise if she thinks that small act is sweet.

"I'm famished! This eating healthy keeps me hungry all the time."

She adjusts the vents on her side of the dashboard, the heat blowing on high in case she's cold in the brisk night air.

"Now, what's this about a surprise?"

Her comment about being famished and her struggle with eating healthy makes me even more eager to reveal the surprise.

"Ah, you'll see soon enough. I've got something special planned for dinner."

I keep the details vague to heighten the anticipation. The drive back to my loft is quick with the synchronized traffic lights. I steal occasional glances at Kacie, her curiosity evident in her expression. As we approach my loft, she leans forward in her seat, flashing me a knowing look when I pull through the entrance gate of my building.

"I hope you're ready for a good meal and a relaxing evening," I tease, pulling into the parking space.

Kacie's eyes light up, otherwise she remains quiet. I jog around to her door, opening it while collecting her belongings to head up to the loft. As I open the door and usher her inside, her reaction to the carefully arranged setting, the candles on the table, the soft jazz music, and the cozy setup on the couch —is priceless. Her eyes widened in surprise, and a delighted smile spreads across her face.

"Wow, Giovanni, did you do all this?" While I deposit her bags on the entry table, she takes in the scene. "It smells amazing in here."

"I thought we could enjoy a quiet dinner together, just unwind and relax."

I lead her to the table to sit while I pour the wine and get the first servings ready for us. She side-eyes me.

"You mean sex."

"Not necessarily. But just for the record, I'd never turn down a chance to be with you."

My hands curl around the edges of her coat, her perfume tantalizing me. Even though I masturbated twice today, I could easily take her again and again if she let me. My cock standing at attention agrees when I poke her from behind with it.

"*Never.*"

She laughs at my emphasis while slipping out of her heavy winter coat. A cold front is blowing in tonight, and I can't think of a better way to keep warm than burying my face between her ass cheeks and taking her orally.

"Good to know. Although don't be upset, I have some work that needs to be done. With leaving early and all . . ."

Her arms rub up and down the sides of her body, trying to chase away a chill, and I walk to the thermostat to make it warmer for her.

Early.

She's already put in more hours than most this week, so leaving at the normal work time is not early. However, she shouldn't have to apologize to me for being so dedicated. That's not how I want our relationship to be. Not beholden to each other like my mamma is to my dad. Ugh.

"Good, I needed to work too."

My hands find her hips, pulling her toward me to give her a succession of kisses.

"Work?" Her eyebrows wrinkle at my statement. "Tell me more."

I give her a couple more kisses, then step away to get everything on the table so we can sit and talk. Something about the homeyness of having her over, eating together, and sharing our day fills me with contentment. As if I've found the peace and settled feeling, I didn't know I needed so much. I briefly think about yesterday with Seb and what he said about Chloe.

I'm beginning to see why he feels so passionately for her. It's what she gives him. What Kacie gives me is freedom. Freedom to be myself without being clingy or pressuring me to change. If I were to tell a woman my age that my family is pressuring me to go into medicine, she would join their side. But with Kacie, she just wants me to be happy and do what I love. It's a night and day difference.

"Giovanni? Are you okay? Is it work?"

Her voice pulls me back from my thoughts, and I realize I've been lost in reflection.

"Yeah, I'm more than okay. Just thinking about how nice it is to have you here to share this evening."

Kacie returns the smile, a look of warmth in her emerald eyes as she sits at the table.

"It's lovely to be here," she says. "Your place always feels so welcoming, like a haven from everything else."

"You called it a cocoon."

"I did. It is."

I light the candles again before serving the dinner, plating it for us. The aroma of the food, the candlelight flickers between us, and the soft music adds to the cozy atmosphere.

"As for work," I continue, answering her earlier question. "I spent the day training clients and got in a good workout myself.

I want to compile a list of competitions to enter leading up to Mr. Olympia in the fall. It's something I've been putting off, but with you needing to work, we can do it on the couch together."

The relief that coats her expression says it all.

"That would be lovely. You're the most handsome colleague I've ever had."

The jealous streak from before is back when she says it.

"Tell me about this Ethan guy. I sense some competition."

Her loud laughter bursts from her, reminding me of Seb. She clutches her chest while shaking her head.

"Ethan? Oh, Giovanni, there's no competition there. He's married, *with kids.*"

Married with kids doesn't stop some guys I see at the gym bragging about their side pieces. But I appreciate her naiveté that marriage vows are always honored. Her reassurance eases the irrational flicker of jealousy that momentarily flares up in me. I realize how silly my concern must seem to her.

"I guess I don't have to flex my muscles to scare him off then."

"No flexing necessary. You're the only one I'm interested in."

"Good. I have to say, planning this evening for us was the highlight of my day."

"This is just wonderful. No one has ever done anything like this for me. And the flowers . . . those were lovely too. Thank you, Giovanni."

Her hand finds mine on the table, giving it a light squeeze before releasing it. My heart leaps in my chest. She appreciates all the little things I do for her, bringing me a sense of pride and fulfillment that's hard to describe.

"You're welcome, Kacie. It's really nothing compared to how I feel about you."

I mean every word—doing something special for her feels as rewarding for me as it does for her.

"How do you feel?"

She sets her fork on her plate and leans forward. The softness in her expression makes me want to blurb it out.

"Well, I guess I'm trying to say that you've become a very important part of my life quicker than I expected. I feel this strong connection with you, something that's hard to put into words."

"It's like every time we're together, everything just feels right. You understand me in a way that no one else does. It's more than just attraction. It's like we're in tune with each other."

I fight the urge to drag her chair over to mine and set her on my lap.

"I feel the same way, Giovanni. It's not just about the fun times we have. It's the conversations, the way we can be ourselves around each other. It's rare to find someone you can connect with on so many levels."

"Exactly. And it's happening so fast. I'm having a hard time wrapping my mind around it. But then, that's why I wanted to make tonight special. To show you how much I appreciate you and enjoy being with you."

"It has been quick. However, that doesn't diminish your feelings. You've already shown me in so many ways, Giovanni. Just being here with you, sharing these moments, it's special to me too."

My gaze drops from those intense emerald eyes to her plump lips and down to her full breasts that mostly sit on the edge of the table.

"I'm trying to keep my word and not drag you into the bedroom right now," I grit through clenched teeth, my fingers moving toward her hand.

"Who says you have to keep your word?"

12

KACIE

The smolder on his face and how he's been looking at me while confessing his feelings is nothing short of blistering hot. Something that should be rewarded by him dragging me into his bedroom and conquering me.

"Kacie, don't you dare look at me like that."

His warning is cut short when he releases my hand to grasp the lip of the chair and effortlessly pulls me next to him. It's the sexiest move he has made without touching me at all. Wetness starts pooling between my legs, and I lean into his body.

"How am I looking at you, O.G.?" I taunt, using his new bedroom nickname, which has his eyes darkening.

The space between us disappears. I find myself drawn irresistibly toward him, my lips parting in anticipation of his kiss. I know he loves to be in control. I love it too. There's an undeniable electricity in this power dynamic between us.

It's playful yet sincere. Containing mutual respect and desire. As I lean into him, feeling the warmth of his body, I sense his control, a quality that he wields with care and confidence. And in this moment, I enjoy it just as much, willingly caught up in the intensity of our connection.

"Kacie."

His hand cups my face. I lean into his touch when his thumb strums my lips back and forth. If this is no, then he doesn't know the definition of the word when his lips replace his thumb. His hand moves to my neck, angling it up to give him deeper access to plunge his tongue into my mouth. I moan, relishing the feeling of this and reaching out to touch his chest when he captures my hand and moves it off him. I break the kiss immediately, giving him a curious look.

"Don't give me that look either. I'm on fire for you, and my resolve is fading fast."

The struggle is apparent by the rasp in his voice and in my hand when he thrusts it against his hard shaft.

"Oh."

"Yeah, oh. You have no idea how much I've replayed last night. But I'm trying to be considerate of the work you said you needed to get done tonight."

His declaration sends a tantalizing shiver through me, igniting a fire as well. The intensity in his dark eyes is mirrored in the fervency of his voice.

"Thank you for being considerate."

My voice is barely audible over the racing of my heart. His nearness, the warmth radiating from his body, envelops me in an alluring mix of comfort and longing.

"But I think I can manage to get my work done later," I add, feeling a boldness take hold while stroking him over the outside of his clothing. He releases a long groan, the corners of his mouth turning up at the good feeling.

"Are you sure? I don't want to be a distraction."

"Sometimes, a little distraction is exactly what I need. Especially when it's as enticing as you."

The air around us seems to throb with desire and restraint. It's a thrilling game, each push and pull drawing us closer in a rhythm of mutual attraction. Seconds tick by of us staring, my hand rubbing his shaft and contemplating our next moves.

"Let's eat first. You already missed out on dinner last night because of my greediness. I wouldn't—"

"*Our* greediness," I correct as his hand slides to my shoulder and starts rubbing the tight muscles, eliciting a groan of a different kind from me. My hand is still on his cock while I enjoy the goodness radiating from the tension being rubbed away.

"Kacie, these are way too tight. And there's a couple of knots."

His fingers work their magic until he bores into a spot that has me shifting away in pain. His hand falls to my back, rubbing soothing circles as if in apology.

"How about a proper massage after dinner?" His voice is warm with the promise of relaxation as he removes my hand from his shaft. "I think you could use one."

I nod, feeling a rush of gratitude.

"Dinner, massage, and sex. That sounds perfect."

"I like where this is going. Let's enjoy this meal. I want to make sure you're well-fed after your long day." His tone is caring, and his wink is suggestive. "Plus, you'll need a carb load for your cardio workout."

I laugh. My priorities of working tonight fade as I push aside my caseload for another night of fun with him. A long, drawn-out night of fun, I hope. When I think dinner will be quick and easy, Giovanni turns dinner into another romantic affair. He picks up a fork, skewering a piece of grilled salmon and holding it to my lips. I open my mouth, letting him feed me, and savor the rich, flavorful taste of the fish.

There's something deeply intimate about this gesture, and I relax further into the moment. We share the same fork, and between bites that he carefully feeds me, we engage in light conversation about his day and his clients while looking at the skyline surrounding us. He asks about my day, but I want to escape work and not think about it anymore. He gets the hint when I respectfully decline.

The dinner progresses slowly, with Giovanni taking his time to ensure I enjoy every bite. It's not just about the food, but the experience—being cared for, the gentleness of the moment. It's a side of him that I find both endearing and attractive.

A gentle giant, if I were to be honest, and yet something I might not ever voice to him. He might not like that since he's more sensitive than I initially realized, and I'd never intentionally hurt his feelings. Once we finish our meal, he stands and offers his hand.

"Ready for that massage?"

"Shouldn't we clean all this up first?"

"No. I've been very patient, but watching that sauce glisten on your lips has me wanting them to glisten with something else."

"Oh."

My eyebrows raise at his blatant intention. His usual gentleness, juxtaposed with this sudden boldness, catches me off guard. Not one for being very good at giving men oral sex, a sudden wave of nervousness runs through me.

"I mean, if you're comfortable with that," he quickly adds, noticing the change in my expression.

His tone is now softer, a reminder of his constant consideration for my feelings. He has always been respectful and understanding, creating a space where I feel safe and valued. This moment, while unexpected, doesn't change that.

"Yes, I'm okay with it. Just . . . maybe guide me a bit on how you like it?"

I feel insecure about stating the obvious, but surely men can tell experience from inexperience. If I set the expectations low, he won't be disappointed. Or we can move on to other things if he is.

"Of course," he assures me with a look of relief and desire mingling in his eyes. "We'll take it slow. I just want to be close to you, Kacie."

I appreciate his honesty and his willingness to communicate openly. His sensitivity, far from being a weakness, is something I've come to admire deeply. He interweaves our fingers, sending a comforting squeeze through his into mine as we walk down the hall to his bedroom.

There is no music this time, only the soft light from the bathroom cascading across the bed as if my performance takes center stage. It's a little daunting. Not even remembering the last time I gave a man oral sex, I release his hand to reach for his shirt.

He tsks before saying, "I promised you a massage."

My mind is so preoccupied with the other thing that I forgot he's working on my muscles first. My shoulders sag in relief and I cast him an easy smile.

"Of course. Where do you want me?"

"On the bed, face down."

He throws back the bedding to the luxurious sheets and adjusts the pillows.

"First, you need to get naked."

He raises a suggestive eyebrow before returning to me. His hands are eagerly raising my blouse above my head, groaning when he catches sight of my breasts and deposits kisses on the top of each one. His fingers quickly unfasten my bra, tossing it onto his dresser before dipping to catch a nipple in his mouth.

The heat from his mouth creates a tingling sensation in my core that wants so much more than a massage. His tongue flicks my nipple into a hard bud, then applies pressure, causing me to shrink against the forceful suction he's administering. It's too much attention to one area and not enough to another. I reach for the hem of his shirt, tugging at it to come off. He takes immediate action by whipping it over his head and onto the floor to return to suckle at my other breast.

My body arches toward his lips while he traces a trail of kisses between them. I moan and writhe as his tongue swirls my sensitive peaks. One hand holds onto his shoulder while the other grips his soft hair, urging him to go lower. I'm greedy, wanting oral from him without having given it yet. He's been generous so far, and with how pleasing he's been to me, I want to be equally pleasing to him.

His hands wander down to the waistband of my skirt. With one swift tug, he pulls it down, revealing my legs and the delicate lace panties I'm wearing. His gaze lingers on them for a moment before he reaches forward and slides them off, exposing my slick folds.

"Step out."

His voice is raspy as I step out of the ring of my skirt, panties, and shoes with his assistance. Standing naked over him while he kneels is empowering and unsettling. But it's all forgotten when he locks his eyes on my swollen lips, taking in the sight of me. Without hesitation, he leans forward and flicks his tongue against me, tasting me. His fingers separate my lips, exposing my sensitive bud to him, and I gasp in pleasure.

"Good girl," he murmurs against my flesh, our gaze connecting when my hand slips from his shoulder. "You're already wet for me."

"I am."

I can scarcely breathe when the sharp points of his mustache scrap against my delicate flesh.

"I want to do everything."

His eyes continue to bore into mine as I make requests. I have no idea how I'm going to handle them. He doesn't say anything. He merely continues to spoil me with his hot breath and skilled tongue. My entire body trembles, needing more.

His calloused hand slides up the back of my leg, stopping at the base of my butt and pulling my cheeks apart to reach my warm pussy. It's shockingly intimate, accessing me from behind rather than the front, and my brain doesn't know how to process it.

His fingers press into me, forcing my legs further apart and opening to him. My eyes close, my head falls back, and I relax into his expert fingers and tongue. I'm straddling his hand, suspended between riding it and rubbing my clit on his face. The more friction I create, the sloppier his actions get until he's diving deeper, plunging his tongue roughly into my clit and making me the center of his attention.

He strokes every sensitive spot, sending waves of pleasure through my body. My hips buck against him uncontrollably as I lose myself in the euphoria of his touch and my orgasm. I ride it out until his tongue flattens against me with long swipes lapping up my cum. When it's too sensitive to the touch, I pull away.

"That was amazing."

I open my eyes to see those dark orbs staring at me.

"Yeah, it was. Now get on the bed."

He stands swiftly, his knee popping at the fast action, which he ignores. His hand catches under my elbow, helping me to the edge of the bed.

Before lying down, I ask, "Why did you do that? Don't get me wrong, I loved it, but I thought I was supposed to do you first."

His hands plant on his hips, the V in the front of my face a promise of what's to come, and my nervousness is making a comeback.

"Well, first off, I love tasting you, and I've wanted to do that all day. More importantly, you looked worried when we walked in here, and I wouldn't say I liked it. I wanted to put you at ease. You always have the right to say no, Kacie. We agreed to me being in charge, but I won't ask you to do things you don't want to do. There's no fun in that for either of us."

His eyes meet mine, and I can see the sincerity there. He's right. We agreed he would take charge, but I never expected it to mean this much. He's genuinely concerned about my feelings and comfort, making me feel appreciated and cared for. All the books talk about this when they say partners need to communicate. It's all he and I do, and I'm very fond of it. I appreciate his perspective and give him a bright grin.

"Let's have more fun."

I flop onto my stomach, my body making a flatulence sound against the sheets, which has me mortified. He belts out a laugh so loud that I'm forced to chuckle along with him.

"You're adorable, Kacie."

I prop myself on my elbows to look over my shoulder at him. He's busy staring at my butt while laughing. It makes me feel silly, fun, and carefree all at the same time. What a glorious feeling to be truly accepted, weight gain and all.

"I'm going to go get my oils. Make yourself comfortable."

I comply, lying face down on the bed, feeling the softness of the sheets against my skin and the fluffy pillow under my head. The soft light from the bathroom offers just enough illumination, creating a sensual atmosphere. It seems like only a few seconds when music strums through the speakers in his ceiling.

I sense his presence by the side of the bed until it dips under his weight. He straddles me, his bare cock poking into my butt, and I squirm in anticipation of everything yet to come.

I hear the subtle sound of him dispensing massage oil, and then I feel the warmth of his hands on my back. His touch is firm yet gentle. His skilled fingers work their way across my tense muscles. The sensation is relaxing and invigorating, easing the stress and tension from the day.

"Let me know if the pressure is too much."

"It's perfect," I hum, melting under his touch.

His hands move confidently, each stroke and knead bringing a deeper relaxation. My nervousness dissipates as he works on my shoulders and neck. His ability to tune into my needs, to put me before him, is a gift in and of itself. I can't recall ever meeting such a selfless guy. The fact that his family can't see this in him is beyond me and something I want to help him with.

The massage continues, his movements in tune with the melody of the music, and just as I'm about to fall asleep, his hands sweep down to my butt to massage my cheeks. He mutters about holding tension in where the leg joins the body, moving my knee out, and manipulating the hip joint until I'm moaning in a different type of pleasure.

I've never had my butt, hip, and inner outer thigh massaged like this, but damn if it doesn't feel almost as good as an orgasm. He continues to explain that sitting for long hours causes the muscles to tighten, thus becoming shorter—one of many reasons why sitting is the new smoking.

I'm half listening, thoroughly enjoying, and when he hits a deeper section with his elbow, I inhale a quick breath. It's an odd mix of pain and pleasure, and the more he rubs out the hurt, the better it feels until I'm putty in his hands.

When that side is fully squishy and stress-free, he moves to the other leg and starts the process over. If he plans on having sex tonight, it might have to be in this position, as I'm floating on clouds from the release of stress everywhere in my body.

"You're amazing," I slur against his pillows, fighting and falling asleep with how relaxed and weightless I feel. It's almost beyond words.

"It does feel great, huh?"

His question floats somewhere behind me until that elbow finds the deep hip pocket, and I'm sucking in the air again.

"Relax, Kacie. I promise you're going to feel like a million bucks tomorrow."

"I feel like a million bucks now. Seriously, you're going to have to have sex with me just like this because I don't think I can move."

It's half jest and half-truth.

"That can easily be arranged," he says without missing a beat. "Is there anywhere else you are holding tension that I can rub out."

"My pussy," I blurt out, then hold my breath at being so blunt and forward—extremely uncharacteristic of me.

"Is that so?"

He taps his hard shaft against my ass cheek as if I didn't already feel the snake slithering across my body when he changes positions or directions.

"Definitely."

My boldness continues. I blame it on the utter uselessness of my body. Not wanting to do any work other than lying back and having him make me feel amazing in every way possible.

"Good girl. Get me ready, and I'll give you what you want."

My insecurity raises a feeble attempt at making me worried about oral but fails with how many good sensations course through my body compliments of him. When his shaft steps into my line of sight, I know what he wants, and I wish to return part of what he's already given to me. I prop myself up on my elbows and scoot to the edge of the bed while licking my lips. When I reach out to touch him, he tsks again at me.

"Only that perfect mouth, Kac."

He moves closer, his thick, muscular thighs spreading slightly when he leans toward the bed. His shaft is hard, angled right at me with a drop of precum waiting to be licked. His hands remain by his side, patiently waiting for me to start.

I take a deep breath, circle my mouth, and latch onto him. He's warm and a bit salty. The vein on the underside presses against my flattened tongue as I take him as far as I can and then gag.

His hand caresses my cheek as I pull back, wanting to start again.

"Relax. There's no need to take all of me. Start with the tip."

His fingers are featherlight, moving down my neck and toward my breast before falling away. I start again, closing my eyes and setting a rhythm that works for me. Not too deep, but still sexy and sensual in my head. Not having to use my hands makes it easier to focus on one thing. The grunts and groans pouring out of him are confirmation I'm on the right track.

"Very good girl."

I open my eyes to lock onto his. Molten dark chocolate irises, pleased and proud, sends a thrill through me.

"Keep up the rhythm, and let me know if you need a break."

I resume my task, feeling more confident now that I know what to expect. I focus on his taste, seeking out the subtle flavors of his skin and the musky scent of his arousal. As I lick and suck, he responds with more groans and subtle shifts in his hips, encouraging me further.

I explore his shaft, circling the head with my tongue and then swiping down the length of him, tracing the vein and the sensitive spots. His breath hitches, and I know I'm hitting the right places. I can feel his pulse throbbing under my lips, and his taste is becoming more and more familiar.

As he comes closer to his release, he grips my head, guiding me to take more of him in my mouth. I obey, opening wider and taking him deeper, relishing in the salty taste of him and the feel of him hitting the back of my mouth.

"Fuck."

His hips buck into my face.

"Such a good girl for me."

I can feel his shaft throbbing against my tongue. I know he's close by the pressure of his hand on my head and his wildly bucking hips. I want to taste his release. I bob my head faster, sucking harder and licking every inch that will fit in my mouth.

"I'm coming, Kac," he warns me, his voice strained. "Hold it in your mouth, don't swallow it."

I hum my acknowledgment, not taking my mouth off him. I want to experience him in this way and to make him feel as good as he does to me. With a deep, guttural groan, his muscles tense, and his cock pulses in my mouth. I can feel his hot, salty release coming, the heat bursting against my tongue and throat.

It's a lot more than I expected, and I'm having trouble containing it all while he keeps thrusting while riding out his climax. I watch in awe at his stunning face, lost in the pleasure that I brought him, and I couldn't be happier. When his eyes find mine, it's scorching hot. He grabs the base of his cock when removing it, dragging some of his cum onto my chin.

"Show me."

I oblige, opening my mouth and showing him the remains of his release on my tongue. A pleased smile passes over his lips, his hand stroking my hair until it settles against my face.

"That's exactly what I envisioned when you had that sauce glistening on your lips at dinner."

I swallow it down, pleased I could live out his fantasy from earlier tonight and proud that my first blowjob in years is a huge success. I flash him a little smirk, then show him my empty tongue, which elicits a growl from him before collapsing on the bed next to me. We share a kiss, our tongues mingling with the taste of him, and I can feel his erection hardening against my side as I break away.

"Glad you like it. Now someone said if I'm a good girl, which I was, I get what I want?"

I elbow him, watching his chest rise and fall while catching his breath.

"No rest for the weary, huh?"

"Not a chance when that snake is already trying to bite me."

"Your wish is my command. Stay just like that. I'm taking you from behind."

13

GIOVANNI

Her dark eyebrow arches and her lips part slightly as if she's about to ask a question, but then she seems to change her mind. I find her natural curiosity endearing, but there's something even more appealing about her silent compliance. It's as if her intrigue about the unexpected outweighs her usual investigative nature. This shift in her, choosing the thrill of surprise over immediate answers, feels like a victory for the trust we're building together. I appreciate her willingness to go along with the moment, and trust me. I'm determined not to spoil it by offering explanations she hasn't asked for.

I maneuver behind her, leaving her precisely as she was during the massage, with the only exception being a pillow stuffed under her hips to raise her slightly. When she begins to rise on all fours, I make my usual disapproving sound that has her lowering back down to the mattress. I reward her by kneading her ass and separating the plump flesh to get a visual of her delicious holes. I love that her skin tone is darker around them. The contrast in watching my cock penetrate her tight pussy is an attraction that makes me want to bust the second I'm inside.

Without feeling the wetness of her soft lips, I let a long string of saliva drop from my mouth to the center of her taint. As much as I'd love to take her anally, I'm a generously large size, and most women are unwilling to try once they see my cock. It's a delicatessen that's rarely offered and rarely successful. Hurting Kacie is absolutely out of the question, but with her comment that she wants to do everything, maybe we'll try it sometime.

With one hand still separating her cheeks, she stacks her arms on the pillow and rests her cheek against her forearm, completely trusting me to care for her as she closes her eyes. It boosts my confidence, and my cock swells further. I rub the salvia with my thumb over her pussy lips, which are wetter than I expect. Some women get turned on when giving head. I suspect Kacie is one of them. If that's the case, we're going to warm her up with a lot more oral to get her in the mood.

"You're very wet."

She doesn't open her eyes or raise her head, she sighs. I'll keep testing her to get my real answers since she's unwilling to share.

"Do you trust me, Kac?"

"Inexplicably."

Her light voice is muffled against the pillow. Otherwise, the sea of silky smooth skin awaits me, and I lean forward to plant kisses down her spine. She squirms, light whimpers seeping out of her when I return to stroking her drenched pussy lips. I open her wider, knowing it will take some work to get inside from the angle. Yet, it will be worth it when I feel how tight she is and when she takes all of me straight to her cervix.

I reach into the drawer to grab a condom and roll it on, adjusting my legs over hers before pressing the tip of my cock against her slick entrance. It resists the intrusion, the space too compressed by her thick thighs, and a smile ghosts across my face. I love curvy women, having my face or cock getting lost in their folds is the best. It's a hidden gift that they don't even know about. Most women want to lose weight to fit some nonsensical standard. They might not be so concerned if they only knew we wanted to be smothered by their voluptuous figure.

"You're so sexy like this."

I skim a hand over her ass, beyond her waist to her shoulder, giving it an encouraging squeeze, and then back down. She moans, pliable under me and patiently waiting for me to do whatever I want to her. That thought resumes my focus on getting the tip in her, and once that happens, the rest follows pretty easily.

I spread her even further, nudging her legs out a bit more to allow me in. Then, with my thighs positioned on the outside of hers, I'll collapse them together when I'm all the way in. I level another line of spit to her plump lips as I push into her, her tight muscles giving way to me and eliciting a long moan.

"I've never done it this way."

She lifts onto her elbows to glance over her shoulder. Her dark curls, silky caramel skin, and those sparklingly green eyes heighten my lust for her. I stare at her, into her, trying to communicate the growing attraction I have for her both physically, mentally, and emotionally. She's the total package, everything I could want, and much more. Our sexual compatibility is the icing on the cake. Unbelievable, in fact.

"Do you like it?"

I like that we always check in, ensuring the other feels good and enjoys how things are going. My nightmare would be to have done something she dislikes and never see her again. Losing her is fast becoming my greatest fear.

"I do. You're so deep. It's as if I can feel every inch of you."

I flash her a knowing smile.

"I know. Now be a good girl and relax so I can go all the way in."

Little does she know the way her body is holding her upright is tightening her legs and lower body, pausing my progress of going all the way into her pussy. When a small O shapes her lips, she resumes her current position, her body relaxing, allowing me to slide home. Our shared groan when I bottom out at her cervix is hot, and I pause to relish the feeling before drawing slowly back out.

"Yes." Her voice is hoarse with desire. "Feels amazing."

I can't hold back my grunt as I start to move. My hips piston forward with a slow, measured rhythm. She grabs hold of the pillow, her nails digging into the fabric as my thrusts push her forward. Her hips arch upward, invitation clear, and I thrust deeper, feeling the snug heat of her pussy enveloping me completely.

"Yes, you do."

My grip on her hips tightens, the force of my cock plunging into her ripples across her flesh, and her body moves with considerable force toward the headboard. She throws out a hand, bracing herself against the carved wood as I take her over and over again. Her tight walls feel like velvet against my cock, clutching me tightly when I clench my legs over hers.

I grab another pillow and stuff it on top of the other, which bends her waist even more and angles her butt higher. She moans at the change, her hand rolling into a fist against the headboard. I'm thrusting down into her, steep and unrelenting until she screams out my name. I pump faster and harder, my sweat dripping onto her back without her noticing how loud and long she screams. Her pussy expands and contracts with pleasure, the rings clenching me harder and making me almost climax and then releasing to allow me to plunge harder.

I'm practically straddling her, my cock so deep I never want to come out when I see her asshole unexpectantly gape. It's a pleasant surprise, one I'm more than happy to fill to test the waters and gauge her reaction. I don't stop pumping into her, hard and fast, while I wet my thumb and slip it inside. She moves forward in surprise, a glance over her shoulder, and I give her a mischievous wink.

Trust and surprises. I'd never hurt her. She knows that unexpected actions can be very pleasurable if done correctly. I'm in and out before she can utter a word, which she doesn't, as another orgasm rockets through her. I keep my thumb on her hole, circling, teasing, and removing it altogether. It's strategic —the way I'm taking her. Giving her what she wants, taking what I need, and sampling what lies ahead.

"Did you like that, my good girl?"

My voice is thick with desire, even to my ears. And when she wiggles her ass, I almost lose it. Maybe she's too shy to say it or too lost in her climax, but I don't waste any time rewarding her with my thumb pushing inside her. She moans my name repeatedly as I plunge my cock down into her until my balls tingle and my climax rolls through me with a shudder.

Sweat continues to drip off me, mixing with the perspiration beading at her lower back while riding out the amazing sensations sweeping over me. She is motionless, having stopped trying to fuck me back to receive and enjoy instead. My thumb slides from her gaping hole when my body comes to a stop. She's panting into the pillow, her breath harsh and ragged. Sudden worry fills me, and I sweep her tight curls, blocking her face to check on her.

"Kac?"

A brief smile appears on her lips, but her eyes are closed. I internally panic that it must have been too rough for her, and I fear I might have scared her off. My mind starts racing with guilt and regret. But then her eyes snap open, and she grins mischievously at me.

"If that is plundering, I'll take more, please, and thank you."

Relief surges through me. I move backward off her hips to ease the stress I put on her back, and my cock slides out of my favorite place.

"I worried I got a little too carried away with you."

I squeeze her cheeks, kneading them before sliding my thumbs to her waist to use our sweat to rub away the possible soreness.

"It's this juicy ass of yours. All I want to do is dominate it."

With me kneeling at her legs, she twists her upper body, revealing those equally delicious breasts of hers. The thought of her blowing me in between them makes my cock twitch.

"Conquered, dominated, plundered. All synonymous terms at this point."

She waves a carefree hand in the air before smoothing back her wild curls. I move to the edge of the bed, standing to give her space to stretch while I get rid of the condom.

"Not too much?"

I await her answer as I roll the full condom off my cock and decide I'm going to paint her with my cum next time.

"No, O.G., definitely not too much."

She flips onto her back with a groan, bed lines crisscrossing her body from the sheets that I molded her into.

"But there at the end, with the two pillows and how deep you were, then the finger, well, that was spectacular."

I stare at her on my bed, comfortable and casual to let me play with her how I want. Her legs are splayed, her tight pussy nestled in between them glistening with her multiple releases. The way her skin shimmers with sweat in the bathroom light. How her heavy breasts slip to the side of her body, beckoning my lips, hand, or cock to be nestled in the middle of them.

Her full lips smile at me while her eyes dance with happiness. It's nearly too much to take, and I close my eyes for a few seconds to commit it to memory. My new mission is to make her look like this every time I see her.

"What are you thinking?" she asks in her sweet melody.

I open my eyes to see she tucked a hand behind her head, otherwise, she hasn't moved an inch.

"That I want to make you this happy always," I tell her the truth. I want it always to be this good between us.

"I don't know if it's *always* achievable, but we can aim for the majority."

She looks up at me, her eyes bright and enchanting, and I squat down to give her a few kisses.

"Would this tough-as-nails ADA accept majority rules?"

I kiss the bridge of her nose and her forehead before standing.

"No, she wouldn't. Let's aim for always."

Leaving her with my parting words, I stroll into the bathroom to start the water warming for her towel while I dispose of the condom and use the facilities. I don't hear her come in over the loudness of my pee bursting from my still hard cock. It never goes down when she's around. I find it an interesting problem. When I finish up in the water closet, I'm surprised to see her dressed in my shirt at the sink.

"What is this?"

I pluck at the fabric, not unhappy seeing her in my clothes. After all, she's mine, and I'm hers. I'd rather her be naked so I can see, touch, and fondle as I see fit, though.

She gives me a guilty smile in the mirror's reflection while washing her hands and wiping away a clump of mascara stuck to her cheek. I stand behind her, circling my arms around her to wash my hands. Not protesting being smashed up against the counter while I work the soap through my fingers, she leans her body into mine while tilting her head.

"Giovanni, I hope you don't mind me saying this. And please know I'm not trying to intrude in your business, but I've been thinking about what you said about your family. The pressure they put on you to enter a field you don't want to pursue."

I'm completely caught off guard. Her dwelling on my problems is new and takes me back. I'm so used to having to go it alone, treading water in the middle of the ocean, knowing help won't be coming, that I'm not sure what to say. I turn off the water and step back to dry my hands.

She turns to face me, her hands gripping the counter and causing her elbows to jut outward. Her expression turns focused, the sharp intellect of a seasoned ADA coming to the forefront. She takes my stunned silence as acceptance to proceed.

"Here's what you could do. Put together a comprehensive business plan for your fitness career. Include your achievements, client testimonials, financial projections, and how the fitness industry is growing. How your bodybuilding competitions will help build your brand and raise awareness of your business. Facts and hard evidence. That's what will speak to their pragmatic minds."

I listen intently, impressed by the clarity of her suggestion.

"That's brilliant. Show them it's not just a passion, but a profitable and sustainable career."

She nods, her eyes alight with her strategic thinking.

"Exactly. Add market research, your competition wins, and maybe even a business model for your gym and supplement line. Present it like a case. Clear, logical, and compelling. Make them see the potential returns on their 'investment' in you."

The idea resonates with me deeply.

"I never thought about it like that. Presenting it in a way my dad understands, in his language of business and ROI."

She gives me a confident smile.

"You've got a strong case, Giovanni. You need to lay it out for them. And I'm here to help you structure it, to make it as convincing as possible."

Her offer to help, combined with this solid, actionable plan, fills me with a newfound sense of purpose and hope. Kacie is more than just offering support. She's giving me a tool to bridge the gap between my world and my family's. Not only does she care about me, but her wanting to help tackle my problems has me embracing her.

"You have no idea how much this means to me, Kac."

My voice clogs with emotion as I rest my cheek on her head. I ignore the fine strands tickling my skin as I hold her. Her hands slide around my waist, clinging to me as tightly as I cling to her.

"Of course. I want to see you succeed, Giovanni. Your happiness matters to me."

Her voice is muffled against my chest, but it rings with sincerity. I tighten my embrace, overcome with gratitude and affection.

"Your belief in me gives me the strength I didn't know I needed," I admit, clearing my throat.

Her offer fills me with an indescribable feeling of warmth and support. As we stand holding each other, I feel like everything in my life is starting to fall into place with her by my side. Eventually, she breaks the embrace, wanting us to clean up before we begin working. I furnish her with a pair of basketball shorts draping down to her knees but fitting her figure snugly.

We return to the living area, ready to start working on the plan. As we sit down, laptops open, her sharp mind and keen insights come into play, helping me frame my arguments and gather the necessary data.

The way she effortlessly blends her professional acumen with her interest in my life makes me appreciate her even more. Once she has the general business plan template how she likes it, she sets about her work on the opposite end of the couch, citing privacy reasons for sitting too far away. I understand entirely, choosing to enjoy how easily and effortlessly we can transition from passionate lovers to working partners. It's a rare combination—something I'm enjoying immensely.

"How about a chickpea protein brownie? I know late-night snacking isn't on either of our meal plans, but I think we burned off about a thousand calories there."

I toss my thumb toward the bedroom when our eyes meet.

"More like you burned ten thousand calories, and I just laid there."

She winks, extending her fist for me to bump. It's the first time she's done it, and I secretly love it.

"But it sounds interesting, so why not."

"Now you're talking!"

14

KACIE

I'm standing in the courthouse hallway, leaning against the cool marble wall, waiting for my co-counsel to arrive to go over our docket. It's going to be a long day. In several cases, we couldn't get a plea deal on return to court with more motions filed.

As I wait, the stillness of the early morning gives me a moment of calm before the flurry of activity fills these halls. My phone vibrates in my hand, a welcome distraction from making small talk with passing counselors. It's a message from Giovanni.

> Good morning! Still thinking about last night. It was really special.
>
> Hope your day goes smoothly 😊

Reading his words brings a smile to my face, a warmth that slices through the mounting tension of the impending hectic day. I quickly type back, my fingers moving deftly over the screen.

> Thanks, it means a lot. Today's packed with court cases. Wish me luck.

Sending the message, I tuck the phone away as my co-counsel arrives, her footsteps echoing in the quiet corridor.

"Morning," she greets, her voice echoing against the marble surrounding us. "Ready for this marathon?"

I nod, drawing a deep breath.

"As ready as I'll ever be."

Together, we walk toward the courtroom, reviewing our docket and discussing strategies for each case. The day's schedule is daunting—back-to-back hearings, complex arguments, and navigating unforeseen legal twists. As we step into the courtroom, the buzz of activity starts to pick up. Other attorneys, clerks, and clients begin to fill the space, each person adding to the growing hum of voices and movement.

I steel myself for the day ahead, fortified by the memory of last night. The intimate candlelight dinner, the gentle manner in which he fed me, the sensual massage, the patience and encouraging oral I gave him, and the mind-blowing way we had sex. It brings a renewed heat and passion to repeat it and has me fanning my face with a stack of papers.

Receiving Giovanni's good morning text brings to mind the conversations I've overheard among my single women colleagues around the water cooler. They often talk about the significance of getting a good morning message, particularly after spending the night with someone. Now, experiencing it firsthand, I understand the excitement and affirmation it brings. It truly is a wonderful feeling to start the day with such a thoughtful gesture.

"Everything alright?"

My colleague glances at the waving papers, which I immediately stop.

"Yes, just a little stuffy in here. This courtroom always gets too much heat in the winter."

I use the robust central heating as an excuse, even if it's mostly accurate, and why everyone dislikes this courtroom. It's stifling in the winter and freezing in the summer.

"I think it's because the judge is elderly."

I bristle at the remark. It strikes me as a bit off-color and ageist, attributing the courtroom's temperature issues to the judge's age. It's an unnecessary and unfair accusation. However, I choose to hold my tongue, realizing that voicing my thoughts might not be helpful to the victim's cases we are handling today if I get sideways with my colleague at the start of the day.

I return to work, refocusing on the cases while waiting for the victim to arrive. We've come too far in many of them for me to be distracted now, and I push the thoughts of Giovanni to the back of my mind.

The morning passes in a blur of legal proceedings. I navigate each hearing professionally and confidently, delivering arguments with precision and responding to the judges' questions with clarity. Between hearings, I scarf down a protein bar and almonds, a far cry from last night's delicious dinner.

As the day wears on, the cases become increasingly complex. My mind is a whirlwind of legal statutes, case precedents, and strategic maneuvering. Despite the intensity of the day, I find my rhythm in the proceedings, a flow that comes from years of experience in the courtroom.

I'm collapsed in my chair, papers in hand, waiting for the final case of the day. Giovanni has texted a couple of times asking if we can go out tonight after our session at the gym. I initially agreed, thinking a night on the town would be exhilarating. With how long and exhausting this day is, I think a night on the couch with a glass of wine sounds better. I send him a quick text.

> I might be late to our session. It's running an hour late with all the dockets adding extra time.

No worries. You know I'll wait for you.

I smile at my phone. Of course, he'd wait. His patience is one of many things I like about him. He understands that my career comes first and respects the importance of it.

I'm excited to see you.

He adds, and I chuckle, garnering the attention of my co-counsel, which I wave away with a shake of my head.

You just saw me last night.

Yes, but I can still be excited to see you.

I'm flattered. It's refreshing how open he is with me.

Not sick of me yet?

Not a chance, Kac. If anything, you're addicting. I've always had a thing for milk chocolate.

I cover my mouth while laughing, which is not the appropriate response in court. Since we are between cases, I can get away with it a little.

Oh my, I don't know what to say.

Do you know what goes well with milk chocolate?

I can't hide my smile when I drop my hand to respond.

What?

Me!

I was thinking more along the lines of food. His response makes my smile even bigger. The courtrooms stir to life around me, and I shoot off a quick text that I must run but will text him as soon as I'm done. He closes with a kiss emoji before I lock and stow away my phone.

As the victim and her family arrive, I quickly greet them. We gather in a private room, where I carefully go over all the details we've discussed in previous meetings, ensuring they're fully prepared for the hearing ahead. I focus on making them feel as comfortable and informed as possible, aware of the emotional toll a day in court can bring.

The court proceedings commence with a solemn undertone despite the rumbling of the gallery behind us. The judge's gavel rattles a couple of times to quiet the chatter, which is a bad omen. A disruptive gallery brings unease to the proceedings and usually leads to emotional outbursts that can jar the victim's testimony, which is the last thing we need today.

The victim, a slight figure with a quiet determination etched into her features, is seated at the front of the courtroom to give her testimony. Despite the tremble in her voice, an unmistakable strength resonates through her words.

She does very well as I lead her through the practiced line of questioning, focusing on me and the jury. Her eyes never venture to the defendant, whose demeanor shifts alarmingly fast. His brows knit together in anger, his jaw clenched tight, and his hands, rough and calloused, curl into fists on top of the table. My eyes move from him to his attorney to the bailiff against the wall as the courtroom becomes tense.

When I ask her for details of the attack, he suddenly bursts forward, eyes wild, hurling threats as he lunges forward. The room erupts into chaos, chairs scraping against the floor as people jump up in a panicked rush. My heart races, pounding against my ribcage. My hands, usually steady and sure, tremble slightly as I race toward the victim.

Her face is pale, her eyes wide with fear, and she is quickly whisked away to the judge's chambers by a sturdy, uniformed officer. The judge, a middle-aged woman with a stern countenance, follows closely behind them. The jury members, caught off guard by the sudden turmoil, are quickly escorted out of the courtroom by a court officer. They are led back to their designated deliberation room, away from the chaos of the courtroom.

The victim's father, his face red with rage and revenge, vaults over the low courtroom barrier. His movements are swift and desperate as he attacks the defendant. The ensuing scuffle is a blur of bodies, blood, and yelling while two bailiffs work to break it up.

Chairs are askew, and papers are scattered over the floor as the gallery breaks out in chaos with more fighting between the victims and defendants' families. My co-counsel runs toward me, standing before the judge's bench, trying to project calm coolness as I grip the hardwood.

More officers pour into the courtroom to restore order to the gallery as the bailiff hauls the two men to their feet with blood-soaked clothes, a broken nose on the defendant, and a black eye on the father. Both are placed in handcuffs and dragged away.

As order is slowly restored, I feel a gradual unclenching of my muscles, and my breath becomes deeper, more deliberate. With a hurried assurance of future contact, the defendant's attorney rushes out in the wake of his client. With a brush to my shoulder, my co-counsel draws my attention to the victim returning to the courtroom. The judge and the officer accompany her.

Her posture, arms wrapped around her body, and the tears flowing down her face speak to the scariness of the incident. I gave her a quick embrace, replaced by her mother and family surrounding her and whispering words of support. The judge ceremoniously adjourns the court, even though the officers have cleared the court and the jurors are still gone.

"That was . . ." my co-counselor starts but then tapers off.

"Yeah, let's get started filing the necessary motions."

We collect our belongings, leaving behind the disarray. As I pick up my belongings, I pull out my phone to text Giovanni. Regretfully, I inform him that our plans for the evening must be canceled due to the unexpected workload that has arisen from the attack on my client and the subsequent altercation involving her father.

I linger for a few moments, anticipating his typically prompt reply. When it doesn't arrive, I head toward the elevator, resigning myself to a night of work in the office. I'm already mentally preparing to order takeout, a fallback to old habits I had hoped to avoid. As I press the elevator button, I silently promise myself that this will be an exception, determined not to let this one hectic day draw me back into a routine I'm striving to change.

With the morning light long gone and the afternoon sun streaming through the gym, I feel better after sleeping in and taking it slowly after the late night at the office. Giovanni is already here, working with his usual clients, which gives me plenty of time to saunter in here and get warmed up. I choose a treadmill at the far end of the gym with sightlines to where he works in the free weights with a muscular man named Marco.

I'm busy tapping the machine's buttons when I feel a presence on the treadmill beside me. As I start my incline walk, I glimpse a woman whose appearance stands out amidst the sea of gym attire. She embodies the punk rock spirit. Her hair is a vivid shade of pink, her arms are adorned with a tapestry of tattoos, and her face and ears are accented with piercings. She exudes a sense of bold confidence.

Just as I'm about to focus on my routine, she turns my way with a friendly smile.

"Don't ya hate how all these machines seem to be set on Fox News? Are they trying to condition us or what?"

A cynical snort escapes her as she points to various treadmill screens with the same programming. I never really thought about it, as I always chose machines with the television screens off so I can listen to podcasts instead. Never one to discuss politics with anyone, especially with my position at the DA's office, I remain neutral in my response.

"Oh, I'm not much of a television watcher."

My eyes move from her to Giovanni and his client as they leave the free weights area to cross the gym toward his desk at the front.

"Ah, more of a trainer watcher."

Her teasing draws my gaze away from him and back to her, trying to my obvious embarrassment at being caught.

"I don't blame you. He's popular around here."

"Oh, you know him?"

"Yeah, I see him around a lot. Hard to miss, right? I'm Bex, by the way. Well, my given name is Rebecca, but don't ever call me that."

She extends her hand in a friendly shake before changing the television station on her treadmill. I crack a smile at the gruffness that comes out when explaining her name.

"Hi, I'm Kacie Yacob, you can call me Kacie."

Her grip is firm when I take it. The callouses speak to the

hours of gym time, as do her defined muscles bulging out everywhere.

"Like the Sunshine Band."

Her reply catches me off guard. I have no idea what she is referencing.

"Excuse me?" I ask when her hand moves out of mine to adjust the speed of her machine.

"Band stuff. Anyway, it's nice to meet ya. I've seen you around here with him. You're a lawyer, right?"

Her tone casual yet genuinely interested. I'm slightly taken aback by her directness and knowing my profession.

"Ah, I overheard him bragging about you when I was working out next to him and his buddy, Marco."

It's sweet that Giovanni was speaking highly of me to his friend. However, I'm unsure how I feel about her eavesdropping on their conversation, although certain areas in the gym are relatively small.

"Uh, what exactly was he saying?"

I never discuss the cases I'm working on, nor would Giovanni ask, so Bex knowing I'm a lawyer makes me curious.

"All good things, don't worry."

She gives me a playful wink, which doesn't answer the question. My expression must reflect my distrust when she adds, "He was just going on about how you're dedicated to your job as an ADA, that's all. Must be tough."

"What is?"

I lower the incline on my machine, struggling to keep up this conversation and exercise at the same time. Meanwhile, Bex is speed walking at twelve inclines with no problem.

"Working for the city, getting paid shit. My old man is a public defender, so I grew up around that crap. Vowed never to follow in his footsteps."

She scowls when she says it, which is not an uncommon

reaction. However, I'm curious about who her dad is, as if I've gone up against almost everyone in this city.

"Who is your father? Perhaps I know him."

When she rattles off his name, I suck in a breath. He's not a public defender assigned by the court. She has it all wrong. He's a highly sought-after and handsomely paid defense attorney with extensive practice. His office is across from the Lyric Center Building, a place commonly known as the hub for lawyers in the area.

He's more than just a prominent figure in the legal community. Her dad built a lucrative career for himself and his firm. He owns a large, prestigious building in downtown Houston, a testament to his success and reputation. The building is easily recognizable, adorned with a striking mural of Lady Justice on its west side.

His accomplishments in the legal field are impressive, and it's clear that Bex doesn't have the complete picture of who he is professionally. But at this moment, I'm not correcting her.

"Anyway, the legal world is dog-eat-dog. But it's good of you to upset the apple cart, being a woman and a minority. I bet the men really hate that—especially my dad. I hope you stick it to him for getting bad people off. This town's going to shit for these idiot judges letting murders bond out and the bastards like my dad making it happen."

Bex's blunt remarks catch me off guard, but they're not unfamiliar. Throughout my career, I've faced my share of stereotypes and battled against the prejudice that comes with being a woman of color in a predominantly male-dominated field. Her comment about 'sticking it to' those who bend the law, including her father, reveals a common misconception about the legal system and the role of attorneys in it. The bonding process could be enhanced, but that requires the legislature to get involved, which takes time and is another common misconception. One I heard more and more with the elections coming up.

"Well, I do my best to try to get justice for the victims and their families," I respond carefully, thinking about the recent courtroom incident.

The memory of the victim's father, driven to violence by the harrowing testimony and provocation, flashes in my mind. It's a stark reminder of the emotional complexities and moral dilemmas we often face in pursuing justice.

"The law can be complex with lots of precedence. Sometimes the lines between right and wrong aren't as clear-cut as we'd like them to be," I continue, trying to relay the nuanced reality of my work.

Bex nods, her expression showing a mix of understanding and skepticism.

"I guess. But I'm glad you're in there fighting the good fight."

I appreciate her effort to understand, even if her perspective is somewhat simplified. The conversation with Bex, though brief, underscores the varied viewpoints people hold about the legal system and those who work within it. At least she didn't go on the attack about how it all needs to be overhauled, citing other countries as examples to support their claim. I've heard that argument more times than I can count.

A few minutes pass while I drink my water bottle and wipe the sweat from my face before resuming our conversation.

"And what about you, Bex? If you don't mind me asking, what do you do?" I inquire, opting for a classic and safe conversation starter. It's the question commonplace in various social settings, from charity galas to casual encounters at the local bakery.

"I'm an artist. Anything from oils and water to spray paint and graffiti. That and being a musician."

Bex shares snippets of her life—her band, her art, and her adventures, painting a vivid picture of a life lived boldly and creatively. Her stories starkly contrast my structured world of law and order, and I find myself captivated by the diversity of her experiences.

It's a refreshing change of pace when she talks animatedly about painting during her downtime and getting her physical stamina up for her upcoming tour. I find myself smiling more often than not at her wild tales. It's clear she took the path as opposite of her father as possible.

We talk for quite a long time, exchanging numbers before Giovanni finishes up with his client and makes his way over to us. His approach is marked by his usual confident stride and bright smile. I can't help but feel proud to be associated with him.

"Hey, Kacie," Giovanni greets me with a warm smile. "We ran long. Sorry to keep you waiting."

"It's okay. It gave me time to make a new friend here."

I gesture to Bex, ready to make introductions when Giovanni does it.

"Hi, I'm Giovanni."

He extends a friendly hand toward her. She grips his hand hard like she did mine, which causes a flash of surprise to wrinkle across his face that goes unnoticed by her.

"Bex."

"Nice to meet you." His eyes are briefly drawn to the intricate rings adorning each of her tattooed fingers. "Those are some impressive rings."

She glances at her hands, a nonchalant shrug accompanying her response.

"Thanks, though they're a bit of a hassle with my guitar. Scratches up the surface," she says with a hint of ruefulness, but then quickly adds with a smirk. "But hey, it's all part of the look, right?"

Her casual attitude and the easy way she brushes off practical inconvenience for the sake of her personal style are both amusing and emblematic of her free-spirited nature. Her stark contrast to my conservative demeanor and her carefree attitude is surprisingly captivating. I find myself genuinely drawn to her, appreciating the refreshing perspective she brings.

"Yep, you have to fully embody who you are."

Giovanni's words couldn't be more accurate when I look at his physique and the embodiment of his bodybuilding dreams we worked on the other night. I glance down at my body, the extra weight, the oversized t-shirt, and sweatpants, and wonder what mine says about me. Undisciplined and out of shape is what it screams. When I raise my eyes to Bex agreeing about embodiment and explaining a recent tattoo mishap, I catch Giovanni staring with a slight inquiry in his expression. Who's the overly observant one now? When her story comes to a natural conclusion, Giovanni turns his attention to me.

"Are you ready to start?"

Something in his tone warns me of what's to come, and that's the question remaining on his face.

"I sure am."

I press the stop button on the treadmill, welcoming the pause despite knowing the importance of a proper warm-up to prevent injuries. Giovanni extends his hand to me, and I take it, aware of Bex's observant gaze on us.

"Hey, let's grab a protein shake after your workout sometime," she offers while toying with the case of her earphones.

"I'd like that."

I smile warmly at Bex, realizing that I've just made my first gym friend and, in fact, my first new friend in quite a long time. Her invitation is a pleasant reminder of the unexpected connections that can arise in everyday places.

"Cool."

As she plugs her earbuds back in, she adjusts her treadmill settings, transitioning into a brisk sprint. Her vibrant pink hair is a colorful contrast against the gym's neutral backdrop. I find myself glancing back at her a few times, impressed by the speed and intensity of her running.

With that, she puts her buds in, lowers the incline, and increases the speed to start sprinting. It's impressive, and I look back at her several times as Giovanni leads me away.

"What was with that look back there?"

His body bumps into mine, drawing my attention back to him.

"What?"

"You looked her up and down and then did the same to yourself, then frowned. I want to know what you were thinking because I feel it's not good."

We pause in the hallway that leads to the group fitness classes, the sounds of the gym—the clanking of weights, the rhythmic thumping of treadmills—fading into a softer hum. His hand gently cups my elbow, a reassuring gesture that prompts me to stop and face him. I let out a small sigh, feeling a bit exposed.

"I was hoping you wouldn't notice that, or at least not mention it."

His expression softens, understanding and empathy evident in his eyes.

"Hey, it's okay. You know you can talk to me about anything, right?"

I take a moment, hesitating to divulge more insecurities that he already knows, which makes it even more embarrassing to admit.

"It's just . . . seeing Bex, so confident and in her element, ripped to shreds in her tiny gym outfit and then me in my baggy clothes made me a bit self-conscious."

Giovanni's grip on my elbow tightens slightly, a gesture of support.

"You're here, putting in the work, and that's what matters. Everyone's journey is different, and comparison only sets you back. You're strong, capable, and making progress. That's something to be proud of."

"You're required to say that as my trainer."

Giovanni chuckles softly at my response, his eyes twinkling with a different emotion as he pulls me around the corner and away from the busyness of the main gym floor. He backs me against the wall, his body flush with mine. His hard cock pressing into my soft stomach when he tilts my chin upwards to look him in the eye.

"Maybe as your trainer, but I'm also your lover. And I can tell you that I love your body."

His hand slips up my arm, grazing the side of my breast over my shirt.

"I love the weight of your breasts in my hand as I pump into you from behind. I love spreading your delicious thighs and finding your sweet spot. And you know I love your round ass. It makes me want to take you right now in the sauna."

His bluntness is out of character and makes me horny as can be, especially when he moves his hips to press his cock harder against me.

"I know a byproduct of improving health is your physical appearance. But make no mistake, you're stunning to me as you are."

The desire coursing through my body is beyond belief with how open and accepting he is of me. I feel stunned by the way he's looking at me right now.

"I could kiss you right now," I blurt out, my hands lightly cupping his sides. I'm unsure how much his colleagues know about us. The last thing I'd want is to get him in trouble with Mr. Daniels.

"Kiss me, is all? I'm hurt."

He taunts me with a suggestive eyebrow, and I know he's joking even though we both want more.

"Maybe I'll take *you* in the sauna."

My hands move to his hips, thrusting them toward me to where I'm pinned against the wall.

"I'd love to see that happen."

He steps back, forcing my hands to fall away when the group fitness music stops pulsing, and the door swings open to chattering people leaving the glass.

"Now, let's get this workout in since I have a surprise in store for you."

"Another surprise?"

With a twitch to his mustache, he leans forward and whispers, "Yes, now be a good girl and get that sweet round ass out to the gym floor."

15

GIOVANNI

Feeling disappointed about not seeing Kacie last night would be putting it mildly. The moment she sent the text canceling our workout and spending the night—which was going to be a first for us —I felt deflated. I completely understand that her work is her priority, and I'd never want to get in the way of that. So, I texted her back, suggesting I could bring her dinner or anything else she might need to make her evening a bit easier.

But her brief response, a simple 'no, but thank you,' left me feeling even more downhearted. I know we're in a good place in our relationship, but her succinct replies didn't do much to alleviate my disappointment.

My moodiness carried forth into today, Frank noticing and commenting on it. I brushed it off as having gotten a bad night of sleep, something he bought. We exchanged brief texts this morning between my clients, but finally seeing her in person and her making a new gym friend relieved me. But spending time with her during our workout fixed the rest. As I walk her out to her car, the afternoon sun warm against the crisp, cool air, she touches my arm to stop me.

"Are you all right?"

Those beautiful green eyes stare up at me, the lip balm she put on, complaining of chapped lips glistening in the sunlight and begging me to kiss her obscenely in the middle of this parking lot.

"I think so."

I'm not at a hundred percent, but when she sees what I have in store for us, I know I'll return to normal. Her hands move to her waist, planting against her hips while the breeze blows her silky curls away from her face—another nudge from the universe to kiss her and not care if my boss sees.

"That's not very convincing."

Her eyebrows draw together, and a hand moves to block the sun from its glare.

"You were rather quiet during our workout, especially after all that sexy talk in the hallway."

I look away at the jet fuel lines crisscrossing the sky. How do I admit I missed her last night after knowing her for a week? It screams of desperation and comes off as a little clingy. How do I tell her I had my hopes crushed at the last-minute cancellation that was not her fault and was far more important?

It all sounds selfish in my head when I go through the reasons. Not to mention my physical response to her, dealing with a raging hard on with every squat or walking lunge that she did, it took all my concentration to will it to go down, especially with other women around that quickly notice that kind of stuff.

"Giovanni?" Her hand is light on my arm, the cadence filled with worry. "Are we okay?"

I turn to her, meeting her worried gaze and drawing her close, not carrying what my boss might think or say.

"We're more than okay, Kac. I'm just being a baby because I missed you," I admit, putting my pride aside to douse her worries as they are more important than my idiotic feelings. "I know it's all fast, and I shouldn't feel this way, but . . ."

I shrug, hoping that communicates the rest. Her dazzling smile is fast and efficient in its delivery while her hand tightens on my arm, the nails pressing in slightly.

"Please don't think that way. I was feeling the same last night. I'm sorry if my responses were brief, but the office was absolutely chaotic, and I was surrounded by people almost the entire evening. I was so exhausted when I finally got home that I collapsed into bed. I didn't even have the energy to take off my makeup."

I can't decide if I dislike her explaining this to me because she shouldn't have to justify herself to anyone. Or if I love that she's so open and honest, feeling the same as I do.

I don't know what to say, so I hug her instead. Her head tucks under my chin, her hair caressing my neck when she rests her cheek against my chest. I love the feeling of her in my arms. All those curves she worries about and frowns at are my absolute favorite, and I need to make it a point to demonstrate that more.

"Are you still spending the night?"

A wave of insecurities ripples through me. My confidence is a little shaken by the understandable but sudden cancellation. I'm cautiously eager for the surprise I have in store for her. The idea came to me when we were working on my business plan, which is entirely unrelated topic-wise. When she leaned back and stared at the large industry fan anchored to the ceiling, I knew exactly what I wanted to do to make our first sleepover memorable.

"I wouldn't miss it for the world."

She shifts in my arms, breaking me out of my thoughts, and I lose my grip on her.

"Okay, I'll pick you up at 7 pm."

I dip my head to sneak a kiss in, which she doesn't return since I'm in and out faster than she can respond.

"And dress casually."

Her eyebrows furrow as if I told her to wear a ball gown or something.

"How casually?"

She looks down at her baggy t-shirt and sweatpants, which would be okay with what I have planned. However, knowing she worries about her appearance far more than she should, I provide her with the best answer possible.

"Hmm, trying to get a hint from me, are ya?"

I tickle her ribs, and the worried brow disappears into laughter as she attempts to dodge my fingers. When she grabs both hands to hold in hers, I'm enamored by the easygoing humor we share.

"Okay, okay. Um, it's going to be outside, so dress warmly and wear comfortable shoes. We'll be doing some walking."

Kacie tilts her head, her eyes narrowing slightly as she contemplates this information. I squeeze her hands reassuringly before she lets go.

"Don't waste your time guessing. You'll never get it," I taunt, knowing we both enjoy the little surprises I dole out for her. "I got to get back inside. See you in a little while."

Leaning in, I give her a few more affectionate kisses, followed by a playful smack on her butt. Her reaction is immediate, howling with laughter, a sound I'm starting to like more and more. With a final chuckle, she starts to walk away. I watch her momentarily, appreciating her easygoing nature and how things are progressing with us.

The rest of the day flies by as my clients stream in and out at designated times. I accidentally cut my prep time short by saying 7 pm, which only gives me half an hour to drive home, get ready and be at her place. We trade texts the whole time, and when I mention being a few minutes late, she suggests meeting me at the curb. It's not very chivalrous of me not to pick her up at her front door, but I don't argue. After all, it's about what makes her comfortable, and I appreciate her understanding of the time crunch.

"Is this okay?" Kacie asks when I greet her with a kiss on her cheek on the curb and take her overnight bag to put in the backseat of my truck.

She's bundled in all black, even down to her boots—her red headband holds a hint of color aside from the nude shimmer on her lips, which immediately draws my attention.

"You look good enough to eat."

I would kiss her that delicious-looking mouth right now, but I learned long ago that women don't like guys messing up with their makeup and being forced to reapply it.

"I'll take that as a yes."

She chuckles, getting into the truck and adjusting the vents while I round the back to drop in beside her. It's a quick ten-minute drive. When I park next to the column painted with waves blue and green waves of the ocean, she gives me a knowing look.

"Isn't this place for kids?"

The leather seat creaks when she shifts around to look out the back window. The blue and green neon lights of the ferris wheel glow on her face.

"Nope. Let's go."

I'm out of the truck and opening her door before she can protest. Not that I expect her to be game for everything I've asked her to do. Expecting this to be no different, I practically drag her to the carnival games on the lower level of the property.

"Our reservation isn't until 8 pm, so that gives us an hour to play games, go through the shark exhibit and the ferris wheel, and get our picture taken at the photo booth."

The exuberance in my voice is unmistakable, and I lead us over to the ticket booth.

"You have it all planned out."

She chuckles, but the way her eyes roam around the Aquarium, a popular downtown tourist attraction, lets me know she's never been here before. I couldn't be happier about this idea and her other surprise later tonight.

"I do."

Determined to make the most of our evening, I buy a hefty stack of tickets. Kacie raises an eyebrow at the number of them in my hand, a playful smirk forming on her lips.

"Planning to own a piece of the carnival with all those tickets?"

I flash her a confident grin and twist the end of my mustache like a spy.

"I've got a mission tonight. I'm winning you a giant stuffed shark, no matter what it takes."

"What am I going to do with that?" she asks, the music from the speakers mounted all over the park, almost drowning out her light voice.

"Take it to dinner, of course."

I interweave our fingers before dragging her away from the dancing water fountains with kids screaming and running through them on this cold winter night.

"Now let's go."

Our first stop is at the ring toss game. The challenge seems straightforward enough. I pick up a ring, feeling the cool metal against my skin. My first few attempts at tossing the rings over the bottles miss entirely and prove trickier than expected.

"You sure about that shark?"

"Just getting started."

I focus on my next throw. The ring flies through the air in a perfect arc and lands snugly over a bottle—success at last. Kacie's applause adds to the festiveness. The air is crisp with the scent of popcorn and cotton candy, which I offer to buy her, but she doesn't want to spoil her diet, something I neglected to think about, getting caught up in the moment.

Next, we try our hand at the balloon dart game. I hand Kacie a dart, and she aims, her tongue peeking out in concentration. With a precise throw, she pops a balloon, and we both cheer. I follow suit, hitting a balloon on my second try.

"This is more like it," I say, fist bumping her.

We move from game to game, laughing and joking with each other. At the basketball shooting game, Kacie surprises us with her unexpected skill, sinking several shots in a row. I can't help but admire her form and the easy way she handles the ball.

"Looks like I'm not the only one on a mission."

"Don't you know I played center in college?" she says as the ball rolls off her fingertips, sails through the air, and falls with a swoosh.

"Really?"

She burst out laughing, shaking her head and collecting more tokens for us to turn in for the giant shark hanging from the ceiling of one of the booths.

"O.G., I'm five foot three. Do you think I ever played basketball, much less at the collegiate level?"

A flush hit my cheeks despite the cool temperatures.

"Could have fooled me."

We continue playing various games, the competitive yet playful spirit between us growing with each win. Kacie's quick wit and my gullibility create a different dynamic between us, a pleasant change from the controlled atmosphere of my loft, where I take the lead.

The evening's crowning moment arrives at the baseball booth, where the objective is simple. Pitch a strike to topple the pin. I hand over a significant portion of our tickets and feel confident stepping up to the line, reminiscing about my high school pitching days.

Shedding my jacket with flair, I indulge in some showmanship, performing an exaggerated wind-up. But to my chagrin, the ball sails wide, completely missing the target. My ego takes a hit, and so does the booth attendant's patience as she scolds me for the excessive force of my throw.

Kacie pulls on my shoulder to give me a sudden kiss for good luck, and then I'm off. Dial down the speed and dial up the accuracy to demolish all nine pins in a row and win us the most tickets possible. She jumps up and down, clapping with glee while I hold out my hand to collect the tokens.

I theatrically blow on my fingers, playing up the part of the confident ace, and Kacie responds by looping her arms around my waist. Together, we stroll over to the prize booth, ready to exchange our hard-earned tickets for the blue and white stuffed killer shark I promised from the beginning.

The attendant hands it to Kacie. Her delight is evident as she takes the stuffed animal into her arms and hugs it, filling me with happiness at how great of a date this is. As we leave the booth, a shark in tow, hands intertwined, I look forward to the shark ride, where we get to sit close and cuddle. Her face beams with happiness when she looks up at me, then shoves the shark's face into mine for a makeshift kiss.

"What should we name him?"

I give her a quizzical look. Naming a stuffed toy? And assigning a gender to it? It's cute but nothing I've ever done before.

"No idea. Where do you want to sit?"

The train is not crowded, especially with it being a random Saturday night in January. I bet this place was packed last month leading up to Christmas. She releases my hand to wander ahead, picking a seat in the middle of the train. She puts the shark in between us, which isn't going to work. I pluck the thing from the space, slide next to her, and stuff it by her outer door. Once I wrap my arm around her, she presses into my body, her back against my chest and her hair grazing my cheek.

"You have no claim of naming rights. Is that what you're saying?"

She loops her arm around the toy as mine is looped around her. Never in a million years would I have thought something as simple as a stuffed shark would make her this happy. I love how it doesn't take much to bring out the joy in her.

"Correct."

As the train fills up, half submerged in the glass-enclosed tunnel, sharks swimming beside and above us. Their effortless movements are mesmerizing, powerful bodies turning and twisting with fluidity. The train conductor welcomes us aboard before the train ambles deeper into the tunnel with him, pointing out the various ones. It's calmer here, away from the loudness of the carnival, and warmer as we travel deeper into the exhibit.

I'm more content to watch Kacie's face, the merriment as she points to different sharks we pass. When she admits to having never been here, I'm surprised and plan to take her on the Ferris wheel next.

Eventually, we emerge from the tunnel, stepping back into the vibrant energy of the Aquarium. We make our way to the Ferris wheel, the city skyline sprawling out before us as we ascend, painting a breathtaking view that grows more impressive with every foot we rise.

But as we reach the higher levels, the biting chill of the elevated air has us both shivering and Kacie's teeth chattering. Despite the stunning view, we're both relieved when the ride ends, eager to escape the cold.

Before leaving the carnival, we pause by the dancing dolphin fountain at the front of the property to take a photo on my phone. Some nice couple offers to help us out, and when we see the pictures—our smiles, the stuffed shark she names Jaws after the movie, and the backdrop of dolphins frozen in mid-leap—it immortalizes this perfect first date.

"I'm cold, and I could really use some food right now," Kacie declares, a slight shiver in her voice.

She lets go of my hand and picks up the pace, the stuffed shark bouncing in her arms as she makes a beeline for the restaurant's warmth. I quickly follow, reaching her side as we approach the hostess stand. As we wait, I gently place my hand on her back, rubbing softly to warm her.

While the hostess scans her seating chart for our reserva-tion, Kacie is captivated by the grand three-story Aquarium dominating the foyer. The myriad of fish swimming inside draws a look of wonder from her, and I can't help but watch the delight play across her face.

We're soon guided up the stairs to our table, which offers a cozy vantage point over the aquatic display. After we settle in and order drinks and salads, Kacie leans in, resting her chilled hand over mine on the tabletop.

"Thank you for bringing me here. This evening has been wonderful."

I envelop her hand with mine, hoping the warmth from my palm will seep into her fingers. The subtle glow from the surrounding tanks casts a serene ambiance over us, the faint sounds of the water and distant conversations creating a tran-quil and romantic backdrop.

"Just you wait. I've got plenty of ideas up my sleeve. The goal is to keep you smiling like this."

Her laughter, light and melodic, fills the air around us.

"You're doing an excellent job so far."

Her gaze holds mine until the server comes with our drinks and breaks the mood. The brief interruption allows us time to discuss healthy dining options, which she asked about during one of our sessions.

With curiosity getting the better of me, I ask Kacie about the courtroom incident from yesterday. Her response is immediate as she dives into the story. She recounts the events in vivid detail, the poor victim's fear and her family member facing charges of his own, painting a clear picture of the chaotic scenes and the reasons behind her late stay at the office.

Her storytelling is so engaging that it carries the conversation through the arrival of our salad and well into our main course of fish and vegetables.

I'm completely drawn into her world. She has the ability to stay calm amid the danger and drama, then shove it all aside to have a clear head back at the office to pick apart the details with her co-counsel.

"Wow, Kac. That's unbelievable."

After hearing what she and everyone went through, my bruised, sensitive feelings from the last-minute cancellation resolved immediately. It makes me feel foolish for getting bothered in the first place. Kacie would never intentionally blow me off. Not that I thought it was that, but her comment about falling into bed makes perfect sense after such a traumatic day.

"Has that happened before?"

She pauses eating her food to think and then replies, "Maybe once, several years ago. But not usually. And here's a strange thought that struck me during my trial. Have you spoken to your dad yet? You're still working on the proposal but haven't mentioned anything to him, right?"

"No, I haven't."

I could have called my dad to talk about it, but without the business plan finalized, I've yet to take that step. Kacie's eyes light up with a new idea.

"Good, because I have someone I think you should meet.

He's a criminal defense attorney, but don't hold that against him."

She laughs at her joke, which must be a common theme of ADAs dislike opposing counsel.

"He's also big into bodybuilding. The guy's huge and somehow manages to fit into these custom suits. I was thinking we could all do lunch. You two could talk about competitions, shows, the whole bodybuilding scene."

The suggestion catches my interest. The idea of meeting someone who balances a demanding legal career with a passion for bodybuilding is intriguing. I rarely come across this. Even Frank is focused on bodybuilding only.

"I'd love to meet him and get some insights, especially from someone juggling both worlds successfully." I give her an appreciative smile, vowing to show my genuine appreciation in bed tonight.

"I'll set it up then. It'll be good for you to connect with someone who gets both sides of your life. And who knows, maybe he could invest in your gym. The guy is loaded."

The inflection in her tone is complimentary and not a hint of malice or envy for being a wealthy attorney. It's another reason she's perfect for the DA's office, which is none to make nearly as much money as private practice. Kacie's motivated by justice, not money. But it's very intriguing that she thinks this attorney and I could hit it off so well that he might be willing to invest in me and my dream more than my dad.

Trying to temper my expectations, I pick up my fork to resume eating.

"I want to avoid getting ahead of myself with the investment idea, but meeting him sounds promising. I'm looking forward to it. I know you're busy, so let me know when you can arrange it."

"I'll call his office on Monday and get something scheduled for this week."

Kacie is already becoming the most important person in my life, and I feel so happy every time I'm with her. But her support of my dreams and achieving them this year is beyond anything I could have ever asked for. All I want to do is rush her home to see her next surprise and take full advantage of showing her how much I appreciate everything about her, including her selfless willingness to help me.

"Stop looking at me like that, Giovanni. I plan on finishing my delicious and healthy dinner before you whisk me away from here and have your way with me."

A heat creeps into my cheeks from my obvious lust for her.

"Well, it's entirely your fault if I'm being honest. If you weren't so delectable, I wouldn't want to take you on this table."

"Or I could crawl under it and make you very happy."

She winks and resumes eating as if she didn't just give me a stiffy thinking about her giving me head in a public place.

16

KACIE

The evening has been nothing short of incredible. I'm genuinely amazed at how Giovanni keeps surprising me. When I thought the night couldn't get any better, he hints at another surprise waiting for us. My office overlooks the Aquarium, and I've often found myself gazing at the ferris wheel from my window, watching it turn while I'm on conference calls.

Despite its proximity, the thought of visiting never once crossed my mind. That's one of the things I appreciate about Giovanni—his spontaneity and knack for gently pushing me beyond the boundaries of my usual routine. His surprises always lead to new experiences, making me step out of my comfort zone in the best possible way.

Full of a delicious dinner, warm from the heat of his truck, and sandwiched between us is our new shark. I'm both nervous and excited about spending the night at his house. I packed my bonnet, eyeglasses, and other things people usually don't see about me, so I'm a little insecure about being this vulnerable in front of him. However, he's already made it so comfortable for me to be myself I wonder if I'm completely overreacting.

He takes the same route as the other day to his loft, parking in his usual spot, and by the time we hit his front door with my bags on his shoulder, my stomach is swimming with nerves. He pauses long enough to flash me a mischievous grin when he unlocks the door.

"OK, if you don't like it, we can take it down, but I think it would be really fun for us, considering this is our first sleepover."

His voice also has a smidge of trepidation, which makes me feel better about the situation. However, I don't think that our nervousness is not for the same reasons. Mine is to be fully vulnerable with someone other than myself. His is probably if I would like his surprise or not.

"I'm sure I'll love whatever you have planned."

His playful use of the term 'sleepover' has a charming inno-cence, contrasting humorously with the more adult nature of our relationship. His boyish excitement adds a light-hearted touch to the evening, making it all the more special.

As he swings open the door, the anticipation builds. He takes a few steps inside, tossing his keys onto the hall table and depositing my bags beside them.

"Wait, close your eyes."

Before I can comply, his hands gently cover my eyes, and I can feel the warmth of his body against my back as he kicks the door closed and guides me forward. His voice is filled with eagerness. A growing curiosity about his plan replaces my lingering nerves.

"Okay, open them up."

As his hands fall away, I'm greeted with a whimsical and romantic sight. The loft has been transformed into an indoor campout with a makeshift teepee in the center. Sheets, suspended from the massive industrial ceiling fan in the center of the living room, cascade down in a dramatic drape, creating a cozy enclosure around his furniture. The white panels stretch out from the center of the fan and tuck neatly out of sight.

He leads me closer to the entrance, where pillows and blankets are arranged in a comfortable nest, creating an intimate retreat. Twinkling fairy lights are draped along the inside of the panels, casting a soft glow. It's like stepping into a childhood fantasy but with a grown-up twist.

There is another opening on the opposite side, including the television displaying a crackling fire, with a tray of fruit and chilling wine thoughtfully laid out, perfect for a cozy night.

The entire setup is charming and ingenious, adding to the cocoon feeling I always feel at his place. He put a lot of thought and effort into creating this unique experience, making me like him even more.

"Wow! This is . . . magical."

I gaze over my shoulder at him. He's beaming, his eyes roaming his creative endeavor before returning to mine.

"You like it?"

"I love it!"

His arms circle me instantly when I lean into him, taking in the memorable sight.

"You always say my place is our cocoon, so I thought to make our own little campout inside our own little world," he says, with a tight squeeze, resting his chin on the top of my head with a contented sigh. "It's too cold outside for real camping, so I thought we could use a little adventure indoors."

His explanation brings a warmth that goes beyond the cozy atmosphere of the makeshift camp.

"You're always thinking of the most thoughtful things to do for me. I don't know how I can top it."

His chuckle vibrates through me, a sound of genuine happiness.

"Well, I aim to impress, but it's not a competition, so no

worries about topping it. This is as much for me as it is for you."

Even though he says it, I'm not sure I completely believe it. He put in a lot of work to make this happen, to make it memorable for me that he didn't have to, and I can't let that go unacknowledged.

"This is some kind of wonderful."

"No, *you* are some kind of wonderful." He lifts his chin and walks us into the center of the teepee. With the twinkle lights surrounding us, he helps me onto the pillows and blankets arranged on the floor before swinging down next to me.

"What do you want to watch?"

"Huh?"

"It's a movie night, so pick something you want to see but haven't."

"Oh, I can't even tell you. I haven't been to the movies in years. I don't even know what's out or who's playing in what."

It would be an embarrassing admission if Giovanni didn't already know how much of a workaholic I am.

"No worries, we'll find something you like."

He picks up the remote, scrolling through a selection of movies. His expression is focused yet relaxed. As he browses, Giovanni occasionally suggests titles, gauging my interest. I appreciate his patience and desire to find something I'll enjoy. It's a small gesture, but it speaks volumes about his thoughtfulness.

"How about you choose? I'm not picky. Most anything will do."

"Are you sure?"

His eyebrow pops up to look at me. With a confirmed nod, he returns to flipping through more channels than I have seen on television. He selects a movie that seems interesting—a classic I've heard of but never had the chance to watch. As the film starts, the screen's light adds a blueish glow to the teepee's ambiance. We settle back against the pillows, and I snuggle into his side.

He offers me some wine, but I decline because I am too full from dinner. The movie starts, holding my attention just long enough for his body's warmth, the night's contentment, and the tiredness from a busy week to overtake me. I'm asleep in a matter of minutes.

"Wake up, Kac."

Groggy and disoriented, I sit up and wipe the drool from the side of my mouth. Giovanni has already changed into some lounging pants with no shirt. The muscles of his chest and eight-pack abdominals are on full display. And when I look up at his smiling face, he's wearing my green bonnet over his hair.

"Let's go to bed."

I rub my eyes, the stinging unrelenting from fatigue. His hands are extended, offering to help me to my feet while I'm still trying to get my bearings. The television returns to the cracking fire and the twinkle lights are turned off.

"I'm sorry I fell asleep."

"Don't worry about that. You've had a long week and an eventful twenty-four hours. It's understandable."

He gives me a sympathetic look, leading me out of the teepee and down the hallway where my bag lays open on his dresser, my night clothes are on his bed, and my toothbrush is on the counter, ready for me.

"How do I look? Is it my color?"

He strikes a ridiculous and endearing pose, the bonnet sitting slightly askew. I can't help but laugh at the sight.

"You could be a model for them."

I play along, too tired to care whether I wear it to bed. I didn't last night when I fell into bed, and my hair didn't look a complete fright today. I might forgo tonight as well. He fakes a thoughtful expression, running a hand over his amazing abs.

"I think it's all about confidence," he says, striking an exaggerated model pose highlighting his well-defined muscles. "You've got to own it."

He struts like a peacock around his bedroom, throwing his hip out like a model and doing some bodybuilding poses with his muscles flexing and rippling under his olive skin. He's certainly stunning to look at, and unexpected humor at the most unexpected times adds to his charm. One of the many things I like about him is his ability to make me laugh and feel at ease, no matter the situation.

"You certainly own it," I concede, rubbing at the tiredness in my eyes and probably smearing my makeup. "I'm so tired. I really don't want to do my night routine."

"So don't."

He clicks off the hallway and bathroom lights before throwing back the covers and diving into bed. When he pats the empty side next to him, I sigh, knowing I still need to change clothes, brush my teeth, and wash my face before retrieving the bonnet from his head.

"I'll get make-up on your pillowcases, and I have to brush my teeth. It's literally the bare minimum," I say more for my sake than his as I try to muster the energy to move toward the bathroom.

"The pillowcases are washable. But I get the teeth brushing. I'll wait here and warm up the bed for you."

He snuggles against the pillows, looking invitingly comfortable while I shuffle into the bathroom. I don't bother turning on the light, letting his bedside lamp illuminate the whole teeth brushing process. I race through it, go to the bathroom, and wash my hands while he's sprawled out in bed, reading an autobiography about Schwarzenegger.

I return to the bedroom, quickly changing into my night clothes in the dim light. Giovanni is absorbed in his book, but he looks up as I approach the bed, his eyes warm and welcoming.

"Schwarzenegger, huh?"

Glancing at the cover of the book.

"Yeah, he's a legend in the bodybuilding world," he replies, setting the book aside. "But right now, I'm more interested in cuddling my girl. Get in here."

Sliding under the covers beside him, I immediately feel the warmth he's gathered in the bed. He plucks the bonnet from his head, his curls tumbling out to carefully gather my hair and tuck it in. It makes me feel so cared for.

"Did I do it, right?"

He leans closer, giving me a few innocent kisses before easing me down to the mattress in a longer, more prolonged kiss. Hovering above me, his eyes are dark with desire, and if I weren't so exhausted, I'd initiate something more.

"Perfect."

"Good."

He suddenly offers me his fist to bump, and he kisses me again once I do.

"Sweet dreams, Kac."

He reaches to turn off the bedside lamp, plunging the room into darkness, illuminated only by the faint glow from the city outside. He wraps an arm around me, drawing me close, and I rest my head against his chest, comforted by the rhythm of his heartbeat.

In the quiet of his room, the day's events replay in my mind —the Aquarium, the carnival games, the magical indoor campout. Each memory is tinged with the warmth of Giovanni's thoughtfulness and the joy it brings me.

Lying there, in the peaceful darkness, in his arms, I find not just a place to rest but a sense of peace, a feeling of being exactly where I'm meant to be. I fall asleep with that lovely feeling overtaking my body.

As the first light of morning filters through the windows, casting a soft glow in the room, I awaken to find myself still in

Giovanni's embrace. His breathing is slow and steady, a peaceful rhythm harmonizing with the early morning tranquility. For a moment, I lie there, enjoying the warmth of being nestled against him, reflecting on the beautiful week this has been with him.

He stirs beside me, his eyes fluttering open. He greets me with a sleepy smile, his arm tightening gently around me.

"Morning, Kac," he murmurs, his voice rough with sleep. "Did you sleep well?"

"Very. Thanks to your cocoon away from the world."

My voice is also laced with drowsiness as I stretch. I haven't slept this soundly in a long time. Not that I live in a bad part of town or a rowdy apartment complex, but there's always some city sound making its' way into my place and waking me up. These lofts are expensive, with massive sheets of windows, and they block out the sounds much better than my place does. Even now, I can't hear any city buses bustling outside his building. He props himself up on one elbow, looking at me affectionately.

"You know, we could always stay in bed . . ."

His curly hair is a mess, sticking out in all directions like a lion's mane. His mustache is slightly crooked on one side as he leans in for a gentle morning kiss. His lips are soft and smooth against mine, lingering momentarily while his fingers caress my cheek. When he moves away, I smile up at him, readying to play with him just as much as his hard shaft against my body is ready to play with me.

"And?" I tease, my hands already drifting down the abs he had on full display when strutting his stuff around the room last night.

"Good girl. I already like where this is going."

As he speaks, I catch a whiff of his clean, musky cologne from last night and a hint of mint from his toothpaste.

"And where is this going, O.G.?"

I blink up at him, my hands stilling at his waistband. His groan of frustration is short lived when he rolls us over and shoves my hips down to plant his erection against my pubic bone.

"A show for me."

He winks, his hand tugging my bonnet away before cupping the back of my neck and drawing me in for a passionate kiss. His lips are firm yet gentle, his mustache tickling my sensitive skin as his tongue dances with mine. He's exploring every area of my mouth as if it's new and exotic. I can't get enough, grinding against him and moaning into his mouth. My desire grows with each stroke of the tongue against mine and every thrust of his cock into my body. I'm yearning for him, wetness pooling between my legs as his hands knead my butt as he likes to do.

He breaks the kiss to whisper, "I need you, Kac."

"I need you, too."

I sit up, more than eager to give him a show, while he stretches to his nightstand to retrieve a condom, something that wasn't there last night when he put his book away. I appreciate this preparation and confidence in knowing this was to come.

"Were you planning this the whole time?"

I point to the condom in his hand, and he casts me the biggest guilty smile.

"Not planning but hoping."

His hand strokes up the side of my body, plucking at the top.

"Now be a good girl for me and get naked. I want to see how beautiful you are."

The praise makes my body tingle with lust, and I place my hand on his chest, feeling the muscles flex as I slide off him. He shucks his lounge pants off and has the condom on in seconds. It takes me a bit longer until an extra set of hands pulls at everything to help me.

"Someone's eager."

I bite my lip as I straddle him, his fingers digging into my skin as if the restraint of letting me lead is almost too much.

"You have no idea, Kac. I've been tempted half a dozen times to wake you in the middle of the night. I've done good holding off this long."

I plant my hand on his stomach, balancing my weight as I loop my ankles over his legs. He holds his cock, lining it up at my entrance while staring at me. His gaze is blistering, his pupils overtaking the gold flakes as I slowly descend onto his erection. We both moan. The feeling of him slowly filling me up is being savored by both of us. I'm tighter in the morning, I have no idea why. When I clench my thighs together to adjust to his large size, he grabs my waist and stops me.

"Give me a sec."

While his hands still my movements, his eyes devour me, greedily zeroing in on my breasts and clit until he sucks his thumb, then plants it flat against my clit. My eyes flutter closed at the contact, savoring the sensation as I lean into his touch. The soft stroking is fantastic. My hips gently rock into the goodness until he suddenly thrusts into me. My eyes fly open as he's buried to the hilt, the hard pressing fullness a contrast to the featherlight touch against my clit.

"You're mine, you know that?"

His hand trails up my ribcage to the side of my breast, cupping it and stroking his thumb in an opposite rhythm to the one at my clit.

It's not a claim of ownership, something I'd never go for. More a claim that I am his and he is mine. He's got me, and I've got him. An exclusivity that we both agree on. I can't help the smile that spreads across my lips.

"Yes, Giovanni, I'm yours."

"Good girl."

The praise, him massaging my breast, the stroking of my

clit, and the occasional thrusting into me has my body tingling, my nerves tight and raw with lust and want. Wanting to be owned and owning him.

"And you're mine," I add, picking up the pace now that he seems more in control.

His calloused hand skims down my flesh, holding onto my hip as I grind into him. Wetness pours out of me from his perfectly timed thrusts. Wanting to put on a good show for him, I leverage the strength in my legs to bounce on his shaft while fondling my breasts. His eyes widen, and his breath stills until a growl rumbles out of him, and he pulls me down to him.

"I *am* yours."

His hand splays on my butt, pushing it down with every upward thrust of his hips. The power and strength coming from his body is intoxicating as he keeps me exactly where he wants me.

It's wild and sloppy, fast and reckless, racing me towards an orgasm that bursts out of me. His hand slips into my hair, curling into a fist while I suck on his neck. I slide my knees higher toward his waist, giving him more access to plunge deeper, harder, and faster. The angle is perfect, hammering me over and over until the tidal wave of a climax builds in me so rapidly that I'm coming again.

"Scream my name," he rasps as his pulse pounds against my lips.

I'm lost in the moment. The way his arms tighten around my body, stealing my breath, his hands gripping my flesh in desperate need, and how my lower body bounces off his shaft. It's sensory overload in the best way. When the blinding good-ness of my powerful climax overtakes me a third time, I don't scream his name but breathlessly mutter it against his sweaty skin.

"You're going to know who you belong to, Kac."

I haven't recovered when he flips us again. With my legs on

his shoulders, his knees on either side of my body, bending me in half to continue his powerful thrusts. I ride out the remnants of my orgasm, my body weightless and my limbs like jelly as sweat drips from him onto my breasts. A smile emerges as he shakes his head, sending droplets all over me. I grip the sheets, trying to hold onto something, when his eyes lock on mine.

"Who do you belong to?"

He leans forward, and the stretch on my hamstrings is intense when I lean up to kiss him, quietly murmuring, "You. I'm yours, O.G."

"Good girl."

He chases my lips, causing my leg to slip to his elbow as he deepens the kiss. His tongue invades my mouth, seeking and exploring the same as his shaft and pulling yet another, more minor orgasm from me. Suddenly, he breaks the kiss, pulls out of me, and rips off the condom. His fist pumps his cock until long spurts of white cum spray all over my breasts and stomach.

Giovanni groans deep and long while continuing to come, dampness collecting on the curls at the base of his neck. He's a vision of perfection with his mouth slacked in bliss, his arm flexing while tightly stroking his cock, and his abdominals clenched. If bodybuilders had a dream pose, this would be mine for him. Privately, of course, as he would say. When his glassy eyes focus on me, a proud expression appears.

"Mmm, you look perfect right now."

I chuckle as his hand caresses the length of my leg, pausing at my ankle to incircle it before releasing it and continuing upwards.

"Covered in your cum?"

I look down at the creamy white fluid pooling in between my breasts.

"Isn't that a little chauvinistic?"

"Definitely chauvinistic."

He winks with a wide grin, his hand still caressing my skin.

"Now, how about a shower? And breakfast. I know this great little smoothie bar we can walk to."

"That sounds wonderful. But I need a minute to catch my breath."

And to savor how I feel right now while replaying everything that just happened.

"Of course. Take your time. I'll get the water heating up."

He bounds off the bed, swipes the condom off the sheets, and walks away to start the shower. His butt is high and tight, over his shredded thighs and proportionate calves. When I first met him, he told me that legs were his favorite workout, and I can tell he's never missed a leg day.

He has the body of Adonis and the face of an Italian God under the halo of chocolate curls. I almost have to pinch myself to believe this is real. A shrill from his phone in the other room has him exiting the bathroom, looking utterly confused.

"Who is calling at this hour?"

He glowers, his expression turning sour at the intrusion.

"Go ahead and jump in the shower, I'll join you in a sec."

Having no idea what time it is other than the sun has risen, casting golden sparkles around his room from reflection off the glass building across the street. I ease off his bed, grabbing my bonnet to act as a makeshift shower cap while being mindful of his cum sliding down my body.

Next to the shower, a pile of towels awaits, and with my hair neatly tucked away, I step into the steaming cascade. The water pours down, soothing my weary muscles—not from Giovanni, but from endless hours at the office, in court, and in meetings. I contort under the high-pressure jets, aiming for relief from every ache.

Giovanni's voice pierces the steam outside the glass, his tone unmistakably agitated. The words are muffled, but the discontent in his voice is crystal clear. Puzzled by what's happening, I stop stretching and speed up, getting clean, keen to finish, and find out what's causing the trouble.

Cutting off the water and wrapped in a towel, I join him on the wide rug, where he's still naked with a hand on his hip. His eyes bore into mine when he switches the phone to speaker so I can hear.

His boss, Mr. Daniels, explains how two trainers are out with the flu, causing overbookings with the ones already scheduled to work. He's practically pleading with Giovanni to work, offering him double time pay and bringing in lunch. Giovanni mutes the line, mid-sentence of his boss still talking.

"Kacie."

"If you need to go in, I understand. He sounds like he's in a bind, or he wouldn't be calling you on your day off," I defend, as Giovanni seems conflicted between continuing our weekend together and feeling obligated to acquiesce to his boss's pleas. "Really, it's okay."

He hesitates, his eyes searching mine for reassurance.

"But our plans . . ." he begins, the conflict evident in his voice.

"I know, but sometimes these things happen."

I place my hand on his arm, trying to reassure him physically.

"I had to cancel on you Friday for work. This is no different."

"That was way different and far more important."

"Maybe, but either way, your boss clearly needs you. He wouldn't call and offer you all these incentives if it weren't important. We can always reschedule our plans."

He nods slowly, the decision weighing heavily on his face as he unmutes the call.

"Okay, I'll go in. Just for a few hours." He holds up four fingers, indicating how many hours we'll be apart.

"Thank you, Giovanni, you're a lifesaver," Mr. Daniels's

voice bursts through the speaker, coated with relief. "See you in half an hour."

He ends the call and I smile supportively.

"Go save the day," I encourage, removing the bonnet from my hair and giving him a quick peck so he can get ready. "We'll pick up where we left off when you're done."

He smiles back, gratitude and regret on his face, before hurrying into the shower. I quickly prepare myself, collecting everything in my overnight bag and waiting for him by the makeshift teepee. He comes out, wrestling to get his shirt on, and catches me smiling. I compliment him again, barring a few kisses, before he slips on his shoes, grabs everything he needs, and walks us out the door.

Upon returning to my apartment, I methodically unpack and prepare my breakfast. As the hours elapse, I work, addressing various motions and emails that have emerged from Friday's incident and require my immediate attention. It is nearly past 4 pm when my phone chimes. Anticipating a message from Giovanni, I am surprised to discover it is from my new friend, Bex.

> Not sure if I should send this to you but if it were me, I'd want to know. I'm sorry.

Sorry?

Sorry for what I wonder as the three dots circle for a couple of long seconds. When the image flashes onto my screen, shock grips me. My heart drops, my hand goes limp, and the coffee mug I hold plummets, shattering on the floor. Hot coffee splatters across my tiles as my hand covers my mouth.

Giovanni is kissing Jenna.

17

GIOVANNI

Rushing off to work, I quickly drop Kacie at her apartment building, offering a brief, apologetic kiss goodbye. The urgency in my step doesn't falter as I head straight to the gym. Mr. Daniels is waiting for me right at the door with stress lines cutting across his forehead. He claps me on the shoulder, a silent thank you for showing up amid the crisis.

The moment I step through the door, it's clear today will be a marathon. Clients are swarming in, each with urgent demands and simmering frustrations. I'm in the thick of it, doing my best to juggle scheduling conflicts and appease upset clients.

It's a delicate balancing act. On the one hand, I'm trying to calm them down, and on the other, rapidly rearranging appointments to fit everyone in. It's evident of the flu's impact rippling through the gym as the receptionist desk is short-staffed and Mr. Daniels, who doesn't usually work Sundays, is checking people in while answering phones.

I move through the gym with purpose, attending to each client's needs. My role is more than just a trainer today. I'm a mediator, problem-solver, therapist, and negotiator. I find myself performing a delicate balancing act, employing diplomacy and swift decision-making in equal measure.

As I guide clients through their routines, I'm acutely aware of the physical and mental demands of the job. My muscles work tirelessly, and my mind races to keep up with the ever-changing dynamics of the day. Each interaction is carefully navigated, aiming to maintain client satisfaction.

Throughout the day, my thoughts sporadically drift to Kacie. Her understanding and supportive demeanor when I left this morning makes me happy and content that I have such a caring woman by my side. I silently vow to plan a special evening to show my appreciation for her patience and understanding in cutting our time short. Maybe dinner in the tent followed by making love to her under the string of lights. Play some romantic movies on the television to set the mood. The image in my mind is giving me a stiffy as I think about it. This morning was great, but a sample snack compared to how much I want to devour her when I get home.

And having her covered in my cum, the white against her sultry skin, makes me want to sink into her the second I see her again. I run a tense hand through my hair, needing to release this horny tension somehow. I jump in to do a few bench presses with my client to demonstrate form over function while using it as a distraction from my thoughts.

If I could catch a break, I'd masturbate in the private bathroom reserved on the second floor. Without that being a possibility, I continue to knock out a few sets with each client to get rid of some of the energy and lust coursing through my body every time I think of Kacie.

The gym's clock ticks onward, and the influx of clients wanes as the day progresses. The noise level gradually decreases, allowing the beat of the music blasting through the speakers to finally register as I take a much-needed break to grab a drink and snack from the healthy bar at the front of the gym. I swipe my smoothie from the counter and turn around to run smack dab into Jenna. She stands before me with a surprised look on her face.

"Giovanni! I didn't expect to see you here today."

She adjusts her long ponytail before flipping it over her shoulder.

"Aren't you off on Sundays?"

I manage to smile, glancing at the clock to see it's after 4 pm. Way past the four hours I committed to when my boss called. I wonder how fast I could get out of here and back to Kacie.

"Yeah, it's been a hectic day. Had to fill in for a couple of trainers out sick," I explain, adjusting my grip on the smoothie. She nods sympathetically.

"You look like you've been through a marathon. But I must say, it's always a pleasure to have you around. You bring a certain energy to the place."

I chuckle, feeling slightly uneasy at her compliment. This is what used to trip me up before. The mixed signals, but now that I have my girl, it just makes me uncomfortable.

"Thanks, I try my best."

I raise my smoothie as a sort of salute, thinking I could drink it on the way home to clean up before reaching out to Kacie to make plans tonight.

"Well, have a good workout."

Her eyes linger on me for a moment.

"Actually, Gio, could we talk somewhere private for a moment? It's a bit personal."

Internally, I brace myself.

Is she facing some personal crisis? Does she need advice or help with something? The role of a trainer often extends beyond physical guidance. Sometimes, we are dieticians advising about proper nutrition or confidants unwittingly drawn into our clients' lives and struggles. Yet, as I stand there waiting, I can't shake off a slight undercurrent of apprehension.

"Please?"

The plea for help in her voice is unmistakable. I shake my head to clear my worrisome thoughts.

"Of course. I'll follow you."

With my snack in one hand and my smoothie in another, I follow her as she leads us toward the back of the gym. As we retreat to the hallway leading to the racquet and basketball courts, the clamor of the gym recedes, leaving me with a heavy feeling of apprehension. Jenna's steps are hesitant, her usual confidence replaced by an uncharacteristic vulnerability. She pauses, takes a deep breath, and turns to face me, her eyes searching mine.

"Gio, I've been struggling with something and don't know who else to turn to."

Her voice is nervous as she stacks one foot on the other. Concerned, I set my snack and smoothie on a nearby towel service cabinet.

"Whatever it is, you can tell me. Is everything okay?"

I'm curious about the sudden change from her happy demeanor last week when she told Marco and me how great her holidays were. I remember feeling sad about her engagement before meeting Kacie.

The vision of her in my bed, underneath me, wearing nothing but a smile, sends a wave of warmth through my body and calms my brain. She nods slowly, her fingers absently playing with the edge of her workout top.

"It's the engagement. I'm not sure I want to go through with it. I feel so lost and don't know what to do."

Her whispered confession has my mouth dropping, then quickly recovering when tears form in her eyes. I'm at a loss for words. Having never gotten close to being engaged and never asking someone who accepted, I'm treading water here.

"I'm sorry."

My brain locks on the only words that come to mind, even if they don't seem enough when the tears drip down her face. She quickly wipes them away, looking down the hallway to compose herself before looking back at me. I run a nervous hand through my hair, the sweat collecting on my palm when it hits the back of my neck.

"And ..." she hesitates, biting her lip. "There's more."

Okay.

I steel myself against the serious tone in her voice. It's clear it's serious. Wiping my sweaty hand down the front of my gym shirt, I let it rest on my hips, preparing for what she's about to say.

"I've... I've developed feelings. For someone else."

Her eyes lift to meet mine, filled with something unspoken. A deep uneasiness forms in my gut, a dread climbing into my throat with the way she's looking at me.

"I don't understand."

She steps closer, her fingers releasing her shirt.

"It's you, Gio. I've got feelings for you."

Me?

Her words hit me with a jolt. These are words that I would have loved to hear last year amidst those dark, lonely, and drunken nights. But now, things are different. In Kacie, I've found not just friendship but a meaningful connection. The openness and trust we share is something I've never experienced before.

She knows my proclivities, understands my struggles, and supports my dreams. Her acceptance and belief in who I am and want to be is a rare gift. This newfound relationship with Kacie is precious, something I cherish and would never jeopardize. It's a kind of respect and partnership I know is worth more than any fleeting temptation. Something I'd never for a line I shouldn't even be approaching with Jenna.

"Jenna—"

Her face crumples slightly.

"I know it's wrong. I'm engaged, and we're about to post our engagement photos in the paper, but I can't help how I feel. When I saw you again after being away for a couple of weeks, it hit me. I'm not in love with him. I'm in love with you."

Before I can respond, she steps forward and wraps her arms around me in a hug. It's meant to be comforting, but then she leans in, her lips finding mine. I'm so shocked that I don't react other than reactively cupping my hands on her waist to firmly push her away.

"No! I'm with someone."

She steps back, her eyes narrowing with a viciousness I've never seen before.

"You can't be talking about that fat old lady. I've seen the way she looks at you. It's not right."

She ignites a flame of anger within me, her tone and implications about Kacie making my hands tremble with barely contained rage. The audacity of her judgment sets my blood boiling. I step closer, my voice low but seething with anger.

"You're completely out of line. How dare you say that about her. Who are you to judge Kacie or our relationship? What we have is more real and meaningful than you could possibly understand."

Her face registers shock at my reaction, but there's a stubborn defiance in her eyes.

"Gio, I just thought—"

"No," I cut her off, my voice stern as I tower over her to drive home my point. "You didn't think. You don't get to comment on my personal life or insult someone I care deeply about."

The air between us crackles with my fiery response. The gym's distant sounds fade into irrelevance. Jenna looks taken aback, perhaps not expecting such a strong reaction on my part. I couldn't care less. She crossed a line admitting her feelings, knowing I was involved, and another insulting Kacie. Whatever acquaintanceship we had is over.

"Our relationship is strictly professional, and that's how it will stay. I'm committed to Kacie, and your opinion is repugnant and irrelevant. If you need assistance, ask another employee of this place. Otherwise, do not approach me again."

She steps back, surprise registering on her face, with new tears filling her eyes as the gravity of her overstep sinks in. I turn away, livid with her and mad at myself for falling for her need for a private talk. I should have known better and assumed it was terrible, but it's not in my nature not to help someone.

Feeling the need to vent the intense emotions swirling within me physically, I make a beeline for the empty group kickboxing class. The moment I step in, I head straight for the punching bag, unleashing my pent-up frustration and anger. Each strike against the bag is a release, a way to cope with the tumult of feelings Jenna's actions have stirred in me.

For a solid twenty minutes, I'm in a world of my own, the sound of my fists against the bag echoing through the room. Sweat pours down my face and body, my breath heavy with exertion and the remnants of my rant. The physical exertion is cathartic, helping to drain the reservoir of my anger and clear my head.

As I slow down, panting and drenched in sweat, a sense of calm settles over me. As uncomfortable as it was, I realize that this confrontation has reinforced the importance of maintaining professional boundaries and the depth of my commitment to Kacie.

Stepping out of the room, feeling more composed, I head straight to Mr. Daniel's office to tell him I'm going home. Heading out to spend the rest of the night in the comfort and simplicity of my life with Kacie sounds like the best idea I've had all day.

The moment I grab my stuff from my desk and toss it over my shoulder, I call Kacie, dying to hear her voice. It catches me by surprise when it goes directly to voicemail. I hang up and try again as I push through the gym door and cross the parking lot. When it does the same thing, I pull it away from my ear and stare at the screen, trying to understand why this is happening.

Concern starts to creep in as I stare at my phone, confused. Kacie not picking up is unusual, especially since we had plans for the evening. I pause by my car in the parking lot, debating my next move.

With a deep breath, I decide to leave her a voicemail.

"Hey Kac, it's me. Just finished up at the gym and heading home. I was hoping to catch up with you. Call me back when you get this, okay? I hope everything's alright."

There's a hint of worry in my voice that I can't quite mask. Slipping my phone into my pocket, I unlock my truck and slide in, still mulling over why Kacie hasn't answered. The drive home is a blur, my mind preoccupied with thoughts of her. Maybe she's just busy, or her phone's on silent. But a nagging feeling in my mind can't shake the concern.

Once home, I quickly shower, trying to wash away the remnants of the day's stress and the gym's sweat. Dressed in fresh clothes, I check my phone again, but Kacie still has not responded. Restlessness settles in, and I find myself pacing the apartment. Our open and honest communication is one of the cornerstones of our relationship, and this silence feels out of character for her.

The evening stretches on, and each passing hour deepens my worry. I try calling a few more times, each echoing the same result—straight to voicemail. I send a couple of texts, hoping for a response.

Finally, as the clock ticks past our usual dinner time and the loft feels unusually quiet, I make a decision. I grab my keys and head out the door, intent on going to Kacie's apartment. Maybe it's an overreaction, but I must know she's safe. Especially with that explosive situation in the courtroom, my mind is going to dark places about the kinds of people she's trying to put away. The drive is quick, my mind racing faster than the car, filled with terrifying scenarios.

As I reach Kacie's building, my heart pounds with worry and urgency. I'm compelled to ensure she's okay, hear her voice, and see her face. This isn't just about missing a phone call anymore. It's about making sure the person I care about deeply is safe. I press the buzzer to her apartment, hoping for her familiar voice to answer.

The buzzer echoes into the stillness, and I wait, holding my breath. Seconds stretch out, each one feeling longer than the last. Finally, there's a crackle from the intercom, but it's not Kacie's voice that greets me—it's silence, followed by a faint background noise I can't quite place.

"Kacie?" I call into the intercom, my voice laced with concern. "It's me, Giovanni. Are you there?"

There's a pause, then a shuffle of movement, but still no response. My heart races, dread settling in my gut. Something doesn't feel right. Without waiting for an answer, I press the buzzer again, hoping for some sign, any acknowledgment.

Minutes pass, and the silence from the intercom becomes increasingly unsettling. I debate my next move, considering whether to call a neighbor or the building manager. Just as I'm about to dial, the door to the building clicks open.

Stepping inside, I sprint to Kacie's apartment. The hallways are quiet, the usual sounds of life in the building eerily absent. Reaching her door, I knock firmly, calling her name again.

There's a moment of silence before I hear a faint sound from inside–a muffled movement, perhaps a voice. My worry heightens. I knock again, louder this time.

"Kacie, it's Giovanni! Please, if you can hear me, open the door!"

The door finally opens, but it's not Kacie who greets me. Instead, I'm met by a stranger with a worried look, probably because of my erratic behavior. I step back, run a hand through my hair to release some of my nerves and start again with a calmer voice.

"Is Kacie here? I'm her boyfriend, and I really need to see her."

My mind races, trying to understand the reason for her silence, her absence, and it becomes painfully clear when she pushes open the door to a pool of dried blood on the floor.

"Fuck, fuck, fuck."

I panic and rush past her to run in and out of each room of her small apartment, looking for her. My eyes momentarily pause on the stuffed shark she named Jaws nestled against her bed pillows. She's nowhere to be found, and all those horrible scenarios that played in a loop in my mind are coming to life.

"Where is she?"

She wrings her hands together, her eyes falling to the floor before returning to mine.

"They rushed Kacie to the hospital."

A sick feeling overtakes me.

"What do you mean? Why? What's happened? Did someone break in? Hurt her? Was it someone connected to that guy Friday?"

The words tumble out in a rush, my fear mounting.

I can barely keep my eyes off the lingering blood on the floor between us, noticing the shattered cup and spilled coffee staining the tiles.

"I don't think so. She hit her head. I happened to be walking by with my dog when I heard a loud bang from her apartment. I kept calling her name, and when she didn't answer, I called the manager. He let us in, and that's when we found her."

I lunge at her, trying to decide if I should hug her or not for insisting on investigating.

"Fuck, fuck, fuck."

Who knows how long Kacie would have stayed there if she hadn't gotten the manager? Probably a long time with how much I worried and paced at my place when I could have been here helping her.

Fuck.

She steps weary of my anxious and erratic demeanor.

"We called 911, they were pretty quick. Everyone just left."

She motions to the door as if I passed them somehow, but I didn't.

"I think with who she is and what she does, a police car escorted the ambulance while they were taking our statements and ensuring it wasn't a crime."

A tiny ripple of relief enters my brain, only to be eclipsed as to why this happens.

"Did the first responders say what happened? How did she hit her head? Was it her blood pressure? Did she pass out? She's been trying to get that down. Been making all sorts of life-style changes and . . ."

Even though there's pride in my voice for her, I stop talking as I realize I'm delaying myself.

"Where did they take her?"

"Memorial Hermann."

She steps back, a roll of paper towels and cleaning supplies next to her.

"I'm going to clean this up so she doesn't have to when she comes home."

I thank her and rush out of the apartment, only to skid to a stop and dash back in.

"Which Memorial Hermann?"

"Medical Center."

I run back out, my mind a scattered mess, trying to piece together what could have caused her to pass out and lose so much blood. Did she hit her head on the floor? Hit it on the way down? I didn't want to ask any more questions of her neighbor when I could be speeding to the hospital instead. The drive is a blur, my thoughts consumed with her. They circle in a loop, each amplifying my worry to the point I want to vomit.

Arriving at the hospital, I park haphazardly in the garage and sprint to the emergency room. The lobby is in absolute chaos, with first responders unloading patients, gurneys lining the hallway to the left, and no empty chairs in the waiting room.

The reception area is equally busy, with a line waiting to talk to the intake people. A police officer is sitting in a glass partition next to the reception area, keeping an eye on the place to ensure safety first. The moans, groans, and people in pain make me fidget with concern for her. When it's my turn, I manage to get the attention of a nurse.

"I'm here for Kacie Yacob," I explain, suddenly feeling out of breath with the panic compressing my lungs. "She was brought in by ambulance."

"Are you family or related to the person in question?"

My eyes flicker to the cop beside her, who is steadily staring down a guy that high as a kite by the doorway. Having been around medicine my whole life, I know exactly what to say to get the information I want. I lay it on thick.

A cousin on her mom's side, which explains the difference in our skin tone, comes to pick her up for dinner and finds out from her neighbor what happened. She nods, believing it when she asks for my identification to scan into her computer system before printing out a visitor badge with my name on it.

"She's being admitted right now. They are getting her room ready while they run some tests on her. She won't be up there for several more hours. When they have a room number assigned, I'll let you know. Otherwise, you can have a seat if you can find one."

She slides my identification and the badge through the

cutout at the bottom of the glass and then points to the crowded waiting area.

"Thank you, ma'am."

Preparing myself for a long wait ahead in one of the busiest emergency rooms in the city, I turn to walk away when she calls my name.

"Yes?"

"She came in with these belongings."

She hands me a clear plastic bag through the partition. Inside are Kacie's cell phone and wallet. But as the bag bumps against the glass, Kacie's phone screen lights up, revealing an image that shocks me.

The image on Kacie's phone screen is a brutal punch to the gut. Jenna and I were captured in a moment that's nothing like the truth. The angle is damning, painting me as the initiator of the kiss. My heart thunders against my ribcage, a mix of anger and panic surging through me.

Fuck

Dread and disbelief swirl inside me. This picture, so falsely representing what happened, threatens to shatter the trust and honesty I've built with Kacie. The newly formed relationship is on the brink of collapsing, sending me into an absolute panic.

I clutch the plastic bag tighter, feeling the edges dig into my palm. My mind races frantically, scrambling for a way to explain this and not lose the person I cherish the most.

Once a place of anxious waiting, the emergency room now feels like a suffocating cage. The buzzing of the fluorescent lights, the murmur of voices, and the occasional beep of machinery blend into the loud chaos in my head.

I pace back and forth, each step heavy and haunted. How did this picture come to exist? Who took it? And most importantly, how will I explain this to Kacie? She knew I had a crush on Jenna. Not that long ago. What will she think? Will she believe me? Believe the last week is more real to me than anything else in this world. The thought of losing her, of her looking at me with doubt and betrayal, is unbearable.

I need to act, to explain everything before this image does irreparable damage, ending us forever. But Kacie's health is paramount. I need to be here for her, to support her through this crisis, and then, when the time is right, I'll face this new challenge head-on. My resolve hardens. I won't let this misunderstanding destroy what Kacie and I have. The stakes are too high, and I'm unwilling to lose her. I do the only thing I can do. Collapse on the curb outside the emergency room doors and wait.

18

KACIE

My eyelids flutter open to a harsh, glaring fluorescent light above my bed. The pervasive, unmistakable scent of antiseptic fills my nostrils that can only belong to a hospital. My mind is clouded, disoriented by the setting. The steady beeping of a machine permeates the silence, an annoyance that I want to stop.

Attempting to lift my head, I am met with a sharp, throbbing pain that reverberates through my skull, compelling me to recline once more onto the sterile pillow. My hand, moving instinctively to my forehead, feels the gentle tug of an IV line embedded in my arm. I'm encased in the confines of a hospital bed, a blood pressure cuff clasping my arm with an uncomfortable firmness.

To my side, Giovanni is slumbering in a chair, his posture one of discomfort and exhaustion. His face, etched with lines of worry even in slumber, is a source of solace and a trigger of upsetting emotions within me.

Flashes of yesterday return with unrelenting clarity. The image that had appeared on my phone screen—Giovanni and Jenna, kissing, stabbed at my heart. The coffee mug slipped from my trembling fingers, shattering on the floor and spilling the contents across the tile.

In an almost surreal sequence of events, I had stepped forward, intent on cleaning up the mess, only to find myself slipping on the slick tile. The room spun out of control as I desperately tried to reach for something to catch myself. I found only air, and then came the harrowing impact of my head against the unyielding stone corner of the wet bar. Pain erupted before enveloping me in darkness.

Now, waking up here, not knowing what happened with Giovanni, somehow aware of what occurred, is confusing. The alarming realization of how swiftly life can spiral into chaos leaves me equally troubled.

My gaze returns to him. His presence is a paradoxical blend of comfort and turmoil. The image on my phone makes me hurt, angry, and fearful that what we had was too good to be true.

His rhythmic breathing, steady and utterly unaware of the emotional storm inside me, spikes my anger.

The urge to awaken him, to demand answers, and to confront the reality of that image is overwhelming, especially as it's why I'm here. Yet, my prevailing trepidation is what if those answers reveal the truth. His crush is his lover, and he's seeing both of us, thus shattering what we shared.

The room's silence is deafening, punctuated only by the constant beeping of the heart monitor and the occasional compression of the blood pressure cuff. A glance at my heart rate looks good, and then my gaze falls to the blood pressure, having registered after the cuff releases. It's not good, higher than the doctor's office. The very source of why it's high is sleeping right next to me.

I'm at an emotional crossroads, torn between self-preservation and returning to being alone or risking my health to be with him. Lying there, I'm caught in an unbearable limbo.

My heart feels like it's being tugged in two opposite directions. The idea of being alone again, returning to my solitude before Giovanni, is a bleak prospect. Yet, the thought of staying with him, risking further heartache and potentially my health, is equally daunting.

I study Giovanni's face, searching for a hint to guide me. But there's nothing there, just the innocent, young features of a man lost in sleep. How can someone who looks so peaceful and devoted be the cause of such turmoil?

He shifts in this sleep, mumbling something incoherent, a frown briefly crossing his features before his long body settles deeper into his chair. I glance toward the closed door and draw curtains when I hear him stirring.

"Oh my God, Kac!"

His eyes are bloodshot, while a faint stubble shadows his lower jaw. His usually neat curls are now a tousled, wild mane, adding to the disheveled, distressed look etched across his face.

Instantly, he's up from his chair, moving toward me with an instinctive hug. But he hesitates, his eyes scanning over the various wires and tubes connected to me, trying to navigate a way to embrace me without dislodging anything important.

"What are you doing here?"

My voice sounds fragile even to me, and he steps back as if my words physically hit him.

"What do you mean what am I doing here? Kac, you're hurt in the hospital. For Christ's sake, why wouldn't I be here?"

He runs a trembling hand through his hair, causing me to understand why it looks the way it does.

"Giovanni . . . we need to talk," I say the dreaded words that are heavy and hard to release. His body tenses, an alertness replacing his initial grogginess.

"What's wrong? Your head? Are you in pain? I can get a nurse. They were in here early, but I waved them off so they wouldn't disturb you."

The caring nature of his looking out for me stabs at the heartache I feel from his betrayal.

I shake my head, feeling a knot in my stomach.

"It's not about my head, Giovanni. It's about us."

My heart pounds, each beat registering on the monitor near me that catches his eyes momentarily. His frown deepens, a crease forming between his eyebrows when they return to mine. That creases his brow deepens.

"Us? What about us, Kac?"

His voice is edged with a growing apprehension.

I swallow hard, the image on my phone flashing in my mind's eye, reigniting the raw hurt and anger. The irritating blood pressure cuff starts compressing to take a reading at the most inopportune time.

"I saw the picture. You were kissing Jenna."

The words are like acid on my tongue. He moves closer to me, his hand slowly extending toward mine, resting vulnerably on the bedsheet. His expression transforms, morphing from concern to guilt.

"Kacie, that picture . . . it's not what you think."

Frustration and desperation for the truth collide within me as I untangle my cold hand from his.

"Then explain it to me, Giovanni. Because it seems pretty clear from my end."

He leans in, his eyes desperate, pleading.

"You've got to believe me. That picture was taken out of context. Jenna . . . she came onto me. I didn't reciprocate, I swear."

Part of me wants to believe him. Believe in the man, I spent the most wonderful week. Yet the investigator in me knows when things look precisely as they seem, and I can't let that go as easily as he wants me to.

"I find that hard to believe with your lips on hers and your arms around her."

And now, because of it, I'm here in this hospital bed. I want to add but don't. There is no sense in pouring gasoline on an already lit fire.

He reaches out a second time, his hand enveloping mine. His touch is warm, but it does little to thaw the ice forming around my heart.

"I know how it looks, Kacie. But trust me, I care so much about you that I'd never hurt you. You're the most precious thing in my life. You've got to believe me."

Desperation clings to his voice, as does the strength of his grip on my hands. He's as distraught about this as I am, the difference being he's the guilty party. Usually, I'm of the adage of innocent until proven guilty and listening to all the extenuating circumstances, as photos can be doctored or taken from various angles. However, when the cuff releases and registers my blood pressure, an alarm goes off, and a nurse scurries in.

"Oh no, this is not good."

She bustles toward me, forcing Giovanni to break his hold on my hand and step aside. He watches her take over, pressing buttons on the machine while a surge of heat races through my body. I push the covers down, wipe my forehead off the perspiration collecting there, and watch as she adjusts the cuff, preparing to retake my blood pressure.

"We're going to retake this. If it rereads this high, I must get the doctor in here."

Giovanni is stonily silent, his eyes wide, his mouth slacks in surprise as he studies her, me, and the numbers on the machine. His hands plant on his hips, pulling his wrinkled shirt tight across his developed chest and looking authoritative like he did in the gym the first time I met him. However, the cheery confidence is lost in his worry, regret, and concern. Neither of us says a word, exchanging glances while the cuff tightens. The bubbly nurse decides the silence is too much, saying.

"Isn't it nice that your cousin has been here all night? I offered him a pillow and a blanket, but he refused, saying he wanted to be ready when you wake up."

Cousin?

It didn't dawn on me how he got here, as I was too fixated on that picture. He lied to the hospital, lied to get his way. Is this who he really is? A liar. Lying to them and me to get his way.

When I raise an eyebrow in silent inquiry, my expression doesn't fall into an apology. It remains stoic as those dark eyes move to the numbers that register when the cuff releases. The nurse looks at the readings and quickly excuses herself.

"Oh dear. I'll be right back."

I angle my head to glimpse the monitor, and what I see sends a wave of fear crashing over me. The numbers are alarmingly high, nearing two hundred. My heart races with anxiety. It feels like my body has taken the reins, making a decision that fills me with a deep sadness. The reality of my situation, reflected in the disturbing numbers on the monitor, seems to dictate a path my heart is reluctant to follow.

The silence that ensues is deafening, filled only with the mechanical beeping of the monitor and my labored breaths. Giovanni's gaze locks onto mine, his eyes a silent plea for understanding, trust, and forgiveness. I muster the strength to speak the words I know are true.

"You need to go, Giovanni. I can't deal with this right now."

His shoulders slump forward when his hands fall from his hips. His expression is of marked pain and instant sorrow. He nods, wiping a hand over his weary face and trying to hide the sting of rejection.

"I'm sorry, Kacie. For the picture, for making your blood pressure high, for . . ."

His voice trails off when he runs another hand through his hair, turning his back to me and looking at the ceiling for answers. When he turns around, his hand returns to his side, and tears rim his eyes.

"I'll go, but just know I'm here for you. No matter what. You're mine, and I'm yours. That's what we said. That's what you said, Kac."

His words hang heavy in the space between us, a poignant reminder of the commitment we just made to each other yesterday. It's startling how fast things change. But at this moment, surrounded by the stark reality of a hospital room, my health, and his betrayal, his declaration feels like a distant echo of a happier time.

As he turns to leave, a profound loss washes over me. His quiet footsteps resound on the floor, replaced by the swooshing of the door. The room feels emptier and more sterile, plunging me back to an old, lonely life I thought I had left behind.

The nurse, a young woman with a kind face and gentle eyes, enters the room first, looking around for Giovanni and then smiling at me. She's followed closely by a middle-aged man dressed in a white coat with his name embroidered across the front. His forehead is marked by faint lines that speak of years spent in medicine. He approaches my bed, hand outstretched to make introductions.

"Ms. Yacob, I'm Dr. Matthews. It's good to see you awake and alert."

He nods to the nurse, who has a bottle of something in her gloved hand, as she scans the wristband below my IV.

"We're rather concerned about your blood pressure. It's considerably high, which is a matter we take very seriously. We hoped it would come down while you rested, but since it hasn't, we will give you some medicine to help."

A knot of worry forms in my stomach.

"Couldn't it be higher because I'm in here? My general practitioner warned me of this, but I've made some changes this week, started working out and eating better."

My voice is shaky, betraying my growing anxiety. He glances at the monitor, then back at me with a measured look.

"This is something you are aware of? Have you been on anything to help while making these lifestyle changes?"

"Um, no. We didn't think it was that serious."

I remember a forgotten call from the doctor's office lingering on my voicemail from earlier this week. Perhaps it was about putting me on meds once they got my labs back?

"It is significant. We need to monitor you closely to ensure your blood pressure comes down to a safer level. That means staying with us for a day or two. Although the changes are positive and necessary for all of us for heart health, avoidance of diabetes, stress, alcohol, and hereditary factors are big contributors."

He launches into potential causes of my high blood pressure while I speculate that a recent and unexpected emotional surprise might be a contributing factor. Dr. Matthews addresses this by explaining that while emotional stress can cause a temporary spike in blood pressure, it typically doesn't sustain high levels over a long duration like mine.

He notes that supportive, healthy relationships can help lower blood pressure and provide other mental and physical health benefits. He is basically debunking my blame of Giovanni and his actions.

Instead, he zeroes in on my career, the same as Dr. Patel did, and it's like hearing a record on repeat. I stay silent when he asks about recent changes in my workload that could be causing additional stress. Bringing up Friday's incident will just reinforce his point. I shift the conversation to my aching head, where they stitched up a gash and concluded that I didn't have a concussion. My fingers instinctively drift to the area, tender to the touch, while he advises me of the treatment plan.

Once they finish and leave the room, I'm alone with my thoughts. Mulling over the new information with what I thought I knew proves and disproves my theories. I blamed Giovanni for this hospitalization, yet hearing from the doctor, it was inevitable without medication. My relationship with Giovanni, which I thought was adding to my stress, might benefit me in multiple ways.

Despondent over everything and feeling exhausted, I lower the head of my bed, noticing my phone and wristlet sitting on the corner of the tray table. How did these get here? Heck, I didn't even think to ask how I got here. Who found me? I gaze at the wall, trying to remember what happened between falling and waking up here with Giovanni, but my mind is entirely blank. I grab my phone, noticing its battery is nearly drained, and there's a string of messages from my colleagues. Quickly, I text Ethan, giving him a brief rundown of my situation, the name of the hospital, and my room number. Then, I dial my co-counsel, leaving a voicemail about my accident last night, asking her to call me back with any updates on our case.

This situation is a complete disaster. Being sidelined like this couldn't have come at a worse time. During my unexpected absence, I fret about who will take over my caseload. My mind meticulously analyzes each case, contemplating their respective statuses, necessary witness confirmations, and upcoming hearings scheduled within the week.

Dr. Bennett's case is of particular concern, given his stringent availability—he can only appear one day this month, which, unfortunately, falls within this week. This unforeseen hospital stay poses a significant risk to the careful planning and coordination of these legal proceedings.

The phone by my bedside suddenly rings, breaking into my thoughts. I answer it to find my paralegal on the other line, and she also gets Ethan looped into the call. Over the next hour, we meticulously review all my cases, discussing each in detail.

My paralegal takes diligent notes as I give instructions and make decisions from my hospital bed. With his usual efficiency,

Ethan offers to step in where needed, helping to alleviate some of my concerns about Dr. Bennett, this week's docket, and other pressing matters. The conversation is exhaustive but necessary, ensuring that everything is under control in my absence and spiking my blood pressure again.

The monitor's alarm blares sharply, prompting the nurse to rush into my room. She quickly resets the machine and then casts a disapproving look at the phone in my hand. Seizing the opportunity, I use her arrival as a reason to wrap up the call.

"I have to go," I say, feeling a twinge of guilt with their well wishes echoing in the receiver when I hang up.

"You really should be resting, not working. It's not helping your condition."

The nurse, still frowning, reinforces her point. I nod in agreement, albeit reluctantly, understanding the validity of her advice. The call has been productive but also a clear confirmation of the strain my job is putting on my health.

As the dining service brings in my breakfast tray, I realize I need a nap more than a meal. The effort of resolving work matters has left me drained. Yet, with those immediate concerns temporarily put to rest, my thoughts inevitably drift back to Giovanni and how miserable he looked when I asked him to leave.

As I ponder Giovanni's explanation—the situation is not as it appears. Jenna made a pass at him, and he resisted. I reach for my phone. With trepidation, I zoom in on the photo for a closer inspection. Jenna's arms are wrapped around his neck while his hands rest on her waist, maintaining a noticeable space between their bodies.

The ambiguity of the image gnaws at me. Is she pulling him toward her lips, or is he willingly leaning into the kiss? The photo leaves room for interpretation, but either way, it depicts him in an intimate moment with another woman. This, by any definition, falls under infidelity, especially since we had committed to being exclusive to each other the same day this happened. This realization exacerbates the throbbing in my skull more intensely than the pain from the cut on the back of my head. My heart sinks further with the realization that I need to end things with him since the trust we shared has been broken.

I place my phone on the tray table beside my untouched breakfast and close my eyes, finally allowing myself to rest since waking up in this nightmarish situation. I'm roused from my sleep by the gentle rustle of movement. Opening my eyes, I see a hospital staff member carefully placing a stunning arrangement of delicate pink roses and white lilies, their sweet fragrance subtly filling the room. The bouquet is adorned with five cheerful 'Get Well Soon' balloons, dancing lightly in the air.

I assume this thoughtful gesture must be from my work colleagues. However, inspecting the accompanying card nestled among the blooms, I discover it's from Giovanni. His sentiments flow across the card, each word imbued with emotion.

"My Dearest Kacie, I know this is a temporary setback in your health, but you're on the right track and should be proud of what you have already achieved. I'm holding onto the hope that you'll give me the chance to make things right. Please know that I'm with you every step of this journey. Together, we'll overcome this health scare and the issue between us to come out stronger. I'm here for you, now and always, waiting for the moment we can be together again. Yours, O.G."

I press the card gently against my chest as I recline back, my gaze fixed on the ceiling. Lost in thought, I reflect on Giovanni, his heartfelt words echoing in my mind. Despite the turmoil, the sincerity in his words is undeniable. His beautiful flowers, balloons, and words are considerate and characteristic of him. He's always been caring and thoughtful, more gentlemanly than any other man I've dated, and far more romantic. The number of surprises this week alone speaks to it.

It's not what you think.

Giovanni's words resonated with a hint of desperation. This realization sparks a thought – perhaps I can do some investigative work right from my hospital bed. With this in mind, I pick up my phone, silently praying its battery lasts long enough for the crucial call I need to make.

I scroll through my contacts to find her number, sitting through a few rings before she answers.

"Bex."

The word is a bark over the music blaring in the background.

"Hey, Bex, it's Kacie from the gym."

I try to sound casual despite the urgency bubbling inside me. I sit up in bed, trying to feel more confident about this discussion.

"Oh, hey, Kacie. What's up?"

Bex's voice is loud against the backdrop of thumping beats.

"Hang on a sec, let me turn this down."

The music gets louder until it's suddenly silent.

"If I'm interrupting you, I can ca—"

"Nah, I'm just working, and the music helps with my flow. Get's me in the mood. Today is graffiti art. It goes best with heavy metal music. It's all about synergy, am I right?"

I'm unsure I fully understand her meaning, but I get that music sets the mood. It reminds me of the various types of music Giovanni played at his place when I was over.

"Yes, synergy."

A needling discomfort stabs my stomach while I beat around the bush instead of coming right out with it.

"I was just thinking about the gym the other day. You seem to have the inside scoop on what's happening there."

Bex laughs, the music dipping back in as she seems to move to a louder spot.

"Sorry, I'm with other artists, so I can't turn down their music. But yeah, I guess. I spend a lot of time there. Always something going on."

"Speaking of which."

I try to sound nonchalant, using the finesse I use on cases when necessary.

"You sent me a picture the other day. Of Giovanni and Jenna?"

"Oh, that."

Bex's tone changes slightly.

"Yeah, that caught me by surprise. Ya know, I wasn't sure if I should send it without knowing the full story. But I thought you could sort all that out with him rather than me."

She's partially correct. I could sort it out with him, but would I get the truth? Deciding to continue my line of questioning, I chose my words carefully.

"What exactly did you see? Before you took the picture, I mean."

Framing this as an impromptu investigation, I steel my nerves for whatever comes next. Bex's voice momentarily fades as she shouts instructions to someone in the background.

"Sorry about that, Kacie. The guy here was about to mess up the painting sequence for this piece we're working on. Once that's done wrong, there's no fixing it. Anyway, I was on the treadmill, like I was when I met you. You know, that's my usual warm-up before free weights. I was looking for you, by the way, so when those two walked by, I thought, hmm, Bex, that's sort of interesting."

"Yes, I ended up working. It was supposed to be Giovanni's day off, but he got called in with so many people out sick."

She grumbles into the phone, snapping her fingers, which causes me to think I'm distracting her.

"Oh, the crud is going around. Yeah, I noticed he was swamped. Juggling multiple clients, sometimes two at a time."

That explanation fits what I know—the long gap where I hadn't heard from Giovanni, probably too engrossed in his work to call or text. I hum an acknowledgment, encouraging her to continue.

"I was fiddling with my playlist and checking out my hair in my phone's camera when I heard her—Jenna. She was either crying or laughing really loud, I couldn't quite figure out which. Then she lunged at him."

I switch my phone to speaker mode and pull up the picture Bex had sent. Staring at it, I try to discern whether she's laughing or crying, but it's impossible to tell with her face plastered to Giovanni's. A fresh wave of hurt washes over me at the sight.

"What happened after the kiss?"

"It was odd, I'll give you that. Giovanni seemed to be holding her and pushing her away simultaneously. Like he was trying not to hurt her feelings or something, that's when I realized she was crying."

Her tone indicates she's still puzzled by the whole interaction.

"The whole scene was weird. Why would you do something like that in a gym? Everyone's always watching everyone else while working out because the music they play is crap, and the TV's always on those shitty news channels."

Calling Bex, I thought, would clear things up. It's only adding to my confusion.

"Huh? Then what?"

I lighten my voice, trying to glean more information even though the background music is getting louder and acting as a ticking clock to this call ending soon.

"I think they argued, or at least he raised his voice at her."

That statement has me raising my eyebrows. In the short

time I've known him, I've never seen him raise his voice or appear flustered, bothered, or angry. This piece of information is very out of character for him.

"Then he walked off toward the group fitness area, and she ran crying into the locker room. I was tempted to go after her and ask what was up, but I figured it wasn't my place to get involved."

Her inflection takes on a casual tone as if shrugging off the significance of the incident.

"I appreciate you sending me the picture and answering all my questions, Bex. I hope this doesn't put you in an awkward spot."

"Hell no, I'd want someone to do the same for me. Men love them and hate them at the same time, am I right?"

She laughs loudly into the receiver at her remark. Personally, I've never been one to subscribe to broad generalizations about any group of people, but I understand how experiences can shape such sentiments.

"Either way, I appreciate your help, Bex."

The conversation comes to a natural end, and just as I'm about to hang up, she adds, "Oh, hey, one last thing. When I next saw your man, he was dripping in sweat, like having run suicides up and down the basketball court, except he wasn't coming from the courts. I didn't take him—"

But before she can finish her sentence, my phone abruptly dies, leaving her words hanging in the air. I'm left staring at the now blank screen. The timing couldn't be worse. The lack of closure adds another layer of mystery to the already confusing situation.

Bex's sudden observation about Giovanni being drenched in sweat, not coming from the courts, piques my interest. What was he doing? Where was he coming from? And why did she think that was such an important detail to share?

The questions swirl in my head as I lay the phone by my

tray. The weight of not just the physical exhaustion, my pounding head, and high blood pressure compounds my mental strain. The room falls silent again.

The aching loneliness that I usually chased away with long nights at the office isn't going to be possible anymore, and with Giovanni possibly out of the picture, I'm left alone with my thoughts. It's the scariest possible outcome.

19

GIOVANNI

Sitting in my truck outside the hospital, my heart feels like it's shattering into a thousand pieces. Kacie's refusal to hear me out, the hurt on her face, and the pain in her emerald eyes—it's all too much. Tears are welling up, but I fight them back.

The thought that I might be causing her health to worsen guts me. All I've ever wanted to do is help her achieve her goals and become the best version of herself that she wants to be. The fact that her blood pressure rose enough to set off alarm bells makes me nauseous.

The fight within me rages, adhering to her wishes, leaving her alone, or showing her how much she means to me and fighting for us. The picture and the misunderstanding will not prevail. I won't lose her so easily and over something that wasn't my fault. Even though she's pushing me away, I know what to do.

The florist's shop that my parents always use is not far from here. I'm so preoccupied with Kacie that I'm unsure how I got here. Nonetheless, I slip from my truck, my steps heavy as I cross the parking lot and enter the shop. An elderly woman greets me as a team of people works in the back of the shop, assembling different arrangements.

"Can I help you with something?"

Her tone is soft like Kacie's, making my chest ache that much more. I shake my head, not knowing what to order.

"I-I need to send something special."

Send an apology. Send get well wishes. Send anything that will work to bring her to talk to me, to listen, and let me explain. I rub my face, my eyes burning from unshed tears and exhaustion.

"Someone I care about is in the hospital."

Sensing my indecision, the elderly woman pats my arm and suggests something her coworkers are creating. She encourages me to follow her to a large bouquet with pink roses and white lilies. I nod, remembering Kacie's comment about loving the lilies I sent to her office and how fragrant they were. While they finished arranging it, she suggested I get started on the card.

How do you condense everything you're feeling inside into a few lines? I stand there stupefied until she sees me struggling.

"I find most things can be said in three lines."

Then she hands me a larger card that can be folded over for privacy purposes.

"In case you need to say more."

I take both sizes to the counter by the window, the sunshine bright on this otherwise cold day. Standing there, I hesitate, unsure how to start. Then, the words flow over the large card, pouring out of me and wanting to say more but running out of space. I deliberate over the close.

Do I write, Love Giovanni? Do I love her? I'm not sure. Do I care for her more than anyone I ever have before? Yes. Does she feel the same? If she doesn't, will I be coming on too strong, too forceful, and scare her away as I wondered back at the apartment when I opened up about my sexual preferences. That seems a million miles away from where we're at now.

Tears blur the words as I reread what I wrote, deciding to use her words from yesterday.

Yours, O.G.

I sniff and swipe a hand over my eyes, trying to gather my composure. Turning back to the florist, I see she's added a bunch of balloons to the arrangement, making it even more special. I hand her my credit card, give her the hospital's address and Kacie's room number, and swiftly exit.

In the truck, I call my boss and leave a voicemail that I'm running late with a friend in the hospital but will arrive within the hour. The drive to my loft is quick, with my mind working through different approaches I could take, trying to solve the problem on my own and then dismissing them as worthless.

The moment I step in, her lingering scent hits my nostrils, adding to my sorrow. The makeshift tent stands like a painful reminder of what was to be a repeated performance, and I sprint past it into my bedroom, imprinted with memories of everything we have done.

My loft is as hard to be in as her asking me to leave. I rush to prepare, forgoing my usual meal prep to escape the warm cocoon I made for us. Getting to work in record time, I go straight to my desk to distract myself with today's clients and schedules. Monday is always busy, and being late and forcing the few other trainers who are not sick to handle my load isn't something I want to happen, but Kacie comes first.

Work isn't the refuge I had hoped for as the day progresses, with flashes of her everywhere. Her sparkling eyes challenging me when teaching her proper squat form. Her laughter as I dance to the music overhead, trying to distract her when she wants to give up.

Her luscious body traversing the rows of equipment as she

did walking lunges. Her collapsing on the floor in the quiet group fitness room gave me a stiffy, imagining her sprawled out under me. Everywhere I look is a flash, exchange, or memory of her, making my stomach tighten.

Marco senses a change in me and asks what's bothering me. I shake my head, not knowing where to start, until he sits in the chair opposite my desk, just listening. Slowly, I unravel the last twenty-four hours, watching the emotion change on his face at different times until he slaps the desk between us.

"I knew I didn't trust her." His head shakes vigorously from side to side. "The way she played you, damn, bro."

He isn't helping by piling on.

"Marco."

His hands are instantly in the air as if I have a gun at him.

"Sorry, sorry. I warned you to stay away, and now this."

"You're still not helping."

The chair squeaks when he moves it closer, his elbow sprawling out on the desk as he leans closer.

"Okay, here's what you got to do. Nothing. Let them both go and find a new woman."

I groan, leaning back in my chair and glaring at him.

"Just go if you're not going to help me."

"I am helping. Chicks aren't worth all this mental mess. Look around this place."

His gaze sweeps the busy floor, and mine follows, curious about what I'm looking at.

"At least a dozen women would go out with you. Probably a dozen more that wouldn't mind a go at that dick of yours. It is still unfair that you got that along with your height and hair."

I death stare at him now, having heard his complaints many times before as he's average, according to him, bald and under six feet tall. All the things that bother him are common complaints from the women he dates.

"Forget it. I got to get back to work."

I stand, done with his nonsense, when he rises, walking next to me as I make my way to the free weights area to tidy up.

"Alright, I got it. Do some big thing. You know all that shit they do in the movies."

The back of his hand hits my shoulder as if his words weren't enough to get my attention.

"Like, uh, uh, Vision sacrificing himself for Wanda. Something like that."

"You want me to die to show Kacie how I feel about her?"

I can't hide the skepticism in my voice as I nod to Frank, who's walking in, ready to start our session.

"Yeah, not literally. Oh, oh, I got a better one. Like in the sappy movie where the dude paints the house for the chick, and then she comes back to him but doesn't remember him when they are old."

"I don't know what you're talking about."

I pick up some forgotten barbells and place them on the rack, rearranging others to have them in weight order while he trails behind me.

"You want me to paint my loft for her? I'm not sure if my landlord will allow that, plus the exposed brick and—"

He hits me upside my head, causing me to whirl around on him. He takes a few steps back, otherwise holding his position.

"No, dumbass, do something big, something that lets her know how sorry you are. Win her back."

"I already plan on that," I say flatly when Frank joins us by shaking our hands with his greeting. "Alright, Marco, thanks for the advice. Frank, how are you doing today?"

Marco frowns when dismissed, shooting me the middle finger behind my client's back and wandering away. The hour spent with Frank is helpful, allowing me to temporarily forget my immediate problems as we talk about the competition from this weekend and how he did. It isn't until he's covered in sweat, smiling and shaking my hand, that they come rushing back to me. They linger in the front of my mind through the rest of my clients until dusk sets in and the gym empties with people going home to their families.

On his way out, my boss thanks me for yesterday and asks about my friend. My responses are clipped with how guilty and terrible I feel. He claps me on the back, saying he'll see me in the morning. I hum an acknowledgment and return to racking my brain, wondering what grand gesture I can do with her in the hospital. Drumming my fingertips on my desk while staring at the darkening sky, it hits me out of nowhere.

I swiftly rise from my seat, snatch up my keys, and bolt out the door, heading straight for my truck. The urgency propels me forward, each step quick and decisive as I jump in, peel out of the parking lot, and head straight to the grocery store to pick up everything I need. For the first time since I left the hospital, a seedling of hope takes hold in my mind and I find myself humming to the tune in the store as I shop.

Once done with the groceries loaded in my truck, I rush home and dash inside to shower. My hair is still wet, the curls almost ringlets when I change into a suit, grab a box from my closet, and drop her gift inside. I rummage through to find some leftover ribbon from Christmas to tie around it and then run the truck. I spritz some cologne on and steal a look in the mirror, feeling confident about what I'm about to do.

With the clock ticking down on visiting hours, I rush to the hospital, steering my truck into a parking spot in a manner reminiscent of the previous night's haste. I quickly gather my bags and stride toward the hospital entrance, keenly aware of the limited time left to see Kacie.

The hospital's fluorescent lights and sterile corridors contrast sharply with my racing heart and hopeful excitement. I navigate the halls with a single-minded focus, reaching her room.

When I reach her closed door, I pause, take a deep breath,

and murmur an encouraging word to myself. This is that grand gesture they always discuss in the movies. I hope it works. Blowing out a long breath, I slowly open the door, ready to lay my heart and tell her how much she truly means to me. My footsteps are light, a slight trepidation in them as I peek around the pulled curtain to find her eyes closed and resting.

I freeze, bags in hand, and caught off guard. I hadn't anticipated this scenario and am momentarily unsure how to proceed. The balloons swish softly against the vent, and the smell of the white lilies permeates the room. I'm pleasantly surprised to see my card opened and lying on the table's edge, pulled close to her bed. Reading it and not having torn it to shreds is a good sign.

Deciding to proceed with my surprise, I step further into the room, careful not to wake her, as I set the bag in the chair I occupied this morning. Unpacking the contents, I start with the dozen mini LED candles representing a candlelight dinner and quietly open the packages. I watch her as I activate each one and set them around her room before shutting off all the overhead lights except the one behind her bed.

I smile at the warm ambiance it creates in this otherwise sterile room. Retrieving my phone from my pocket and the speaker from the bag, I select the playlist from our first night together. The one she later told me that she liked. Careful to ensure I don't wake her until everything is set up, I leave the music on low and set the speaker across the room. Next is the chilled, non-alcoholic sparkling wine with far too much sugar than we should have, but that is a worry for another time. I quietly pop the top and pour it into the only plastic champagne glasses I could find at the store with Happy New Year's emblazed across them.

Once those are arranged on her table, I quickly glance toward Kacie to confirm she's still asleep. Assured she hasn't been disturbed, I turn around to place my gift beside the speakers. Next, I carefully unpack the deli-prepared meal, chosen specifically for its low sodium content and high nutritional value, ensuring it aligns with her health needs.

Two emerald eyes watch me intently when I place it with the plastic utensils and plates beside the sparkling wine. Having been caught red-handed and not entirely prepared for how to start my big speech, I smile.

"Hi, Kac."

Exhaustion is etched deeply across her beautiful features. Her eyes, usually so vibrant and full of life, now appear tired and heavy-lidded. The hospital gown slips off her shoulder, revealing the smooth, silky skin I've always cherished. Her hair, ordinarily well-kept and lustrous, lies somewhat disheveled around her face. It looks like she's had a long day.

"What?" Her voice cracks forcing her to clear her throat before trying again. "What is all this?"

That seedling of hope grows a little more when she doesn't outright throw me out like she did this morning.

"My grand gesture," I say proudly, moving closer to set the food and utensils down.

A soft chuckle escapes her lips, a sound so heartwarmingly familiar yet painfully rare these past days. It ignites a desire in me to keep her chuckling, to erode the tension between us until the memory of the misunderstood photo fades away and she reassures me we'll be okay.

"I don't think you're supposed to announce it's a grand gesture." A faint sparkle returns to her tired eyes.

"Are you sure? Because that movie with the guy, he paints a house for her, and they live happily ever after."

Her head tilts, with a question in her expression.

"What movie?"

"I honestly have no idea," I admit, a bit sheepishly, and then quickly add, "I'm pretty sure the hospital won't let me paint your walls, so I thought maybe another sleepover? Albeit in a different location?"

"And the suit?"

She raises a weak hand and slides down the front, ensuring it's not too wrinkled from the truck since I didn't take my coat off when driving.

"Because it makes me look good, and I wanted to look good for you ... for this date."

My heart races that this gesture, this moment, might be the turning point for us.

"That's very sweet of you. And you do look handsome."

Her gaze travels around the room, taking in everything I brought. An awkwardness settles between us when her eyes return to mine. I fidget, not knowing if I should drive right in on what's happening between us or put it off so I have more time with her in case she decides to end it with me.

"What did you bring?"

She takes charge of the situation, and my shoulders drop in relief. I'll easily let her control this situation as my previous confidence walking in here is ebbing away. I dive in, explaining the meal I brought, how I assumed she'd be on a restricted diet, and discussed everything with the store kitchen manager. She chuckles, and my story grows bigger, exaggerating parts such as the glasses being in the clearance section to keep the lightness going between us.

One taste of the wine has us both making faces and wanting to spit it out. It's absolutely terrible. When she remarks that the wine at my place the other night was so much better, I dump out those glasses, jog down to the vending machine and get us a couple of drinks to pour into our glasses.

She even lets me fake a New Year's Eve toast with our glasses. The mood lightens, and it's starting to feel like us—laughing, teasing, and enjoying each other's company. I couldn't be happier.

As I carefully remove the lid from the prepared meal, a warm, inviting aroma wafts through the room, bridging the gap between us. Gently, I maneuver the tray table across her bed, positioning it just right, and then I take a vacant spot down by her feet.

No sooner does she take a small bite of the dish than her expression changes. Her nose wrinkles and disgust crosses her features while she slowly finishes and washes it down with her soda.

"That bad?"

My fork hovers above the dish, intending to let her eat as much as she wants, if not all of it. Judging from her face, the rest of it is fair game.

"Try it."

"Try it after that face? No way."

I make a big production of setting my fork down, soaking up everything about this evening with her.

"You have to. It's a party code that you must eat the food you bring, don't you know?"

Her eyes shimmer with humor, as they did so many times this week, and my smile falters. I want to get back to where we were. I release a long breath, unbuttoning my coat and loosening my tie to have the most sincere conversation with her.

"Kac, I didn't kiss her."

Even I can hear the sadness in my voice. Holding her fork, her hand drops in response while she stares at me.

"Nor did I want to kiss her. I know I confessed to having a crush on her when we first met, but not anymore. If anything, I'm angry at her. For what she did to me, to you, and us. It's unforgivable."

"Giovanni—"

"Kacie, let me get this out before you ask me to leave again."

I stand up, the confines of the room seemingly shrinking around me. My jacket feels like an oppressive layer in the charged atmosphere, and I quickly shed it, draping it over the chair along with my tie. In hindsight, I should have stayed dressed for her. Yet sweat starts forming at the back of my neck, and a gnawing anxiety settles in my stomach. I desperately need a respite.

Kacie's lips press together, her expression turning more attentive. Her striking green eyes are wide and alert, following my every move as I grip the edge of her bed with slightly trembling hands.

"I don't know how you got that picture, and frankly, I don't even care at this point," I begin, realizing that I came out sounding careless, which is the furthest thing from what I feel.

"What I mean is that I spent the whole day practicing what I'd say to you. Thinking about different ways to start or handle this, but honestly, I couldn't come up with any. Do you know why? Because I've never felt this way about someone before."

I release the bed, running a shaky hand through my drying hair before looking up at the ceiling to figure out what to say. My brain is bursting with so much, going in different directions, that I want to say it all at the same time.

"Giovanni. I know she instigated it." Her soft voice carries more confusion than clarity when I turn around. "Bex told me. Actually, she was the one that took the picture in the first place."

Bex?

Her new friend. Anger throbs in my veins. Betrayal is its companion. Coming from someone Kacie just met and considers a friend is unbelievable. I struggle not to lose my temper and take a deep breath, trying to calm down to focus on what needs to be said. This conversation is far from over, and I need to tread carefully to navigate the fragile situation even if I want to find Bex tomorrow and yell at her the same as I did Jenna.

"Why did she do that?"

I keep my questions short and sweet, even though I want to demand to know every last word she said to my girl.

"She thought I should know. Said she wanted to know if the roles were reversed."

Kacie doesn't sound as convinced by Bex's response, which slightly cools my temper.

"She appears to have sent it out of context. Maybe you should tell me exactly what happened."

Relieve washes over me as Kacie's sensible side prevails. I quickly move toward her bed, guiding the tray table away from her so I can sit on the edge. When my knee lays atop hers, she tries to move away, and my hand on the covers stops her. I don't want or need more space. If anything, I want to be as close as possible.

Not wanting to ruin this opportunity by leaving anything out, I walk her through my day from the second I dropped her off to running into her neighbor at her apartment. She stays mostly silent except for asking a few pointed questions. When I'm done, I take a swig of the open bottle of sparkling wine, needing something stronger than the soft drink, and gag at the aftertaste. Her face, a mask of concentration, smiles slightly as she takes it all in.

"That makes more sense now."

Her words bring a cautious hope to the surface. The tension in the room seems to ease a bit, replaced by a fragility of not knowing where that leaves me and us. I don't hesitate to express my deepest feelings.

"Kac, this past week has been the best of my life. I know it sounds like something out of a movie, but it's the truth. You've accepted me for who I am, something nobody else has ever done. I shared my dreams with you, half-expecting you to dismiss them as frivolous or childish. Instead, you dove head-first into them, helping me draft a business plan and even offering to meet with that potential investor. That's more than anyone has ever done for me, especially in such a short time."

I pause, searching her face for any sign of how my words are landing.

"You've become a part of my life in a way I never expected. When that picture came out, it felt like my world was falling apart, not because of what others would think, but because I feared losing you, the one person who's come to mean so much to me."

Kacie listens, her expression softening, a hint of understanding in her eyes.

"I didn't want any of this to happen—the misunderstanding, the hurt and pain. All I've ever wanted since I met you was to be there for you, to make you happy."

I reach for her hand, gently enclosing it in mine.

"What I'm trying to say is that you matter to me, Kacie. More than I thought possible in such a short time. I don't want to lose what we've started to build together. I want to be there for you, just like you've been there for me."

Her hand feels warm in mine, that connection we have strengthening amidst the chaos Bex caused. It feels like we're on the brink of something new and better than before, this misunderstanding bringing us closer. I hold her gaze, silently hoping my words have bridged the gap and done the job to move us forward.

The soft flickering of the LED candles creates a serene ambiance while the quiet music gently fills the space around us, setting a calm and intimate mood as I anxiously await her response.

"Giovanni, I . . . I've been confused and hurt. But hearing you explain everything, seeing the effort you've put into this evening . . . it helps. It means a lot to me."

My grip tightens over her, wanting to kiss away the pain and hurt this has caused her. I glimpse at the numbers on her monitor, far lower than this morning.

"I'll do anything for you, Kac. And I'm sorry I raised your blood pressure and caused you to be in here."

Guilt washes over me. The numbers I saw flashing on the monitor this morning were downright scary.

"I know, and I appreciate this. But this . . ." She points to her in bed and the monitor. "It's not your fault. Sure, the timing was coincidental, but it has nothing to do with you. It's all stemming from my job. I'm going to have to make some changes soon."

Worry blankets her features. That must have been hard news for her to receive, considering how important her job is to her and the victims she represents.

"I'm sorry, Kac."

My thumb swipes over her knuckles, wanting to take her into my arms, kiss away the hurt from us and the news about her job. All of it. But we are not there yet, and I don't want to misstep.

"Do you know of any hot trainers that can take on a middle-aged woman carrying excess weight and a growing list of health problems?" She jokes, but it falls flat in its delivery. "Ba-dum-bum."

She releases my hand to make the drumming motion that coordinates with her failed joke. I take it as an opportunity to retrieve my poorly wrapped gift from the shelf and return it to her side.

"I'm unsure where we're at or what you've decided. But for transparency's sake, I want you to open this before you decide."

I try to keep my tone light even though I'm terrified of outright rejection at this point.

She gives me a curious look, turning the small box and looking for clues before sliding the ribbon to the corners to open it. Nestled against some white tissue paper is a key. When those emerald eyes raise to mine, they're wide with panic.

"Again, not what you think. I'm not asking you to move in. I realize that's way too soon. But my place is far closer to your building and even closer to the courthouse than your apartment. If you need to take a break or nap, or I don't know, have sex with me in the middle of the day. You have a key to let yourself in."

Her panicked look is chased away with a bright smile, which has me sinking back onto the bed with her.

"Well, the doctor did recommend a stress reliever. He didn't specify what kind, O.G."

EPILOGUE

KACIE

As I step backstage with Giovanni, the world transforms into a tapestry of sights, sounds, and chaos. The air is electric, buzzing with anticipation, excitement, and determination. My heart races, not just with nerves for Giovanni but with the sheer exhilaration of being part of this momentous day in his journey. The one we meticulously planned together in his apartment on that brisk January evening after we had sex.

Bright lights illuminate the area, glowing on Giovanni's perfectly sculpted body. His muscles, resulting from countless hours of training and discipline, stand out against his bronzed skin, oiled to perfection. Around us, competitors move with a sense of purpose, their bodies a canvas of human strength and artistry. Each athlete, including Giovanni, is a warrior in their own right, preparing for the battle on stage, as he put it when we first got together.

The sounds of clanking weights and determined grunts punctuate the pep talks from trainers and families to the competitors. Frank had already done that for Giovanni before leaving to compete in his class. When they were forehead to forehead building each other up, I stepped back, giving them space and privacy. He's in his element, and I can see the fire of competition light up in his eyes. It's a look I've grown to love, one that sparks every time he speaks of his passion and commitment.

"Kac."

It's utterly quiet over the noise of the room overcrowded with competitors, their gear, loved ones, and rows of chairs. Posing oil and sweat hangs heavy in the air when he attempts to reach for me. I edge away, unwilling to mess up his perfectly applied lotion.

"I hate that I can't touch you."

This is not the first time he's said that today. It's his way of saying he needs physical comfort from the emotions he must be feeling, with this being his first competition.

"You can touch me all you want when you win."

I smirk, glancing down at his tiny little Speedo. I have no idea how it's holding in that giant shaft of his.

"How does all that fit in there anyway?"

As if on cue, his thigh angles out in an adjustment that seems to do more harm than good when his hand plunges into the front of the shiny red fabric.

"It doesn't," he grumbles under his breath, something about his muscular thighs, shoving it forward with no space to hang in between them. I merely chuckle, observing him as one of the judges will do.

His body is nothing short of a masterpiece, a testament to his dedication and discipline. Each muscle is defined with precision and sculpted through countless hours of rigorous training. His shoulders are broad and powerful, tapering down to a chiseled chest, sharply defined pectoral muscles, and an unbelievably lean, chiseled waist.

His arms are adorned with veins that map out the effort and dedication poured into every curl and press. His biceps and triceps are like sculpted marble, hard and defined with strong and sinewy forearms—all a testament to the consistency of endless sessions.

His lats spread like wings, the light and shadow dipping in and out of the depth and definition of each muscle group. His quadriceps bulge with power and definition, hard planes that made giving oral sex to him even hotter with my eyes inches from those broad muscles.

His hamstrings are carved round curves tucked under an insanely hard and high butt that feels like a rock when I attempt to pinch it. The calves he complained and obsessed over, taking the most effort to grow, are perfectly sculpted and symmetrical with his overall body and frame.

Beyond this physical perfection, what truly captivates me is the story of us and how his journey became my journey. I remember early morning workouts, disciplined diets, and the countless sacrifices and surprises he's made to prioritize my health and his training schedule. That night at the hospital, with plastic candles aglow and a small box with a key, set the course for the best relationship I've ever had. We're a team now.

Something Jenna understands after a chance encounter in the ladies' locker room where I made it a point—to borrow Giovanni's phrase—is that he is mine, and I am his. She didn't take too kindly of it, having recently ended her engagement. Yet, she nodded, stuffed her earbuds in, and hustled out of there.

Agreeing never to keep secrets unless it's Giovanni's favorite of doling out surprises to me, I told him about the interaction. He gave me an encouraging kiss, saying I deserved to be rewarded more thoroughly when we got home. Any time I stake ownership over him, as primitive as it initially seemed, it makes him feel loved and accepted and very, very horny.

His long fingers pluck at my sweater, plucking me out of my thoughts about him. Glancing down, I notice his things are neatly organized and more compact than before. I meet his gaze with a knowing smile, acknowledging the subtle change.

"And to address what you said a second ago, I plan to touch you all I want when we return home. I already have a tarp down because you and I will play a little slip-and-slide with this oil."

He returns a knowing smile of his own. Honestly, I won't put it past him. He's more resourceful and creative than anyone I know.

"Sounds like you better win, or else I'll have to go home and sleep alone in my dry, warm bed when we get back to town."

I hope this banter soothes his nerves as it helps me to stop looking at the dreaded clock and counting down the time until his group steps on stage. As if on cue to release some tension, he starts a series of stretches, targeting his upper body, neck, and arms.

"I can't believe this day is actually here."

His chocolate curls are trimmed closer than usual, so 'his trap muscles look more defined.' The haircut caught me off guard when he picked me up from work this week. He ran a hand over them, self-conscious that he had his guy take too much off, but I assured him he was still handsome either way. I proved this when I got down on my knees for him, which I'm much more comfortable doing now that I know how he likes it.

"Well, get used to it, O.G. You're just a few competitions and several months away from the main event."

His mouth twitches with worry, the same look he gets every time I mention it.

"And yes, I already made the hotel and travel arrangements."

When I offered to take over the various competition schedules, filing dates, logistics, and deadlines to compile in a spreadsheet, he hugged the life and breath out of me. People are his forte, not paperwork, is what I learned, especially when

I saw his handwriting that first day I met him. It's as illegible now as it was then.

"I don't know what I'd do without you, Kac."

A sigh loosens from his chest, and his lips roll inward, a sign that he's getting emotional.

"Luckily, you'll never know. You're as stuck with me as you are with our pet shark."

Jaws lives at his house, seeing as how that key he gave me is used more often than mine. The benefits of him living so close to my office building and the courthouse are endless, especially when I want to dash over, eat lunch, or fool around with him as part of my stress reducer. It's been especially wonderful since I've lost some weight, my blood pressure is lower, and my bloodwork shows improved numbers.

"Our little family," he murmurs before dipping in for a few kisses as the announcer calls his group overhead. "Wish me luck."

"You don't need it. You'll win."

I taste the tang of sweat on my lips, a constant scent in the weeks of his training. A wave of emotions surges over me. Anxiety, excitement, and an overwhelming awe at Giovanni and his achievements.

He interlaces our fingers, having me walk with him to the line-up, sending a squeeze through our joined hands before I have to leave to get to my seat. Pride swells in my chest as tears well into my eyes.

Swiftly brushing away my tears, I go through the bustling backstage corridors towards the area alive with brilliant lights, shouts of encouragement echoing as competitors take the stage, and the rhythmic pulse of music reverberating from the speakers above.

I weave through the rows and aisles to our seats at the front of the stage, a connection Sebastian secured to ensure we had the best seats in the house, according to him. I first encountered Sebastian and Chloe during a Valentine's dinner at an upscale restaurant in the museum district that spiraled into an impromptu city night on the town for our group of six, including Paolo and Taylor.

"How's Giovanni holding up?"

Chloe's anxious blue eyes flicker to mine momentarily as she asks, concern etched on her face, as she peeks at the competitors on stage and then back to me.

"He's okay, a bit nervous—"

"That pussy, he needs to man up," Sebastian interrupts, causing Chloe to swiftly hit his chest with the back of her hand.

"Sebastian!" Her glare is sharp enough to push him back in his seat as she leans across him to talk to me. "Ignore him."

Chastened, Sebastian retreats, his fingers absentmindedly twirling the end of her blonde ponytail.

"I just meant that I told him he'd take home the title when we hit the gym the other day."

"Well, say that instead to Kacie."

She doesn't let him off the hook, something I noticed at dinner that night. But with how those two look at each other, I can tell they give as much as they get. Especially when he ordered jello shots for the table and tried to eat them off Chloe, to which she murmured something about doing that later. It was enough for me to mind my own business, resume eating, and be thankful that the only thing Giovanni got on me was his saliva and cum.

Paolo and Taylor, on the other hand, were completely different. He was much more thoughtful, having written her a poem and gifting her a small gold bracelet with cookies and cups engraved on it. The significance eluded me, but the tenderness in her gaze as she nestled into him spoke volumes —it was private, a shared secret that belonged to them.

A sudden burst of anxiety breaks hold, whispering doubts

and fears. What if he's not happy with his performance? What if this doesn't go as he's dreamed?

"There he is."

Paolo points. His voice rises above the roar of applause as the line of competitors strikes their poses before the judges.

"He looks incredible."

Taylor says something inaudible over the crowd. All eyes turn to him, waiting offstage as he shifts to the side to watch the other contenders below his weight class. I know he's ready when I see the determination in his eyes and the set of his jaw. No matter what happens on that stage, he's already won in many ways. My love for him deepens, seeing him so dedicated to his passion.

Waiting to enter the stage, Giovanni's breathing is controlled, unlike mine, coming out in shallow breaths with butterflies swimming in my stomach. His focus is unwavering. His concentration is unyielding, and in that moment, I see not just the bodybuilder but the man I love, ready to take on the world.

The announcer's voice thunders through the venue, summoning Giovanni's division to the spotlight like gladiators entering an arena. My heart faces in my chest, my eyes following him as he steps into the light, ready to show the judges, his fellow competitors and the audience the level of his commitment and dedication.

This stage today and a few more in the coming months until he hits the ultimate stage this fall to compete for Mr. Olympia. Tears stream down my face, and when our eyes connect, he winks, that sassy little one he reserves for his strip-tease routine.

The lights accentuate the contours of his well-sculpted physique. He moves with a grace that belies his size, executing each pose with precision and confidence that he and Frank practiced hundreds of times in the mirrors of the kickboxing room at the gym.

From my vantage point, I can see the minute changes in his expression and the slight tightening of his muscles as he transitions from one pose to another. It truly is a dance of strength and artistry.

Around me, the audience reacts to each competitor, but my focus remains unwaveringly on Giovanni. His performance is not just a display of physical prowess. It's a narrative of his journey. Completing his business plan, presenting it to his father, and with a marginal win of giving him one year to succeed as a bodybuilder or go into medicine put that bright and victorious smile on his face.

As the competitors are called for the final lineup, the tension in the air thickens. The judges' deliberations feel like an eternity. My heart races in sync with my bouncing legs, every fiber of my being hoping for his victory, not just for the title, but for the affirmation of his dreams and proving it to his father.

Finally, the announcer's voice breaks through the suspense, ready to declare the results that could change the trajectory of Giovanni's career. A hush falls over the crowd, every eye fixed on the stage. The competitors sway nervously, some continuing to pose while others look around or down at the stage.

As the announcer calls out the fifth to third-place winners and watches them pose for pictures, none of them are Giovanni, and I'm awash in relief and growing excitement. My mind blurs when I hear the second place winner, sending a shock wave through every member of our group and me.

"And the winner is . . . Giovanni Marconi!"

The announcement thunders overhead, and I jump to my feet, whistling and clapping. The crowd erupts into thunderous applause. Giovanni's face lights up with disbelief and then triumph. He looks around, almost as if to confirm that this moment is real. The event organizers pat him on the back, congratulating him on his well-deserved victory while his winnings are detailed as they take pictures.

I can't contain my joy. Tears of happiness mingle with my earlier ones. I cheer along with the crowd, my heart swelling with pride. Beaming with excitement, Sebastian throws his arm around my shoulders and gives me a friendly side hug, jostling me slightly in his enthusiasm.

Giovanni's gaze finds mine, and we share a moment. While it's his accomplishment, I feel deeply honored to have supported him through his ups and downs and his unwavering effort in achieving it. His name is shouted from different directions for pictures. He humbly shakes hands with the officials before they disperse, leaving him to set the items he was awarded on the stage to pose.

The room begins to clear, allowing us the space to exchange hugs with each other while watching Giovanni soak in this glorious moment. While we wait, Sebastian and Paolo cluster together, quickly making plans to celebrate as Chloe wraps an arm around me.

"Ignore them. If you want to steal Giovanni away and celebrate, ahem, privately, then we'll understand."

She winks, followed by a playful shimmy that rocks my body.

"I wouldn't blame you now that the world can see what he's packing."

Her laughter rings out, light and carefree. It's then that Taylor gently touches her arm, bringing her back with a gentle admonishment.

"Ease up, Chloe."

The laughter and friendly jabs continue, adding to the already vibrant atmosphere. After finishing his photo session, Giovanni turns towards us, his face glowing with exhilaration and fatigue. As he makes his way over to us, our group erupts in cheers and applause.

"Way to go, champ!" Sebastian bellows, giving him a robust pat on the back before frowning and looking at his sticky hand covered with the greasy residue from Giovanni's body oil.

"Ugh, what is this shit? Chloe!"

He shoves the palm of his hand toward Chloe as if she had something to do with it.

"What? Go wash it off."

She pushes his hand away from her, and his shoulders sag.

"I don't want to go alone. Come with me."

Sebastian pouts, casting her a pleading look. She rolls her eyes and adjusts the strap on her expensive purse.

"Save me from looking at Gio's wiener in those girl underwear."

"Sebastian!"

She shakes her head and then looks around the group.

"Let me deal with him. We'll be back. Congratulations, Giovanni, you did remarkable up there."

Sebastian keeps his hand out in front of him as if it will ruin his clothes if it gets near him. As Chloe steps away, he says, "Do you remember that time in New York when I grabbed your thong and put it . . ."

His voice trails off the farther they get from us, leaving an awkward moment before Paolo chimes in, "Man, you crushed it out there!"

They swap high fives. Giovanni's dark eyes glisten with happy tears when he looks down at me for a long, lingering moment.

"Thanks, Paolo. It means a lot you guys driving all this way to support me."

Paolo drapes an arm over Taylor's shoulders, drawing her close while they both smile at him.

"Wouldn't have missed it for the world. You've worked your

ass off for this. I even heard Seb grumbling that he couldn't overtake you anymore. But we both knew that a long time ago."

They share a look of agreement. With Seb and his enormous personality away from the group, the two men are much calmer and more in sync. It's a curiosity that they aren't best friends rather than Sebastian being the common denominator. Too much alikeness may be the cause.

"Typical, Seb," Giovanni answers him while looking at me. "Will you come backstage with me to pack up?"

"Of course."

I drift closer, our hands intertwining while the conversation finishes.

"We'll meet you in the lobby, and then we can all decide where to go to celebrate," Paolo says, glancing at his smiling girlfriend, who finally has a moment to voice her congratulations.

"Sounds good."

Giovanni nods, his short curls barely moving with the product in his hair. They walk ahead of us, Taylor whispering something to Paolo that has him turning his head and kissing her. Their affection is sweet, if not obvious, that they only have eyes for each other. I never imagined that dating Giovanni would also mean gaining a lively group of friends, a mix of charming ladies my age and energetic young men.

As Giovanni and I walk hand in hand towards the backstage area, the people we pass offer their congratulations and well wishes. It's a proud moment, walking alongside him, feeling the warmth of everyone's reception to him.

Each congratulatory word adds to that wide barrel chest raised with pride, marking his hard-earned success and the journey it took to get here. The admiration and respect from onlookers is neat to watch as I share in their awe.

We enter the bustling backstage area. The contrast between the lively atmosphere and Giovanni's quieter space is striking. His belongings are organized neatly amidst the chaos.

He breaks the silence with a sigh, a hint of longing in his voice.

"I'm dreaming about a hot shower back at the hotel and just unwinding in bed with you for the rest of our stay here."

He stops, his hands resting on his hips as he turns to me, his gaze intense and questioning. The statement hangs like questions between us, and with a slight chuckle, I shake my head.

"You know you can't do that. They are waiting for you. Wanting to celebrate this first of many wins to come with you."

I step closer, reaching out to touch his arm, feeling the residue of his oil.

"I know."

His hands slip from his hips. An exhausted sigh passes through his lips as the adrenaline wears off.

"I'll get cleaned up and make a night of it. But just so you know, I'm cutting it early to spend the rest with you. That's not negotiable."

His warning rings more to himself than it does to me, as he generally is in charge of our social calendar. I smile, holding out my fist to bump, which he does wholeheartedly, preferring to sneak in a few kisses.

"Alright, let's get going."

As he pulls a towel from his bag to wipe away the oil, I can see his energy levels dipping, the culmination of his physical and emotional exertion throughout the day catching up to him. He moves with quiet efficiency, focused yet clearly tired, with a groan from a back strain still healing while putting on his sweats. He gently places his bags over his shoulder and puts his arm around me.

"Now you can touch me."

I snug up against his side, my hand resting comfortably on his waist as we head out, ready to join the others to celebrate his victory. Before we meet the group in the lobby, I have a surprise of my own for him. Little does he know that waiting just outside the door is a fellow competitor in a different weight class wanting to speak to him.

When we push through the double doors leading into the hallway on our way to the lobby, he's standing off to our right. When I call his name, his face jerks up from the phone he is tapping on. Giovanni's hand instantly tightens on my waist, a silent claim as the attorney I told him about that night in the loft we know both affectionally call the cocoon walks toward us.

"Congratulations, Giovanni. That was an impressive performance." His hand is extended with a broad smile and a casual glance in my direction. "I don't think Kacie has formally introduced us, but I've heard quite a bit about you."

Giovanni, gracious yet visibly puzzled, accepts the handshake.

"Thanks, I appreciate it."

I step in to bridge the gap.

"Giovanni, this is Bruno. He's the criminal defense attorney I told you about. The one that also competes."

Their handshake lingers for a moment as understanding dawns on Giovanni's face.

"Ah, right. Kacie has mentioned that you juggle a very active law practice as well as your bodybuilding competitions."

Bruno returns the smile, releasing Giovanni's hand.

"Yes, that's me. It's a bit of a balancing act but rewarding in its own way. And seeing performances like yours today reminds me why I keep at it."

He fiddles with the sleeve of his athletic jacket when his diamond-studded Rolex snags on the material. The atmosphere between them is of mutual respect, bridging the worlds of discipline, nutrition, and bodybuilding.

"Well, it's impressive. Juggling two demanding fields is no small feat."

Giovanni raises his hand to the strap on his shoulder, adjusting the heavy bag to a more comfortable position.

"Bruno, here, is my greatest rival in the courtroom."

Releasing my hold on his waist, I step back slightly to see his face more clearly, observing the array of emotions flickering across it.

"Friend, now. Kacie thought it would be good for us to meet. It seems we have a lot in common, especially our goals. I've been dreaming of opening my own gym for years," Bruno explains, his enthusiasm evident.

"It's going to be tailored specifically for bodybuilders. We'll have advanced machines designed for heavy lifting and targeted muscle development—something beyond the usual gym equipment. We'll also have specialized areas for compound movements and isolation exercises, ensuring a full range of training options."

He gestures with his hands to emphasize his points.

"And it's not just about the weights. The gym will have spaces for posing practice, with full-length mirrors and proper lighting—crucial for preparing for competitions. There'll also be a focus on recovery, with state-of-the-art facilities like cryotherapy chambers, hydrotherapy pools, and saunas to aid muscle recovery and enhance overall well-being."

Bruno's animated demeanor is the opposite of his fierce, no-holds-bar approach in court. I might not ever view him in the same intimidating light again.

"And we can't forget about nutrition—that's key. The gym will have an in-house nutritionist for personalized meal plans and a cafe serving meals that align with our dietary needs. It's about creating a comprehensive environment that supports every aspect of bodybuilding, from training to recovery to nutrition. A place where we can train, recover, and grow in the most effective way possible."

Listening intently, Giovanni is momentarily rendered

speechless. His eyes widen in awe at Bruno's detailed vision. With a confident nod, Bruno adds a pivotal piece to his proposal.

"I'm prepared to finance this project, but I need someone who understands the sport to set it up, run and manage it. Someone who knows exactly what a bodybuilder needs from a gym."

He pauses, looking directly at Giovanni.

"That's where you come in. I've seen your dedication, both in and out of the gym. You have the knowledge, the experience, and the passion for this."

Giovanni appears taken aback, his gaze shifting from me to Bruno's smiling face, then upwards to the ceiling. It's a familiar expression he often adopts when working to keep his emotions in check. As Giovanni struggles to hold back his tears, Bruno continues the conversation.

"Partners is what I'm proposing. I'll handle the financial side. You'll bring this vision to life, overseeing the general contractor, sourcing the equipment, creating and building the team, and making it a reality."

In shock over the scope of the offer, Giovanni seems to search for words. The opportunity to create and run his own gym is part of the business plan he proposed to his father. Where one man denies his dream, another steps up, sharing and enhancing the original concept of Giovanni's idea.

This moment is a turning point from the disheartening news his family was all too eager to deliver, assured it would force him into medicine and mostly estranging the brothers. Now, I'm witnessing the transformation of his life, and it's more wonderful than I could have imagined.

"I . . . this is incredible," Giovanni finally rasps, the emotion evident in his voice. "I'm reeling . . . I've been dreaming of this too, and after a recent setback, I didn't see how it could possibly happen."

Bruno extends his hand once more, seeking confirmation.

"So, is that a yes?"

Giovanni grasps his hand firmly, a clear signal of his commitment.

"Absolutely, yes."

With their handshake solidifying their new endeavor, Bruno pulls Giovanni into a side embrace for a quick moment before slipping him his business card.

"Give me a call when you're back in town. Kacie, I'll see you on Monday morning. And don't think I'll take it easy on you. My client is innocent."

The intimidating defense attorney mask slides over his face, which I've stared at, debated with, and both lost and won against. He points a finger at me as he steps back from Giovanni, and then, just as quickly, his features soften into a friendly smile.

"Aren't they all innocent until proven guilty in a court of law?" I shoot back, slipping into my lawyer mode, drawing a curious glance from Giovanni, who's still fiddling with the business card. Bruno pauses, then breaks into a hearty laugh.

"Good one, Kacie. Make sure you guys get home safely. We'll be in touch soon." He's still chuckling as he walks away.

Our eyes follow him, waving at someone in the distance and pausing to join another conversation with a group of people. Giovanni's joy is uncontainable as he lifts me off my feet in a whirlwind embrace, spinning me around until the world blurs into a kaleidoscope of colors and sounds. As my feet touch the ground again, he pulls me close for a kiss that's deep, emotional, and filled with the intensity of the moment.

It stirs a desire to follow his original request of abandoning our friends, going back to the hotel, and celebrating privately. With a sparkle in his eyes and a voice choked with emotion, Giovanni pulls back slightly, still holding me close.

"This is it, Kac." Tears glisten at the corners of his eyes as the business card trembles in his hand. "My own gym, can you believe it?"

Wrapped in his arms, my hands rest on his chest, feeling the rapid beating of his heart. I tilt my head to meet his gaze, my face shining with happiness.

"I'm so proud of you, Giovanni. You've earned this opportunity. Your victory today, and now this partnership. It's all so wonderfully overwhelming."

His embrace becomes firmer. When he starts to speak, his voice is thick with emotion.

"None of this would have been possible without you. The victory, Bruno . . . I owe you everything. You've been my rock through everything."

The intensity of Giovanni's gaze and the safety and security of being in his arms reinforces a truth I've known for weeks. I am madly, utterly in love with Giovanni. It's a feeling that's grown with each challenge we've faced.

"I love you, Giovanni."

My whispered words bring forth the tears threatening to fall every since we stepped into the hallway. As they drip down his cheeks, he collapses into me, burying his face into my neck and quietly sobbing.

With my cheek molded into his chest, my arms hugging him as tightly as possible, my tears rise and fall in cadence with the shaking of his shoulders. It's a long while of us holding each other, my heart threatening to burst with the love flowing from me to him.

His head lifts, his arms slack around me, and those captivating chocolate orbs flecked with gold lock onto mine. Tears still flowing down his face when he licks his lips.

"I love you so damn much. I've been waiting forever to find the right time to say it. I wanted to plan this big surprise, prepare a speech, and make it a big deal. Not tell you in some crowded hallway in the middle of one of my competitions."

I'm certain that whatever he had planned would have been uniquely special and wonderful in Giovanni's signature way.

"I'm sure it would have been beautiful," I assure him, trying to ease the guilt, joining the tears on his face. "But sometimes life doesn't go as planned. Sometimes, we have confessions in a hospital room, kiss when the nurse walks in thinking we are cousins, only to be tossed out when visiting hours end. And sometimes, we profess our love in noisy places that smell of sweat and posing oil. Grand gestures or funny places, this is us. I wouldn't have it any other way, O.G."

I offer him my fist to bump, and he taps it briefly before drawing me into a searing kiss, which is definitely his signature way.

"I wouldn't either, Kac."

**Turn the page to read Chapter One of
Kadus and Bex's story in *Kadus*!**

KADUS: CHAPTER 1
KADUS AND BEX'S STORY

"Atlanta, brace yourselves! Kadence is about to drop a rhythm revolution!"

My shout ricochets through the underground club, a challenge to the night, a promise to the crowd. The energy here is like a live wire, buzzing through the air, thick with sweat, sexiness, and my raw desire to win, to succeed at something—even if it's a cheesy rap battle contest, which is not my specialty.

The club is a dark, modern-day speakeasy with its bootleg alcohol, gambling in the back, and half-naked women rubbing up against their men. Shouts from the crowd blend with the music and chaos of this place packed wall-to-wall with people. Neon lights flicker from the stage, casting a seductive glow over the sea of faces turned my way. Their loud cheers fill me with anticipation and heighten my nerves.

I'm in my element on this stage, feeling every beat of the music in my blood. My hoodie clings to my muscular frame, a shadow against the neon lights, while my jeans hang just right, part of my armor. My dark eyes, intense and unyielding, sweep over the crowd, owning this moment.

"Time to battle!" I roar to a chorus of cheers fueling the fire in me. My rival, all swagger and a smug grin, stands to the left of the stage, in the shadows, waiting for his big entrance as the house favorite. But tonight, the stage is mine. I own this bitch.

The DJ spins a hard-hitting beat, a rhythm that echoes in my chest. I lean into the mic, every part of me coiled and ready. My heart hammers, but my voice is a steady blaze, every word a strike, every line a battle cry.

I rap for the dreamers, the fighters, spinning a story of struggle and hope. My words aren't just hard earned lyrics I wrote. They're pieces of my soul, raw and unfiltered—the beat pounds, a relentless drive that matches the intensity of my verses.

As I reach the climax, the crowd surges forward, clapping and banging on the stage for more. It's a storm of awesomeness, and I'm the eye of it—the center of this whirlwind, riding the high of their screams and shouts. I finish with a line that hits like a clap of thunder, sending them into a frenzy.

I step back, breath ragged, eyes blazing. This is more than a victory. It's a revelation. I'm Kadence. Tonight, I didn't just perform. I owned every inch of this stage, every beat of their hearts.

The seasoned rapper, known as "Lyric Master," is a figure who commands respect the moment he steps on stage. He's a bit older, his age showing not in weariness but in the kind of confidence and presence that only comes from years in the game.

He's dressed in a way that merges the classic with the contemporary—a black leather jacket that's seen its share of stages, worn over a simple, clean white tee that fits just right, and dark denim jeans that speak more to his experience than any attempt at trendiness. His sneakers are worn but clean, a testament to his journey.

"Ka DENSE came hard, but watch the throne,
I'm the king of this battle, in a league of my own.
You talk of streets, of struggles and pain,
But I'm the architect of this rap game.

I've walked these paths, paved them in gold,
My rhymes are legends, bold and old.
You're the storm, Ka DENSE, but I'm the sea,
Vast and deep, can't be contained, you see.

Your fire's bright, but my words cut sharper,
I'm the rap game's scribe, the lyrical harbinger.
You bring the heart, but I bring the art,
Crafting verses that hit like a dart.

This is more than skill, it's a legacy I weave,
In the tapestry of rap, it's my mark I leave.
So, give it up, Ka DENSE, you've met your match,
In this battle of wits, I'm the perfect catch."

The crowd explodes even louder than before, their cheers a testament to the rapper's skill and stature. His words hang in the air, a challenge that's both an honor and a threat.

I nod, respect mixed with the burning desire to rise to this challenge. The battle's on, and the night's just getting started. I step forward, the beat drops, and I dive in, each word a strike of lightning, each line sharper than the last.

"Respect to the king, but the crown's up for grabs,
Kadence on the mic, and I'm swinging jabs.
You paved the way, but I'm laying new tracks,
My rhymes are dynamite, and I'm bringing the max.

You're deep like the sea, but I ride the waves,

In this rap odyssey, it's my voice that saves.
Your legacy's rich, but I'm the new age,
Writing my story on this luminous stage.

You've got the art, but I bring the soul,
In this battle of beats, I'm on a roll.
Your darts are sharp, but my words are fire,
Igniting the crowd, taking us higher.

This ain't just skill, it's a revolution,
Kadence is here, the evolution.
So, bow to the king, but hail the new,
In this rap saga, I'm the breakthrough."

The crowd erupts—a wild, uncontainable force, their energy fueling the fire I've ignited. Their cheers wash over me, a tidal wave of affirmation. I stand my ground, my heart pounding and sweat running down my face, but my confidence is unwavering. This is more than a battle. It's the forging of a legend, and tonight, my name will fall from everyone's lips.

Lyric Master smiles and takes a theatric moment before waving his hands in the air for everyone to quiet down, ready for his rebuttal. He nods at me, ready to bring it. His throne is up for grabs, and by the sound of the crowd, it's almost mine. The crowd settles, eager for his response. He clears his throat, and his voice rolls out, smooth and seasoned, the words tinged on the tip of his tongue.

"Ka DENSE came strong, I gotta confess,
In this clash of titans, he's shown he's the best.
I've ruled this stage, had my time in the sun,
But tonight, it's clear, Kadence has won.

He's the storm, the fire, the new voice in town,

With every fierce verse, he's taken my crown.
I'm the sea, I've had my reign, deep and vast,
But every king knows they can't always last.

This battle's been real, a true test of art,
Kadence, respect, you've played your part.
You've got the soul, the spirit, the heart,
In the rap game's story, you're the new start.

So here's to Kadence, the new king on the rise,
His verses hit hard, a truth that never dies.
In this rap saga, he's the one to beat,
Kadence on the mic, he's made this night complete."

The audience cheers, a thunderous applause that shakes the foundation. The rapper extends his hand to me, a gesture of true sportsmanship. I grasp it, feeling a surge of triumph and respect. Tonight, I didn't just win a battle. I earned my place in the legacy of Atlanta's underground. My artist's name echoes through the club, a chant that marks the birth of a new legend. I soak up their love and energy as long as I can before being touched on the shoulder to pass the microphone to the next challenger and exit the stage.

The roar of their applause makes me feel visible, but the high is short-lived. Stepping off the stage, I disappear behind the curtain where other rappers await their turn. As I bump shoulders with some of the guys, clap hands, and wish them good luck, I realize we're all the same. All of us hope a talent scout is in the audience who might discover us.

Desperation clings to me. Maybe it's the stack of overdue bills on my kitchen counter or the eviction notice burning a hole in my pocket. Or maybe the dream feels just out of reach, no matter how hard I grind. As much as tonight feels like a victory and boosts my confidence, it doesn't bring the money I need to pay anyone I owe, much less Trigger Trey.

It was a bad idea to take money from him. Once those crisp bills hit my hand, I knew. Foolishly believing something would have broken out for me. After getting so much love on social media, it felt as though something good was happening in my hip-hop career. When nothing panned out, I knew it was only a matter of time before he'd hunt me down, demanding payment and breaking something in warning when I had nothing to give him. That's how these things work.

As I head to the back door, ready to push out of this place, I spot Trigger Trey's muscle, roughing up some rappers waiting in line, asking about me. A chill runs down my spine as I realize my time has run out. When I start backing up, one of them sees me, points, and elbows the other. He tosses aside the dude he had by the lapels and shoves his way toward me.

Heart hammering, I dart through the groups of fidgeting rappers, their scowls and curses barely heard as I barrel past. The pounding footsteps of Trigger Trey's goons echo behind me, each thud a grim threat of their promised violence. I slip past the curtain, drop into the audience pit, and scan the clearest path to the front exit.

The heat from the pressed bodies of the vibrating crowd mixes with the sweat rolling down my back. In my blind rush, disaster strikes with a sharp, piercing scream. I inadvertently smash into a girl in sky-high heels. Her face twists in pain when I step on her toes. Her fists pummel my body before she's pulled backward by a hulk of a man barreling toward me. His face is a mask of fury, eyes blazing, fists clenched.

Before I can even mutter an apology, he swings at me, and I duck, almost escaping him until he catches the edge of my hoodie, shaking me like a ragdoll in his grasp. Apologies spew from my lips as I glimpse the goons in my peripheral vision jumping into the pit with us. He growls in anger, his fist connecting with the side of my face.

Dazed, I stagger from the impact, the world tilting on its axis. Pain explodes in my jaw, a bright, searing starburst that sends me crashing into the people behind me. They shove me away, unwilling to get caught up in the confrontation.

Trey's relentless henchmen, their eyes locked on me, toss people out of their way. Fear races through me as the boyfriend steps toward me, and a ragged piece of my hoodie catches in his hand. He swings his scarred fist at me. I duck and slip past him to hide behind a group of girls.

My breath comes in ragged gasps, my mind reeling from the blow. The hulking dude is nothing, a forgotten threat as I stay crouched, weaving my way through the swaying bodies and surging beats. I can hear the goons pushing through the crowd behind me, the startled screams of ladies, evidence that they're still hot on my trail. Every shout and scream propel me faster, my fear forcing me to move quicker, further away from the mess I'm in.

I spot the exit, a glimmer of hope that I can make it out before they catch me, and lunge towards it. But the goons are faster, more ruthless. One grabs my arm, yanking me back, his grip iron. The other swings, his fist a hammer aimed at my head. I twist, turning into him, the momentum causing his blow to hit my shoulder.

The crowd's screams merge with my heartbeat, a chaotic symphony. I'm fighting now, not just for escape, but for survival. Every move is instinct, and every decision is split-second. I can't let them take me down, not here, not like this.

With a surge of adrenaline, I wrench free, breaking into a sprint. The exit's within reach, freedom just a few heartbeats away. I can almost taste it, the night air, the open streets. But the goons are relentless, and I know this chase is far from over.

Just as I feel the vice-like grip of one of them closing in

again, the unmistakable sound of police sirens pierces through my chaos. Red and blue lights swirl through the grimy windows, casting a strobe effect across the frenzied crowd. For a moment, everything seems to freeze, the realization of what's happening setting in—they're shutting down this illegal underground bar.

The goon's hold loosens as his attention snaps towards the entrance, where the heavy thud of police boots is now audible. In that split second of distraction, I wrench myself free, using every ounce of strength left in me. My face is already swelling from the first blow, and pain shoots from my shoulder, but survival is a powerful motivator and gets me moving again.

I dive through the crowd, now a frantic mass of people scrambling in every direction. The mayhem works in my favor, allowing me to slip through unnoticed, just another face in the sea of people. The police flood the club, shouting orders, their flashlights cutting through the dimness like searchlights in a storm.

I glance back briefly and see the goons being detained, their faces twisted in frustration and anger. A part of me knows this is just a temporary reprieve, that Trigger Trey's reach is long. But right now, all that matters is escape.

I follow the sea of people pushing through the back exit. My lungs burn from the suffocating surge of bodies, and my face throbs in time with my pounding heart until I'm stumbling into the alley. The cool night air hits me, a relief from the oppressive heat of the club. I take off into the darkness, knowing I can't go home or to Momma's house. Trigger Trey will easily find me at those places, and I can't put Momma in jeopardy like that.

With the sound of the club shutting down echoing behind me, I race toward the only place I know to go—the bus station. To a sister I haven't spoken to in what feels like forever. She's the golden child, the one whose shadow I've always stood in, and the one Momma always held up as the example, asking why I couldn't be more like her.

"Let's hope sis is up for a visit."

**Read the rest of Kadus and Bex's story in *Kadus*
(The Cougars and Cubs Series 💋, Book 4)**

WHERE BEATS and brushstrokes collide to form a colorful love affair.

In the pulsating heart of Atlanta's hip-hop scene, Kadus Yacob's dreams throb with ambition until one event sends him spiraling. Fleeing from a brush with the law, he finds himself in the vibrant chaos of Houston's art world, right in the path of Rebecca "Bex" Hartley.

Bex is a force to be reckoned with—a rockstar by night, leading her band with wild energy, and a bold, defiant artist by day, her murals splashing the city with rebellion, challenging every societal norm.

Kadus, striving to carve his name in the music industry, finds an unexpected muse in Bex, pestering her for help. But Bex is fighting her own war, torn between her art installations, her band's touring schedule, and her family's conservative expectations, she doesn't want or need a nagging kid around. When he steps into her world, a collision of paint, power, and passion ensues, igniting a sizzling connection that neither can deny.

From the underground beats of Atlanta's nightclubs to the colorful splashes of Houston's art district, their connection deepens, painting a love story as passionate and chaotic as Bex's art. Can the rhythm of Kadus's hip-hop beats resonate with the wild pulse of Bex's rock anthems and the vibrant strokes of her artwork, or will it be another one-hit wonder between these two?

Kadus is an electrifying romance that dances across the lines of opposites-attract, blending the raw energy of a hip-hop artist and a punk rock painter. This passionate narrative charts the journey of two unlikely lovers, discovering that true harmony resonates in embracing their differences, melding their disparate worlds of music and art, and igniting a love as vibrant as a mural and as rhythmic as a beat.

Kadus is the fourth book in The Cougars and Cubs Series and is a connected standalone. It is a steamy, reverse age gap, rockstar, hip hop artist, painter and artist, interracial couple, sister's best friend, opposites attract romance.

GET TWO FREE BOOKS

Sign up for my newsletter to ensure you are the first to know about new releases, sneak peek excerpts, cover reveals, book sales, and author giveaways!

The Cougars and Cubs Series 💋
is steamy, naughty instalust
reverse age gap fun.

DOWNLOAD FOR FREE ON MY WEBSITE
www.gigimeier.com

Paolo and Taylor's story is a duel POV, meet cute,
reverse age gap, workplace romance.

The Cañon Series 🖤
is deliciously dark and intensely traumatic.

DOWNLOAD FOR FREE ON MY WEBSITE
www.gigimeier.com

Dani and Tomlin's story is a single POV, slow burn, enemies-to-lovers, forced proximity romance. Check my website for a list of content and trigger warnings.

BONUS CONTENT

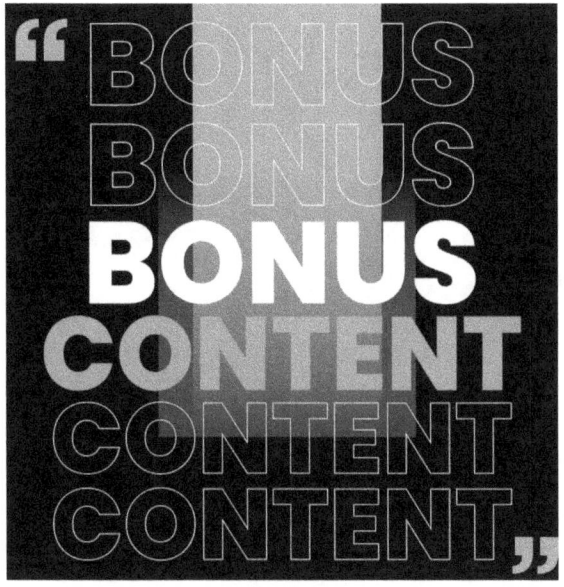

Want more?

I have exclusive bonus and deleted scenes for you on my website: www.gigimeier.com/freebies.

I'm always adding more for my loyal readers as a big THANK YOU for loving my books and supporting me as an author 🌷

IF YOU ENJOYED THIS BOOK

Thank you for reading *Giovanni,* the third book in The Cougars and Cubs Series 💋 . Stick around for *Kadus,* the fourth book in the series and a best friend's brother, rockstar romance.

If you enjoyed *Giovanni,* please consider leaving a review on BookBub, Goodreads, or your favorite retailer to let others know about this steamy, reverse age gap protector, Alpha male romance.

Reviews are greatly appreciated. They help independent authors like myself get our books in front of more readers.

Gigi Meier

ALSO BY GIGI MEIER

Standalone Book

Coyote

Sammie and Carlos's forced proximity

cartel, kidnapped, Military hero, dark romance

The Cañon Series

Tomlin

The start of Dani and Tomlin's

slow burn, enemies-to-almost-lovers

Tomlin Takahashi Duet #1

The Cañon Series, Book #1

Takahashi

The conclusion of Dani and Tomlin's

friends-to-lovers, happily ever after

Tomlin Takahashi Duet #2

The Cañon Series, Book #2

Hamilton

Hamilton and Molli's second chance,

small town, police officer romance

The Cañon Series, Book #3

Isla

Isla and Gabe's opposites attract,

age gap, forbidden love romance

The Cañon Series, Book #4

The Cougars and Cubs Series 💋

Paolo

Taylor and Paolo's reverse age gap,

forced proximity, office romance

The Cougars and Cubs Series 💋, Book #1

Sebastian

Sebastian and Chloe's reverse age gap,

opposites attract, Christmas romance

The Cougars and Cubs Series 💋, Book #2

Giovanni

Giovanni and Kacie's reverse age gap,

protector, Alpha male romance

The Cougars and Cubs Series 💋, Book #3

Kadus

Kadus and Bex's reverse age gap,

best friend's brother, rockstar romance

The Cougars and Cubs Series 💋, Book #4

Marco

Marco and Victoria's reverse age gap,

steamy Latin couple, soulmates romance

The Cougars and Cubs Series 💋, Book #5

Gods and Goddesses Anthology

Eternal Reign

Hades and Persephone Modern Retelling

Russian bratva, kidnapping, touch her and die, slow burn.

ABOUT THE AUTHOR

After retiring from a thirty-year career in corporate America, GiGi Meier is delighted to be writing romance novels about strong female characters and their complicated, swoon-worthy men.

She loves telling stories and figuring out why her characters do what they do. With heartbreaking angst, panty-dropping lust, and enviable love, her stories linger long after you close the book.

When GiGi is not eating over her laptop, she likes to spend time in the pool with her children, walk her furry babies, and film videos for Instagram and YouTube. Whether attending a book club or hosting a game night, she loves connecting with new people and making friends.

Sign up for my newsletter to ensure you are the first to know about new releases, sneak peek excerpts, cover reveals, book sales, and author giveaways!

www.gigimeier.com

www.ingramcontent.com/pod-product-compliance
Lightning Source LLC
Chambersburg PA
CBHW071850220626
47052CB00002B/59